VENUS BESIEGED

What Reviewers Say About

The Richfield & Rivers Series

***Combust the Sun*: First in the Richfield & Rivers series**

"*Combust the Sun* is the first in what appears to be a series in a unique category of lesbian fiction: murder mystery/ relationship. *Combust the Sun* reads well, and that's because life partners Andrews & Austin are writing from what they know, both having worked in movie studios as writers and producers." — *Inside Out Magazine*

***Stellium in Scorpio*: Second in the Richfield & Rivers series**

"Teague's snarky perspective hooks you immediately, carrying you through a high-spirited light noir where the suspense never lets up." — *Curve Magazine*

"If the reader is looking for a well-written, intelligent, and thoroughly enjoyable [novel], *Stellium in Scorpio* is for you. Richfield and Rivers make a wonderful couple who experience the various ups and downs of life with a sense of humour, affection, patience…and an astrology chart." — *Midwest Book Review*

VENUS BESIEGED

THIRD IN THE RICHFIELD AND RIVERS

MYSTERY SERIES

by

Andrews & Austin

2008

VENUS BESIEGED
THIRD IN THE RICHFIELD AND RIVERS MYSTERY SERIES

ISBN10: 1-60282-004-X
ISBN13: 978-1-60282-004-3

THIS TRADE PAPERBACK IS PUBLISHED BY
BOLD STROKES BOOKS, INC.
NEW YORK, USA

FIRST EDITION, FEBRUARY 2008

CREDITS
EDITOR: SHELLEY THRASHER
PRODUCTION DESIGN: J. B. GREYSTONE
COVER ART: BARB KIWAK (www.kiwak.com)
COVER GRAPHIC: SHERI (graphicartist2020@hotmail.com)

Other Books By Andrews & Austin

The Richfield & Rivers Mystery Series

Combust the Sun

Stellium in Scorpio

Chandler & Chase Romance Series

Mistress of the Runes—A Mystical Romance

Acknowledgments

Thank you to award-winning author and BSB publisher, Radclyffe, whose efforts and vision open doors for lesbian literature. We are continually grateful to our personal and extraordinary editor Dr. Shelley Thrasher for her intelligence, patience, and guidance in all our work. Kudos to Barbara Kiwak for her beautiful cover art. And love to BSB publicist Connie Ward for giving so much and for making us laugh.

DEDICATION

To all the animals—angels in fur suits

PROLOGUE

Standing on the flat red rock that juts over the sheer cliff, the only firm ground between her and thousands of feet of air below, the frightened Navajo woman, her body whipped by the wind, a mere updraft away from soaring to her death, begs the shaman to save her from the man who would throw her over its edge.

"Leave her to me," the shaman says, her dark eyes like an eagle's piercing those of the older, diminutive man as she loosens the deerskin cape around her shoulders.

"If you don't do it, he'll come after you." Threatening words from the man who would one day whisper them.

The shaman, angry, suddenly swings her doeskin cape from her shoulders like the wings of a great bird. The deer's last vestige of life fans out and takes the Navajo woman with it, her body sails over the canyon's edge, her cries echo in the night air—silence—the silence of death. Even her adversary is paralyzed by the suddenness of a life ended.

"It is done," the shaman says, clearly demonstrating strength beyond mere threats.

A pause. Turning his back to her, the older man walks on shaking legs to his long, black limo. A tall man with slick black hair steps out and grasps the door handle, holding the passenger door open for him when, from behind, a flash of fur and bared teeth soars through the air, ripping into the tall man's arm.

He curses the animal, slams the door shut, and blood drips from the door seal as the vehicle fishtails on the loose rocks. Tires squealing, it disappears into the night.

The attacking wolf, adrenaline pumping, charges the shaman as if to shred the skin from her body, but at the last possible moment it drops at her feet, resting against her side as she gently strokes its head and whispers to the heavens, "Shimasani, protect us."

Chapter One

I drove down Hollywood Boulevard alongside the dragonesque Grauman's Chinese theater, past a man on roller skates naked except for a red butt thong and full-body tattoos, and spotted the ever-present soul with the tinfoil-covered cardboard box over his head, coat-hanger antennae sticking out of the top, his face peering out of a hole cut in the front, as he shouted, "I would like to thank the Academy."

Worn smooth from trying to sell screenplays to arrogant producers and dense studio development executives, I appreciated the simplicity of putting a box over your head and announcing success.

I punched the button on my cell phone, dialed my house, let it ring, and waited to hear my own voice on the answering machine so I could talk to Elmo. The irony of phoning my basset hound struck me, but only for a second. After all, this was Hollywood, where talking to a dog would get me straighter answers than talking to people.

At the beep, I spoke. "Elmo, it's me. Remember what I told you? Right after my dinner meeting tonight, we're headed for Sedona, so hang in there and don't lick your paws—you hear me? No paw licking. We don't want to end up at the vet again. Besides, if you meet a nice girl basset, she's not going to find a bloody paw attractive. Girls like manicured hands and a nice ass. You've got the latter, preserve the former. I'll be home in a couple of hours." I could almost hear him sigh as I told him I loved him and hung up.

Lately Hollywood had taken its toll on Elmo. Pitching shows all day, I was talked out by the time I got home, so he didn't get much attention. Frankly, I didn't know how to listen to a dog the way Callie Rivers did, so Elmo had been in a basset-hound funk and lay around trying to lick the fur off his paws.

Living with Callie would make us both happy, complete our lives, make us a family, fix everything, I thought, then chided myself for putting the burden of fixing my entire life on my lover. *No fair using love and chocolate as substitutes for therapy.* Nonetheless, when Callie wasn't around, Elmo and I were lost balls in a high wind, blowing around town lightheaded and directionless.

She'll be in Sedona, I thought happily and felt a twinge of excitement below my waist in a spot that seemed wired to the mere mention of her name. I'd seen her only a few weeks earlier in Las Vegas, but that trip was hardly relaxing since murders seemed to follow her like morbid sheep, a fact I attributed to her otherworldly connections and her astrological leanings.

All I cared about now was that Callie and I were going to meet in Sedona and spend a month writing my screenplay, planning our future together, and arranging to live in the same state, city, house so I could wake up to her ethereal blue eyes, wrap my arms around her soft, voluptuous breasts, and start my mornings and end my evenings with the touch and taste of her.

Erotic thoughts of Callie nude, sliding along my own naked form, were clouding my sense of direction, and I missed my turn as I dropped south onto Sunset heading for a large but chic Japanese restaurant to meet Barrett Silvers, the androgynous studio executive who, despite her many faults, was still touted in lesbian-land as one of Hollywood's most fuckable finds, women seeming to line up for the opportunity.

I was reminded of my own short tryst, having gone to Marathon Studios to pitch her my screenplay and ending up in a bungalow at the Bev—where the perks included a massage, wine, and sex with Barrett. Not good sex, just sex, because Barrett liked to make all her writers, right along with their movies. Despite that lapse in judgment, I had remained friends with her because she insisted on it and often sold my scripts, and I hoped it was for more than the talent in my fingers.

Directly in front of me a six-story photograph rose at the head of a curve, making it appear that a young woman with long, tangled hair blowing in the wind, wearing G-string underwear and rose petals for nipple covers, was blocking the road. Beneath her bare feet giant letters instructed, KNOCK ONE BACK, and I realized it was a Vodka billboard. Distilleries seemed unable to sell liquor without involving a sexy woman—obviously they believed getting laid was somehow made better by not remembering most of it.

Minutes later I pulled up in front of the Kotei restaurant and surrendered my Jeep to the valet parker, who took it in exchange for a numbered ticket. How ironic to turn over my vehicle to a total stranger just because he was in close proximity to my destination and wore a logo on his shirt that said Parking. I'd followed men into the woods because their shirt said Guide, let them into my house because their shirt said Delivery, and taken off my clothes because their shirt said Doctor. I was suddenly fretful that a foreign power might buy Van Heusen.

Pushing open the huge teak restaurant door, I was greeted with a riotous whoop from four total strangers wearing dish towels knotted around their heads like Asian Aunt Jemimas, flashing cinematic smiles apparently designed to make me feel welcome, and brandishing knives that could have been onboard a schooner with Johnny Depp.

"Kangeiiiiii!" they chorused, and diners' heads turned. A group greeting was bad enough at a surprise party, but ridiculous at a restaurant. A woman, petite even by Japanese standards, bowed slightly and without a trace of an accent said, "Konnichi waaa, Miss Teague Richfield. Please follow me." Barrett had obviously described me to the woman who waited to lead me through this dark labyrinth of soy sauce and sushi.

I followed her past polished teak tables filled with dining duos, then a virtually empty room with banquet-style dining, finally down a hallway with small signs jutting above each door, and stepped back as she gestured toward a room marked JUICHI, smiled, and backed away, exiting down the hallway.

The door opened with only the touch of my palm, and Barrett Silvers came into view through a dim haze of candlelight. She lay back on big, colorful silk pillows, one leg outstretched, the other bent, the knee used as a resting place for her long, languid, French-cuffed arm. She held a saki glass and her gaze revealed that she'd already been partaking heavily. She was a stunning study in raw sex appeal: her dark Adonis hair framing her chiseled features and her long body completely relaxed and at rest, like a large cheetah lounging between meals but poised for the chase.

"You look good," she said, editing out any perfunctory "Hello, how have you been?"

She knows she looks good. In fact, I think she's talking about herself more than me.

"Did they run out of adult tables?" I asked slyly, checking out the Japanese-style dining table only eighteen inches off the floor. "Elmo would love this place. He likes his doggie bowl at about this height."

Barrett made me nervous, her intent always unknown and her actions unpredictable. It wasn't a good sign that we were dining in a small private room consisting mostly of pillows.

"I brought a copy of the treatment and the notes from our conversations with Jacowitz," I said, referencing the famed director who, thanks to Barrett, had bought the story I'd pitched him and agreed that I would write the screenplay. I also hoped invoking his name would slot Barrett's mind back into a business groove.

Barrett smiled, reading me. "Why don't you sit down, relax, and have a drink. We'll talk about the project in general and then cover the notes." Her tone was light, as if to say my nerves were unwarranted, nothing untoward was going to happen. Dropping to my knees, a position not uncommon for a writer facing a studio executive, I leaned onto the large red pillow to my left—not an easy move for my five foot seven frame. But Barrett had managed it, and she was a few inches taller than I.

A knock at the door had me nearly executing a backflip to see who was behind me. A Japanese girl entered and set another opaque earthenware bottle adorned with painted flowers on the table, along with two fresh glasses and a tray delivered by the Japanese boy padding behind her. What a difference an ocean makes—in their country she would be walking behind him; however, once they crossed the Pacific he was not only trailing her, but carrying the dishes.

Scanning the tray of uncooked seafood, I spotted amaebi, hamachi, masago, ebi, and, thankfully, a couple of California rolls—because despite having tasted nearly everything in life, I drew the line at raw fish.

"You will knock if you want?" The Japanese woman spoke uncertain English while she indicated a place on the wall about two feet off the floor behind Barrett, bearing a symbol I presumed to be the international sign for knocking knuckles. Barrett thanked her, and the two servers bowed and backed out of the room, heads bent as they uttered "Tanoshimu," which I'd been told meant something like "Enjoy yourself"—a phrase that always confused me, as it seemed to invite masturbation.

"So you're headed for Sedona," Barrett said. "I offered you my cabin—"

"Yes, thank you, but Callie made arrangements."

The mention of Callie's name sharpened Barrett's voice and sent it slicing through the air like a knife through cream cheese, cutting the small talk. "I've had another conversation with Jacowitz since he'll be out of pocket soon in Paris. His only concern in the first draft..." she paused to sip from her glass "...is making it sensual enough for foreign audiences."

"I think it's a very sensual story—"

"A young novice counseling a psychologically abused wife—interesting character studies but no heat—doesn't automatically generate steam. Mull over a way to make them more sexually exciting."

"I don't want to whore out the story."

"Never said that." She sipped her drink again and I gulped mine, which burned my throat and stomach immediately upon arrival.

"What is this?"

"Shochu. It shouldn't burn. Take another drink or two and see if it goes away. Shochu is usually mixed with something, but this is straight."

Another sip and I realized the burning was starting to recede, along with the room, and my heart rate had doubled. I blinked and reached for the bottle again, this time to examine the alcohol content on the label—50 proof. "I think I saw this when I was a cop. The guys drinking it were under an overpass."

"Are you avoiding my notes on the story?" Barrett asked, all business.

"Absolutely not. More sex. Sexier. Unexpected sex. Sex within two minutes of the open, sexier a half hour in, huge sex an hour later, sex—"

"The problem with you, Teague—you argue." Barrett's tone was soothing as she handed me a bite of something. "Mirugai."

For all I knew, mirugai meant calm down.

"From my vantage point, it's called not rolling over. Studios and directors buy a screenplay based on the treatment, then before you can turn those ten pages into a hundred and twenty, they begin giving notes. How can you give notes on something that doesn't exist yet?"

I took a bite of the slippery thing Barrett had handed me, spontaneously slapped the remainder of it onto the black lacquer plate in front of me, and slugged the slimy sea creature down with shochu, nearly gagging on the combination. "What the hell was that?"

"Mirugai, giant clam."

Slamming down more shochu, I was emboldened. "Maybe my attorney should contact Jacowitz and remind him that our deal says I write the screenplay, not rewrite the treatment."

This is how it always starts. Love your work, bought your work, so that I can destroy your work and start over. Having played this game for years in a city where people were more scared than horses in a hail storm and followed what everyone else did, herdlike and horrified, taking more chances in bed than they ever did on the screen, I'd apparently chosen tonight to have a breakdown brought on by seafood and saki.

Seeing I was agitated, Barrett took the drink out of my hand and finished it, sipping from the same side of the glass where I had drunk, reminding me without telling me that we had a shared and intimate past that connected us whether I liked it or not.

"The drink is supposed to relax you, but you might be allergic to it." Barrett reached back and thumped her fist against the knuckle block.

Seconds later, the Japanese girl returned and politely awaited Barrett's command.

"My charming friend needs something more soothing."

The girl nodded and left as I got to my knees and staggered to my feet. Telling Barrett I'd return in a moment, I headed down the hall to the bathroom.

This has gotten off to a great start, I chastised myself, looking at my slightly blurred face in the ladies' room mirror. My green eyes weren't quite as sparkly after I'd drunk the shochu, but my punked hair was in place. After using the facilities, I washed up and pulled my green T down under my green cord blazer and pants. When in doubt I gravitated to military colors; perhaps Hollywood reminded me of a battle that never ended in a war that couldn't be won.

Try to be nice, for God's sake. This script will become a movie... will become a movie...will become a movie, I chanted in my head as I strode back down the hall, more off balance than the *Andrea Doria* as I re-entered the private dining room where Barrett was standing, asking if I was alright.

I made a mild attempt at apology, blaming the alcohol. She agreed it wasn't the right drink and offered me the one on the table.

"Nihonshu, a refined version of saki and only 16 percent alcohol. Let's see what this does for you." I knelt and she knelt beside me, on my side of the table, and poured me a glass. We sank down on the pillows facing each other.

"To better days and happy endings." I raised my glass, quoting Melissa Manchester.

"Or you could 'make my day,' as Clint always says." She smiled, toasting me with her own connectedness.

"Listen, I'll be in Sedona for several weeks. We'll stay in touch, and I'll let you see how it's progressing and get you and Jacowitz comfortable with the sex scenes," I offered, trying to be conciliatory.

"Fifty pages at a time?" she asked, and I knew I'd given too much. Now she would be dogging me, wanting to see every scene. "I want to see how it...builds," she said and reached for my shirt, heretofore safely tucked, and flipped it out of my pants, running her hand across my skin and over the top of my bra.

"Barrett," I protested, but my breath was faint and so was I. She unzipped my pants and jammed her hand inside between my legs, using that leverage to pull me into her lips. I pushed back but felt weak, almost drugged.

"Think of it as research." Her fingers fought to slide inside me and her mouth enveloped mine.

Barrett's inability to kiss and the flashing images of Callie and her warm, soft lips and blue eyes saved me. I shoved Barrett away, pulling my pants together and struggling to get to my feet.

But she had me off balance and pulled me down to her unzipped fly murmuring, "Start by eating this."

While I was zipping up my own pants Barrett had apparently been unzipping hers and placing a California roll in the...*what... groin area?* It was resting there like a beached crab. I'd heard the slurs of women and fish but had never contemplated a woman wearing a crustacean in her pants.

"Barrett, for God's sake, let go of me!"

But she was out of her head, either from the drink or the fantasy or her close proximity to a woman. She had a death clutch on my lapels and was using my weight to pin her to the ground so she could writhe up against me. My muscles had failed me and I was struggling to extricate myself, which only seemed to make the sensation more pleasurable for her. As sexual as the next woman, I was nonetheless turned off by trying to turn her off.

"Fuck me, baby," she breathed, then repeated it like a mantra with each hip thrust, trapping my knee between her hot thighs and grinding into me. "Are you the young novice I spoke to on the phone?" Barrett's reputation was not only tied to her promiscuity but to reciting an author's work during the most intimate sexual moment. "Take me places with your mouth my husband would never dream of going."

The word "husband" threw me, despite the fact that somewhere in my head I knew Barrett didn't have a husband. I'd always made it a point never to get involved with a woman whose betrayed lover had chest hair.

When she began to moan and climax, I was unable to escape, and her verbalization of extreme pleasure was reaching Beverly Sills proportions. I clamped my hand over her mouth, thinking our position reminded me of a takedown on the police force rather than an act of consensual sex. *How can sex be so one-sided and so unsexy?*

Suddenly she ratcheted up her hip movements to Tilt-A-Whirl force, groaning loudly, then exploded and went limp, unconscious. Silence—stillness. Scared, I spoke her name, took her pulse, shook her—nothing. My heart raced. *Omigod, has she had a heart attack having sex virtually with herself and died on me like some old guy in a sleazebag hotel?*

I took her pulse again, and it was weak and fluttering. I banged on the wall block and started CPR. The Japanese woman stepped inside the door, startled when I looked up frantic.

"Get an ambulance!" And I resumed trying to breathe life back into her. Images of that day at Orso's flashed through my mind when Barrett was having lunch with me and I had to call an ambulance. *Note to self. No more dining with Barrett, assuming she'll ever be able to dine with anyone again*

Moments later the paramedics arrived, and after much talking into their radios and taking vital signs and quizzing me, they finally gave her a shot of Benadryl and loaded her onto a stretcher.

When the sushi fell out of Barrett's pant leg, the female tech glanced my way and began quizzing me anew. "What was she doing right before it happened?"

"She was drinking and very animated." Only a partial lie or partial truth, whichever way you chose to look at it. I wasn't about to say that Barrett Silvers had humped me like a horned toad and then stopped breathing.

The shot of Benadryl seemingly having done its trick, Barrett was already coming around on the stretcher and demanding to be let off, refusing IVs and further assistance. The young male paramedic allowed her to get up, saying something in the food or wine could have caused the reaction.

Barrett asked me for a pen and, her grip still weak, managed to write a wobbly signature that dismissed the paramedics. Then she signed a waiver for the restaurant that assured any lawyers who cared that whatever had happened wasn't their fault. *For a studio executive, she gave up her rights pretty quickly*, I thought, but I wouldn't want my body taken to an L.A. hospital either, unless my parts were so badly damaged they were arriving under separate transport in an ice chest.

The sexy dining alcove now looked like an episode of *ER* with torn paper, tape, tubing, and other paraphernalia mingled among the lotus blossoms and orange slices.

The medics attempted a quick cleanup and loaded up to leave. I was relieved when the room was cleared and Barrett asked me to drive her home, having come by cab. She put her arm over my shoulder, the full weight of her tall frame heavy and unsexy. The weight of a woman hanging on me, drunkenly rather than affectionately, felt different—both physically and psychologically.

A nervous Japanese restaurant manager who wanted to be on record, I was certain, as having been of assistance, followed us to my car.

Helping Barrett inside, I felt sorry for her, but I also had the same reaction I surmised men had—awaking in bed with someone who looked sexy after six martinis, but now not so good over a couple of eggs. Barrett's pleated and pressed black slacks were wrinkled, her patent loafers had a gouge in one toe, which must have occurred as they hurried to load her on the stretcher, and she looked worn smooth, her loose silk shirt with the French cuffs sadly stained.

I drove slowly, not wanting to jar her, and when I asked occasionally if she was alright, she nodded. As we pulled up in front of her Las Feliz home, she reached over and took my hand in her slightly larger one, the gold pinkie ring somehow exotically sexy on her long slender fingers.

"I enjoyed the first half of the evening," she said, but her words sounded like a perfunctory wrap-up to a date that hadn't ended well. "I'll call you and see how you're doing. Think about the notes from Jacowitz, will you?"

How in hell can she still be talking business, I wondered as she opened the car door, and then I realized business was all she had. I started to get out and help her but she waved me off, some shred of pride left.

As I watched her walk up the steps, I was sad. *Who in the world will Barrett Silvers ever meet who understands her? Where will she ever find love? There's no one on the planet who can handle her or make her want to be faithful, yet deep down that's probably what she wants.*

Early in my life I might have taken on that task simply to save her, despite having to sacrifice myself in the process, but I'd gotten my money's worth with a shrink on that topic, so the most I could give Barrett tonight was a ride home.

Quickly my own love life clicked in, and I wondered if this whole bizarre evening constituted being unfaithful to Callie Rivers. I had tried not to let Barrett have sex on top of me, if that was the proper phrase. I hadn't enjoyed it and was embarrassed by it. Nonetheless, Barrett Silvers had climaxed against my body. What should I tell Callie, and was telling even required?

Callie Rivers was psychic, so wouldn't it be entirely up to her to figure it out, get a call from the cosmos, a visual from Venus, or whatever? Did I have to walk into the cabin and blurt, "Hey, honey, by the way, while I was having a business dinner with Barrett Silvers she put sushi in her slits and humped me like a hound, but it was one-sided"? What earthly good could come from sharing that piece of information? It was bizarre, unexpected, and over.

But the big question still remained: when is telling required? After all, even Catholics go to confession voluntarily.

CHAPTER TWO

An hour later, after brewing coffee so strong I had to almost chisel it out of the pot, I drank two cups before loading Elmo, luggage, and laptop into the Jeep and heading out under a full moon for Sedona to get as far away as possible from L.A and Barrett Silvers. Leaving now would put me in Sedona Sunday at dawn, a day early, and give me time to settle in before Callie arrived the following morning.

Within minutes, we were heading down Riverside Drive in the dark, hooking up with Highway 15, then connecting to I-40 in Barstow and breathing room, as I finally escaped the ubiquitous Valley traffic. Elmo swayed and paced across the flattened backseat of the Jeep, having trouble keeping his footing as I swerved in and out of the chain of headlights.

"I was attacked," I told my faithful hound and he let out a mournful moan. "Barrett lies in wait for me every time, like a damned vulture. I shouldn't have gone. But how do you not go when she's the studio exec on your movie and wants to meet? I didn't do anything…*she* did it."

Elmo cocked his head to look at me.

"What?" I asked defensively. "Look, here's the truth. I don't live with Callie yet—but of course I want to. So that raises the question, when am I considered married?" I broke out in a sweat and began ripping my sweater jacket off as fast as I could while driving eighty miles an hour down the freeway holding the steering wheel with my knees. Lately I'd begun having hot flashes when there was nothing worth flashing about.

Elmo flopped down on the console between the bucket seats, apparently knowing from my tone that this was going to be a long night.

"Straight people have a wedding date after which they're never to look at anyone else, much less fuck anyone else. Forget that the groom might have a bachelor party the night before and screw three hookers and a beauty queen. That's still okay until twelve hours later when he walks down the aisle and is never supposed to do it again—never even think of hookers again, or talk about hookers, or beauty queens, or anyone else but his wife. Now does that make sense to you? What was different in those twelve hours that made him not guilty and then guilty?"

Elmo's sigh sounded somewhere between bored and exasperated.

"Hold on, I'm getting to the point." I reached into the glove box and handed him a cookie to make him a more attentive listener. He chomped down on it, in a slow, thoughtful crunching as if letting me know he was hearing me out, which I appreciated.

"What's different? I'll tell you what's different: the walk down the aisle. An aisle, a long corridor of carpet, suddenly alters right and wrong—get it, *alters*? It interjects morality into what was formerly just sex. The walk down the aisle announces to the world that you have decided to be monogamous forever.

"Where's my aisle? Where is the point at which I'm supposed to be completely hers? I need a marker. Is it after I told her I loved her? Is it after we had that first fabulous night in bed? Is it after we move in together?

"Lesbians have no aisle. The aisle is a finish line. You cross it and you're finished. Straights know that."

Hearing a muffled gurgle, I glanced down to find Elmo snoring.

"I listen to you day and night, thanks to Callie's coaching, and I'm getting moist snores."

Grabbing a Kleenex I daubed at his large black nose and then patted his tricolored fur suit. Elmo never even twitched. I turned on the radio to hear a deep-voiced country singer croon that he would be happy to walk through hell on Sunday to ensure that his lover remained in the garden literally fertilizing the flowers—demonstrating what monogamy can come to if both parties don't buy into it. Patting the white milk bone on Elmo's caramel-colored head, I continued what I suspected was a dogalogue—one-sided dialogue with a dog no longer listening.

"Dogs don't have to worry about the deleterious effects of random sex, unless it's getting hung up during the deed and having some stranger turn a hose on you." Elmo roused and looked up with worried eyes, perhaps seeing images of himself in a compromising position. "Don't panic, it rarely happens. Stick with girls your own size and you'll be fine," I assured him.

Driving from the Valley to Sedona at nirvana-speed—a velocity that exceeded the ridiculously low limit inflicted by governmental bodies but not fast enough to induce a donut-dunking HP officer to fire up his red light and come after me—I was momentarily content.

Callie Rivers's sweet soul and sexy body were finally on my horizon. She had ducked and dodged and given me every excuse for our remaining long-distance lovers, but now I felt certain I had her on the brink of living with me. We'd been together in Tulsa, L.A., and Las Vegas, talking, laughing, and making love in enough places and circumstances for the test drive to be over—the test drive Mother had always warned against when I was growing up.

"Sleeping with a man before you're married comes to no good end. Why buy the cow when the milk's so cheap?" Mother told me from the time I could walk, oblivious to the troubling analogy of daughter as cow. Looking back I realized the advice was sound and effective. I *never* slept with men—thus keeping myself on the market and the value of my mammaries high.

We stopped only once for gas and a bladder break at a time-worn service station whose faded sign obfuscated the name and whose gas-pump handle had endured more hand grabs than a rock star's crotch. I bought a Hershey's Almond Bar, and Elmo nudged me when we got back in the car, wanting a bite.

"You know Callie believes chocolate can kill a dog," I said as

Elmo swung his head suddenly and bit off a third of the candy bar. His eyes glistened in basset ecstasy.

"Damn! You know I hate to eat after you because of where your tongue's been."

Elmo kept his head down but cut his eyes up at me.

"True, but I brush my teeth," I said in response, and bit into the candy bar, knowing Callie would pass out before she would ever eat after a dog.

"Don't do this in front of her, or neither of our mouths will experience pleasure again."

I knew the scenery from L.A. to Sedona by heart and played it in my head like a virtual tour because it was too dark to see anything. When we began to climb slowly up the mountain to Flagstaff, shadows of the topography announced the world had changed. Despite the darkness, I could almost feel the mountains ahead.

The turn south on I-17 began a winding trip down into the canyon an hour before sunrise. No light glanced off the red rocks, and only shadows fell on the forest trees. Nonetheless, I was lighthearted and hopeful.

I would write a powerful screenplay and make love with Callie Rivers in an erotic frenzy that would grow exponentially by the day. And after the screenplay was written, I would take her home with me and we would live together forever. I would be so happy that the mere thought of another woman would simply be blown out of my head right through my ears.

I conjured up euphoric visions of our new domesticity, our concupiscent coupledom, and our mutual joy pegging off the bliss meter. I envisioned our dropping dry cleaning off…together, grocery shopping…together, going to vet visits and dentists' appointments… together. I intended never to let her out of my sight.

"That solves monogamy right there," I said to Elmo, who was snoring.

We drove farther down into the woods, the road hugging a crystal-clear body of water until we came to a horseshoe curve, then a steeper descent down to a creek and a series of cabins indiscernible from the road. Gliding slowly off the highway onto the soft dirt and then crunchy rocks, I rolled to a stop in front of a cabin, reached into my jeans' pocket, and pulled out a key with a tiny white tag dangling from it that said Cabin 11.

A small, rustic, red log cabin, buried back off the main road, peeked out of the tall pines. I put the parking brake on, grabbed a small flashlight out of the glove box, and told Elmo to hang tight while I figured out if this was the right place. Serene and beautiful, it was also a bit spooky in the predawn. Callie had rented the place from someone she knew and mailed me the key and directions.

Shining the light on the plaque by the door I read ELEVEN. This was definitely the place. I put the key in the lock, opened it with a ten-degree turn, and heard it click, making me wonder why whoever owned the place had even bothered, since I could have jimmied the feeble mechanism with a credit card. But this was Sedona, hardly the crime capital of the world.

No light switch inside the door, so I eased across the room looking for a floor lamp and bumped into furniture along the way.

That's when I heard a swish ahead of me, like weather stripping at the bottom of a door scraping the floor, and a shadow played across the door frame. I dropped to a crouch to make myself a smaller target. *Who is it? Maybe the back door was unlocked and a transient is sleeping here.*

Elmo barked loudly from inside the car, apparently trying to warn me of someone at my back. I spun on the balls of my feet, still crouched and facing a hundred and eighty degrees in the opposite direction. Seeing no one, I completed the circle until I was facing the back porch again where I froze, my heart poised to leap out of my chest. *Someone's in the room with me.*

Whoever it was had entered through the back door and was nearly on top of me. Stabbing my hand into my jacket pocket, I grabbed my gun and yanked it out, bounced to a standing position, and pointed it in the direction of the back door.

"Don't move or you're fucked! Turn on the lights!" I shouted to the intruder, who obviously knew the room layout, where I didn't.

"Fucked?" A soft chuckle. "I'll take you up on that—and forget the lights."

I recognized Callie's sultry voice. "What are you doing here? You're not due until tomorrow," I said, delighted to be near her under any circumstance, and laid my gun down on the nearest flat surface.

"I was on the back porch having a drink and waiting for dawn, and something told me my lover was coming."

"You scared the hell out of me."

"I have since the day I met you." She slid into my arms in the dark and covered my face with kisses.

"I could have shot—"

Her mouth muffled my words as she renewed her kisses and reached under my shirt to unhook my bra. Her hands were down the back of my pants pulling me to her, strong and sure of what she wanted, her mouth searching mine as if she'd lost her life there and was determined to find it.

As we kissed, she walked me backward through a doorway and pushed me onto a narrow double bed with squeaking coil springs buried deep inside the old mattress that had obviously seen plenty of action over the years and still had the strength to bounce us when we flopped onto it, making us laugh like kids.

"Wow, this'll be like making love on a trampoline."

"Hang on and don't lose your place," she said and put her hot mouth on my breast. Her fingers searched for me and I tried to adjust to how quickly I'd gone from highway to heaven. "Have you missed me?" she asked as I pushed my body into her, so insane I couldn't remember my own name.

"Incredibly," I managed to whisper.

"Good, because you belong to me, and I want you to remember that. I just got out of the shower. Why don't you hop in and I'll be waiting for you right here." A seductive tone belied her functional intent that anything she put in her mouth would definitely be washed first—be it fruit or friend.

I broke free, dashed into the bathroom promising to be back in sixty seconds, stripped by the dim glow of the bathroom night-light, jumped into the two-by-two tin box, and cranked the rusty metal shower nozzle that squealed on my behalf as the ice-cold spray temporarily shocked all thoughts of sex right out of my brain. I immediately understood why Eskimos, obviously too cold to disrobe, only rubbed noses and undoubtedly adopted children from Brazil.

After jumping out and toweling off, I dove damp and naked into bed beside Callie.

"You smell great." Her warm arms around me, she picked up where she'd left off. I marveled at how good I felt every time she touched me and wondered if our lovemaking would always remain as intense and incredible as it was right now.

Suddenly my mind jumped its track and fixated on the idea that this would be the last woman I would ever touch like this—not that I wanted to touch another woman, not that Callie Rivers wasn't the most phenomenal lover on the planet, it was simply that this was… *it*, that moment when I'd gotten what I was looking for. I'd come to earth to find love and here it was and now it was done. The thought of my perpetual quest for love being done, over, finished made me break out in a sweat.

"Are you okay?" Callie whispered. "You're tense."

"Sorry," I breathed. "Must be flying down the highway all night, thinking I was about to be shot by an intruder, then jumping into an ice-cold shower."

"Clear your mind, darling." Callie kissed my closed eyes, down my nose, and onto my lips and suddenly, thankfully, I mentally re-engaged and slid my knee between her legs. Arms around me, she kissed me—that hot, wet, wild kiss that uncoupled all my synapses—the touching of tongues igniting a lust that began at my loins and exploded through me, an insane heat that would make me do anything, promise anything, searing common sense right out of me and soldering my soul to hers.

Our hearts beat in the same rhythm, our breathing simultaneous; wired and wanton she slid in and out of me in a rhythmic pulsing that increased in speed and intensity until I thought I would pass out from pleasure. Then, trembling, my body begged her to do it again. Sexually spent, I lay still, attempting to breathe as she gently stroked my chest and hips. "I think you missed me."

"I can see that you're very proud of yourself." I smiled, slowly rolling her onto her tummy as she protested, insisting I should relax and enjoy the feelings she'd created while I assured her there were other feelings I would find equally thrilling.

Straddling her back, I held her hips tightly between my knees and let my hands begin at the base of her head, massaging her delicate ears and beautiful neck muscles before straying briefly to brush my hand between her legs. Then on the way back up I squeezed the muscles in her arms and released them slowly, massaging down her spine, every bone, and intermittently stroking between her thighs, finally focusing on her small soft buttocks, massaging their round perfection with my right hand, while I slipped my left hand underneath her and performed a slowly orchestrated, erotic kneading.

Her body responded immediately, telling me she could only give in as I slid on top of her and inside her, pushing with my pelvis against her back with every stroke of my hand as she moaned and surrendered with one final thrust of her small and sensual body. Rolling off her, I lay by her side, loving her, I now believed, like I had never loved anyone.

"I want this every night," she whispered.

Dappled sunlight came through the window and for the first time I could see Callie clearly—her gorgeous blond hair in damp curls, her eyes dreamy, and her body thoroughly sated. She kissed me and clung to me.

"I swear I could stay like this for weeks and never sleep or eat," I whispered.

"We have to get Elmo. He's been in the car for over an hour, unless you've lost him."

"He needs a girlfriend." I sighed at having to leave. "I'll go get him and the luggage. Don't move. I want to come back to you exactly like this."

I got out of bed and grabbed my jeans off the rocking chair in the corner of the small bedroom as a dark figure whooshed past the window like a shadow, a person without form. I gasped and drew back.

"Someone's outside," I whispered and threw my clothes on as Callie reached for hers. "I don't think we locked the door." *I should be a hell of a lot smarter than that. What kind of crazy fool goes to a cabin in the woods and leaves the door unlocked? Someone who's in love*, I thought.

"There shouldn't be anybody around here. The cabins are all empty until midweek for Thanksgiving."

"Well, there is. *Damn, I left my gun in the other room.* I crept into the dark living room and groped from surface to surface until I felt the barrel of my .38, palmed it, headed for the back door, and swung it open, pinpoints of morning light penetrating the valley darkness. Seeing no one, I dashed for the car and clicked open the lock to check on Elmo, whose teeth were chattering.

"Relax, I'll be right back," I told him. Striding around the entire cabin, with the gun aimed midair, I searched for signs of humanity. When I panned down to the ground I spotted the fresh tracks. Large paw prints like those of a dog, but too big for anything but a wild animal.

"Teague, are you alright?" Callie stood on the porch above me.

"Check out the size of these prints." I pointed the flashlight at the ground only now beginning to take on light.

"Looks like a wolf," Callie said quietly.

"So you know what a wolf's paw prints look like, because I don't."

"Yes, a wolf." She stared into the woods but her mind had traveled much farther, searching the ethers for answers while I was left to examine the ground.

By now Callie's connection to the cosmos and the messages she received through some intergalactic-wireless-weirdness were almost routine to me. No longer shocked by her comments about messages she received from the dead or the near-dead, I accepted her and all she knew, felt, or divined.

I guess that means I'm finally ready for her. I thought about our very first meeting when she'd admitted we were destined for one another, but insisted I wasn't ready.

"Go back inside while I get Elmo. I don't want you wandering around with a wolf in the area."

Callie didn't obey, her antennae always up for signs she was being bossed, commanded, or diminished.

"Please, for me," I added quickly.

This time she stepped back inside the house and I went to the car, hooked Elmo up, and let him sniff around the pine needles and relieve himself before I unloaded the luggage. It only took me about ten minutes but Callie, unable to stay inside, was once again standing on the porch staring into the woods.

"In Native American cultures, the wolf often represents wisdom, death, dying, rebirth, and outwitting the enemy. It also confers the ability to pass unseen." Callie seemed to be remembering things she had heard long ago.

"Passing unseen worked for this one. So, based on the size of those tracks, the wolves here must get as large as bears."

"Wolves can be a totem—a personal-power animal for tribal people."

"Why are they roaming around at dawn instead of off getting a latte at the lake?" I said as I retrieved kindling from the cabin porch and carried it inside for a fire. Callie preceded me, holding the door open so I could make several trips.

I immediately located a small desk and hooked up my laptop, creating a space where I could work and see the creek; put a few bottles of wine in the small fridge, along with the cheese; then stacked crackers and other items I'd brought in the cabinet. I was happy to see Callie had already provisioned it; she was far smarter about what foods we needed to actually create a meal.

My idea of food was singular in nature: crackers I could eat out of a box, cheese I could slice and eat out of a package, or a frank I could eat wrapped in nearly anything that would bend and be digestible.

Callie's language about food always sounded less like eating and more like dating—broccoli *went with* cream sauce and *complemented* the filet, asparagus *picked up* salmon's flavor and could be *accompanied by* brown rice, and certain foods *could absolutely not go together* or the evening would be ruined. The whole idea made me smile, and I sneaked up behind Callie and kissed her on the neck.

"What are you smiling about?" She turned, giving me her full attention, and gazed into my eyes. "What were you doing right before you left L.A. to come here?"

Her intense focus took me by surprise. I froze. *Does she know about Barrett, has her cosmic connection kicked in? Maybe she mentally saw me with Barrett.*

"What do you mean?" I replied, aware I sounded guilty.

"Just that. You told me you had a meeting last night with Barrett about the script."

"I did meet her. We went to dinner just before I left to come be with you."

"Is she why you left L.A. early?"

"What do you mean?" I realized how completely stalling and stupid I sounded, but she'd caught me off guard. *She came at me obliquely, so she knows something's up.*

"This is a pivotal time for women, Teague. We have to be very careful. People will try to steal women's power."

I saw it first and, following my startled expression, Callie whirled in time to see it too—the shadow-shape flashing past the window despite the fact it was morning now. Its timing was bone-chilling as we spoke about danger to women, but my salvation because it obliterated the Barrett topic.

Reaching again for my .38 on the desk, I swung the door open suddenly and almost tripped over the newspaper, which made me relax. *Newspaper boy,* I thought, not wanting to find danger lurking in this quiet town at a time when I was focused on my lover and my work. The shadow was obviously benign and merely associated with the delivery of a morning rag with a masthead reading *The Sedona Sands.*

Callie took it from me, rummaging through its pages while answering my other questions about who owned this cabin and how she'd found out about it, explaining that she'd rented it from a woman she'd met one summer who now lived near the reservation.

From where I was standing I could see the picture in the newspaper: a crime scene with police standing around some shrubbery next to a cliff, torn pieces of material on one of the bushes, and an inset photo of a wolf's head. The headline read WOLF KILLING STILL MYSTERY.

I leaned in to read the body copy about the possibility of wolves roaming the area in packs and residents who insisted they weren't taking out the trash at night without toting a gun. There were other quotes from animal-rights activists who insisted that stories like these turned people against perfectly peaceful animals who were already endangered due to overdevelopment of their native habitat.

Callie looked perplexed and finally said, "Women are under attack from men, not wolves—"

"And you know that because—"

"I feel it."

I tapped the inset photo of the wolf's paw print. "As much fun as it is to blame things on guys, I don't know any whose feet are triangular with four toes." But Callie was preoccupied and went to the computer she'd set up on the countertop, its surface made from a long, lacquered split log. The counter separated the kitchen from the large main room whose floors were six-inch planks of darkened wood worn smooth from decades of boots scraping across them.

Slivers of light sliced through the panes in the big wooden window casings, defying the orange burlap draperies. The invading ribbons of light wrapped around me and across the burnt-orange leather couch and armchair and splayed across the arrowhead-shaped slats of a weatherworn oak rocker that had most likely set the tempo for more leisurely days.

"Are you looking at an astrology chart, because every time you look at the planets my love life goes south."

"I'm looking up wolves. Did you know they can travel twenty miles a day searching for food?"

"I do that when I leave the Valley to eat in Bev Hills," I said, kissing her to distract her.

"And their jaws exert 1500 pounds of pressure per square inch so that they can break open the bones of large animals and eat their marrow."

"I *don't* do that. I don't even like to take a nutcracker to a lobster claw."

From her expression, I could tell Callie was about to chastise me for constantly horsing around, but before she could deliver the message, my cell phone rang and I answered to Barrett Silvers's voice.

For the first time since I'd known Callie, I felt like I was sneaking around on her. I had nothing to hide but, because I feared Callie thought I was concealing something, I began behaving as if I had something to cover up, and before I knew it, I was code-talking.

"Hi. Good. Same here. Yep. Safe trip. Good. Really. I'll start work tomorrow and let you know." My words came out cryptically, and I sounded, even to me, like I was in covert activities for the CIA. When I hung up, Callie was staring at me with a questioning look—the kind that asked if I had anything I'd like to share.

"Barrett Silvers wanting to know if I'd gotten here and if I'd started writing."

"Doesn't sound like strictly business," she said as a statement of fact, then picked up the newspaper and headed for the deck.

"Damn," I groaned softly. "Look," I began as I blocked her path to the porch, "Barrett's a very strange woman and she has the hots for every writer she works with and I'm simply another writer she'd love to screw if she could but—"

"You've forgotten I'm psychic."

"Your being psychic is irrelevant because I didn't sleep with her."

"Did you have any sexual contact with her?"

As I was about to deny I had, my mind flashed on Bill Clinton when his squirming psyche, bad timing, and the need for an immediate response forced him to utter those infamous words, "I never had sexual relations with that woman." I felt empathy for Bill.

If I could have Tivoed the entire Barrett telephone scene, I would have been able to point out to myself that cryptic phone conversations could only result in my ending up like horny politicians. From Callie's expression, I intuited that the only acceptable cryptic phone conversation might be to tell a neighbor her house was on fire or to give quick instructions on how to staunch bleeding. Otherwise, I had better talk long enough for Callie to determine what I was talking to another woman about. Her obvious jealousy seemed out of character for a psychic woman whose desire to be with me had seemed, from the beginning, intermittent at best.

"This is so unlike you," I said, remembering the best defense is a good offense.

"No, it's exactly like me. You've asked me to commit to you, so I'm asking you how truthful you've been."

At that moment I realized, for me, truth came in Starbucks' sizes. I could serve up a tall truth—"She likes me." Grande truth—"She kissed me." Or venti truth—"She fucked me." I couldn't go venti; the words wouldn't come out of my mouth.

As if saved by the gods, I heard a knock at the door and we both turned and looked toward the sound, then at one another as Callie opened the door. Standing in the doorway was a tall, broad-shouldered woman of indeterminate age, with long straight hair that flowed over her right shoulder like black, silky fringe.

Wearing deerskin pants, a pelt slung serape-style over one shoulder, and an array of interesting teeth and feathers strung around her neck and down to her waist where a knife with a bone handle was stashed in a scabbard hanging off a braided leather belt, she reminded me that I hadn't seen anyone dressed like that since Scout Cloud Lee appeared on *Survivor*. The woman in our doorway was pretty hot looking in a woodsy kind of way, charismatically exotic due in part to the long, straight Cher-hair.

"You knew to arrive early," the Indian woman said.

"I felt you calling me," Callie said softly.

That remark stuck in my head like an arrow as I stepped forward to ask who she was and what she wanted, but Callie added, "How have you been?"

The long figure seemed riveted on her.

"There are problems..." She glanced at me and became silent.

"Come inside," Callie said, and I felt as if I wasn't even in the room with the two of them.

"You will come to the ceremony tonight," the woman stated rather than asked, not offering to take off her pelt, which I assumed was the equivalent of an overcoat, but then who knew.

"I ..." Callie paused, uncomfortable, and for the first time they both looked back at me, the Indian woman not moving or offering to introduce herself, Callie finally taking charge of the formalities.

"Teague." She waved me forward. "This is the woman whose cabin we're renting—my spiritual teacher from summers ago. She is Manaba, some call her Shaman. She is a spiritual healer trained under her powerful grandmother, Eyota, a Navajo elder."

Manaba nodded and I did the same. She took her eyes from me, as if not only through with me for the moment, but perhaps for an entire lifetime, and locked her gaze back on Callie.

"Tonight, dusk, the ceremonial ground."

Callie pursed her lips almost imperceptibly, seeming to indicate she understood.

Pausing as if wanting to say something more, Manaba suddenly changed her mind, turned, and left.

Callie stayed at the door with her back to me for a good ten seconds, the energy between them obvious from the way their eyes engaged and their bodies threw off electricity. To say I didn't like what I saw was an understatement. I didn't like anyone but me sending sparks Callie's way.

"You have a connection with Barrett," she said, not bothering to face me, seeming to reside in my head these days, refuting what I had never said aloud.

It's fine for me to have a connection with Barrett because it means nothing, but I don't want you having a relationship with anyone but me.

"Male view," she said quietly about my thoughts.

"So tell me more about LaBamba," I said, intentionally twisting her name.

"Manaba. It's Navajo, meaning 'Returns to War.'"

"She's going to have war alright if she keeps looking at you like that." I made a mental note that the shaman wasn't getting near Callie.

Chapter Three

"So what did she *teach*?" I asked casually, instead of what I really wanted to know—namely why the fuck Pocahontas was staring at my lover as if she were corn pudding.

"Energy flow and creating a balance between the land and its people. She's unique, like the Berdache, transvestite males valued as spiritual leaders and recognized for their wisdom and nurturing."

"Manaba is a transvestite?"

"Teague, do you always have to snatch key words out of our conversations and create your own meaning, or could you listen to the entire paragraph?"

"Sorry, not trained in paragraphs, proceed."

"Manaba is not a transvestite, to my knowledge," Callie said, clearly trying to regain her composure. "Navajo Berdache tradition was made up of people who were both male and female by nature, and they were awarded an elevated status in their people's culture. We don't know very much about Native American lesbian culture, but I was making the point that with Manaba's talent and the respect her people have for her, she might be *likened* to the Berdache."

"Oh," I said, slightly hurt by her criticism. "So how did you meet the shaman?"

"I attended a workshop on Navajo culture, and a young Native American woman told me about Manaba and introduced me to her. I spent time studying under her."

"Literally?" I couldn't keep the snide tone out of my voice.

"Why don't we make a pact not to quiz each other about our sexual past?"

"So your past with her was sexual?" My ears were getting hot and I was instantly jealous.

"Let's enjoy the present." Callie kissed me so impulsively she knocked the attitude right out of me, a wanton, feral kiss that made me grateful for whatever had made her this sexual in the present.

Nonetheless, I was suspicious of the timing: was she really this hot for me, or had seeing Manaba made her hot and I happened to be handy, or was she faking hot like a red herring to get my mind off the idea of her being with Manaba? Having personally done all three of those things in other relationships, I was on the lookout for them, despite being aware that the guilty almost always accuse the innocent.

About the time I decided to erase the brain cells of my mental blackboard and focus on lovemaking with Callie, she pulled back. "You need to start writing. That's what this trip is all about. You have deadlines."

"We could continue this in the bedroom and then I could write."

"Sexual tension will make your writing better."

"Then I should be Hemingway," I groaned, pulled away reluctantly, and headed for the computer. Accessing my documents I found the file entitled *The Coming Out of Mrs. Carmichael* and began typing the opening scene where Angelique, the young novice, is on her knees confessing her sin of sexual desire.

She tells the priest she knows it's not right and maybe it's because she's away from home and lonely, and she intends, before God, to spend more time at her work, counseling those who need to find salvation, and less time contemplating foolish thoughts. The priest tells her she has sinned, but God will forgive all sin confessed with a true heart, and he gives her a penance of fifty Hail Marys.

The novice crosses herself and leaves the chapel, nearly colliding with a woman fifteen years her senior, looking frail and tired, but beautiful beneath the scarf tied around her head. The woman, her taut, anxious expression indicating she is searching for something, asks the novice to help her, saying her mother has sent her to get counseling because she has an ongoing problem with her husband—she doesn't want to satisfy his needs.

It was dusk before I looked up from the computer and saw Callie lounging on the couch staring at me, Elmo stretched out beside her, having taken my place. His big jowls on her clean shirt, a fact she'd chosen to ignore, demonstrated her love for the lightly snoring hound. I ran my hands through my hair and smiled at her.

"Good start," I said of my efforts and read her several pages from the screenplay.

"You shouldn't have the novice cross herself—it means she's placing a burden on herself. Crosses carry sadness and—"

"Cal, she's a mother inferior. She's got to cross herself, it's required," I said somewhat crossly.

"Whatever." Callie gave up, not caring about a fictional character burdened by religious luggage. "You've been writing for hours. How about a break?"

"Depends on the kind." Stiff and cramped from sitting so long, I got up and went over to the couch and carefully helped Elmo down, then crawled in beside her. "Is it an exercise break, or a food break, or..." I rubbed my fingers across her breasts, "a lovemaking break?"

"It's a we're-leaving-the-cabin break. I want to take you with me to the ceremony on the red rocks tonight."

"You mean with Manaba Sasquatch?"

"Don't use derogatory terms about women. She doesn't invite many people outside of her students to the ceremony."

"And she's remained true to that, since she only invited you and not me."

"She invited us both."

"No, she didn't, but that's okay. Let's go." I shrugged, trying to hide the fact that I was jealous of a woman who looked like she shopped at a tannery and whose jewelry implied she'd had a head-on collision with a very large bird.

I placed a dog bone next to Elmo's flattened jowls, pressed wide by the wooden floor, and whispered, "In case you wake up hungry." I kissed him good-bye.

❖

Driving through the red canyons, I marveled at the rock walls' mesmerizing patterns, colors, and petrified swirls, demonstrating that forces much larger than man had been at work in heaven's basin for centuries. The wind whispered past the rock striations that marked a time when the water rose halfway up their stony faces, and rays from the setting sun hit jagged angles of the cliffs, creating dramatic shards of shadow and light, a reminder that we were but a grain of sand in the cosmic picture.

Twenty minutes south of town, tall rock plateaus, scattered among sage and sand, beckoned the faithful to red-rock climb. Farther on and a quarter of a mile down, where nothing lay but a trail of loose red dirt, the true natives were trekking toward the mesa that bulged out of the orange moonscape ahead of us.

I parked the car and locked it, taking a bottle of drinking water for us, and we headed toward the plateau.

"In the middle of these three mesas is a powerful Indian vortex. Supposedly the natives climbed the mesas and looked down on the sacred ground below and offered up their prayers to the gods," Callie said over her shoulder.

"The climbing part's the killer piece."

"The energy of this place was so intense that tribes traveled for days to scale the rocks and worship here, but they wouldn't stay after dark."

"And we're going up here after dark because…?" I asked nervously.

"Because we are gods too." Callie smiled at me in her enigmatic way, and for a moment, staring at her phenomenal shock of blond hair and her exquisitely carved features, I thought she was a goddess and I was her follower. Much like the Japanese boy trailing his pretty counterpart at the restaurant, I tagged along obediently as Callie scampered up the gradual incline.

As rock became ground and the incline steeper, it was apparent that no path existed up this rocky ceremonial slope, only tiny footholds carved out by the shoes of other climbers more skilled than I. After several minutes, I stopped to breathe and made the mistake of looking down.

"This is worse than flying! One wrong step and we're toast."

"Always look up." Her warning held true for much of life, and she extended her hand. I refused to take it, afraid I would make her lose her balance in the gathering darkness.

"Keep your hands on the rocks," I warned. "I'm right behind you."

Moments later the footpath began to widen and level out, and I relaxed for the remainder of the walk to a large flat area. A series of medium-sized stones delineated a circle about forty feet in diameter with a bonfire in the center, small bundles of what appeared to be herbs lying beside the fire, and a painting I couldn't quite decipher drawn in the sand.

"I think this will be a Holyway to restore health, or an Evilway."

"Which I assume wards off evil, which you don't believe in, so this could be only an exercise in rock climbing," I muttered as Callie approached the circle and sat on the outer edge of the wheel facing north and pulled me gently down beside her.

The darkness folded in on us and none of the women, most of whom appeared to be Native American, seemed to feel the need for introductions.

"So is any food served…" I asked, and she gave me a look that I was pretty sure said she hoped I was kidding. "Well, how would I know?"

"Breathe deeply," Callie ordered softly, and I took in three large breaths, which relaxed me to the point of yawning.

I was able to gaze over the northern vista and marvel at what I was seeing. The darkness removed all illusion of depth, erasing the valley below and pulling the white clouds through the sky as if on strings, making them almost appear eye level, revealing the world according to eagles. The sky seemed as close as an old friend, the night like a soft black blanket on my shoulders, and the heat from the fire a mother's loving arms. In that moment, I saw and embraced the night sky the Native Americans knew.

A rhythmic drumbeat began, and a sound equivalent in pitch and texture to a hundred rattles filled the air while the women chanted what sounded like a blessing. Their voices rose and fell amid the roar and crackle of the fire, the wind shifted, and a wide veil of smoke drifted in our direction, creating strange images. The north wind caught the smoke and made it look like a huge bear rushing at me; then a horizontal gust strung the smoke out like taffy into an ephemeral band that looked like a flowing stream, and finally a new puff of smoke behind it and a wolf's head emerged—kaleidoscopic desert imagery.

Suddenly Manaba appeared in the fire—not by the fire, or near the fire, but *in* the fire—standing there full form and calm and as real as Callie next to me. The flames encircled her, the embers glowed under her shoes, the smoke caressed her. Callie restrained me to keep me from jumping to her rescue.

Her voice was strong and rhythmic and hypnotic, and I heard the drumbeat gather force and become fierce for the first time. The sound of something like rain rattles jigging to the rhythm of the drum grew louder, and Callie whispered that Manaba was asking for protection.

After a long time had passed, words that sounded like *Sa'ah naaghéi, Bik'eh hózh* filled the air, and Callie explained that if the ceremony had left out anything, saying these words was like errors-and-omissions insurance.

A second drumming seemed to kick off prayers for the Native American woman who was killed by the wolf.

"Did Manaba know the woman who was killed?" I asked Callie.

"Her name is Nizhoni."

"I think I drank something that sounded like that at the Japanese restaurant." At Callie's disapproving look I added, "I'm not kidding. It means *saki* or something like that."

"*Nizhoni* means beautiful."

The drumbeat grew louder, and the twenty or so women around the fire rose as if on cue and formed the Indian version of a line dance, stomping and chanting in ritual lockstep that picked up in speed and intensity. Then Manaba pulled Callie into the smoke and danced with her—an erotic dance that made a seamless piece of their bodies.

Rising to separate them, I was jealous that Callie would dance with someone other than me, aware that the two of us had never danced together and feeling even angrier that the first time I saw her dance was with Manaba. Then Callie tugged my arm, pulling me back to a sitting position, and I realized she was beside me, dancing with no one.

"Were you up there for a moment, dancing with her?"

"Not in a real sense, it's spiritual."

"I think she's after you."

"She's calling on me to be one with her search."

"Yeah, well, I don't like what she's searching for, which I think is you," I said, sounding like some grumbling husband with a limited vocabulary.

Bright lights swung across us like search beams and the drumbeat slapped to a hard stop, the rattles dopplered into silence, and the dancers wandered off away from the circle as a four-wheel-drive vehicle slowly inched its way up the southern edge of the plateau. My mind grappled with how a car got up a hill so steep it challenged a jackrabbit.

A short, wiry cowboy of a man in his late sixties stepped out of the SUV and strolled over to the fire where the dancers were breaking up.

Tipping his hat to Manaba, he said, "Saw the fire and wanted to make sure you women were safe up here, particularly after the wolf killing. Former Senator Cy Blackstone." He introduced himself to a seemingly disinterested woman attired in Navajo dress, before attempting to take Manaba's hand in a gentlemanly gesture, but Manaba stepped back from him.

He had his cowboy hat pushed back on his head, so the light from the fire caught the craggy folds of his leathery face and a set jaw that bespoke a resolve about life that neither reason nor affection could overcome. His jeans tight fitting, belt buckle flashing silver in the flames, and his black ostrich boots dusty but new, he was a crossover cowboy—the kind who could push cattle or congressmen, rope steers or statesmen—a comfort cowboy who rode the range in a Range Rover.

"Now that the woman…" he paused to glance around him before continuing "…was given a decent burial, I could sure use a favor."

Manaba's face revealed nothing. In fact, if you were looking for evidence that she knew him, had expected him, hadn't expected him, disliked him, or loved him, it was a dry hole. Nonetheless, he seemed undeterred as he kicked up the dirt with his toe and ducked his head, not unlike a schoolboy thinking of asking a girl to dance.

"Lotta the natives think this deal is like last time and they're spooked, not wantin' to show up at the site. You go on camera and talk, it'd settle things down. Hell, even the whites are sayin' that your grandma's callin' the wolf down on 'em. Mall means a lot of jobs—jobs for Indians too. You think about it. In light of what you and me are tryin' to do, you give it some extra thought. It's important to our protecting people you care about. Protection is the key to freedom—ask any dating boy."

He chuckled and cast his eyes around the circle at the women. "Didn't mean to interrupt." His tone said the opposite. In fact he'd probably made a special trip up here to interrupt and, beyond that, even delighted in interrupting. The sly way he sank into his own hip, pulled his hat back down over the ridge of his brow, and spat into the fire, the sacred fire, spoke all anyone needed to hear.

"Well, night, Ms. Manaba," he called over his shoulder with a laugh, as if stringing Ms. and Manaba together was funny, and kept on talking as he walked. "Oh." He stopped and turned back in bad Columbo style, acting as if he'd thought of something. "You decided where you're gonna be movin' your meetings? Mall construction's going to be coming right up here pretty quick. This is going to make a beautiful restaurant, don't you think? People dining and looking out over this cliff. They'll be standing in line for days. Progress, Manaba, progress. If we live long enough, we collide with it. I hope all you ladies will take care and enjoy your evening."

Manaba stared at him, muttering something I imagined was designed to turn him into a toad.

Callie intercepted him. “Mr. Blackstone, did anyone ever find the wolf’s body?”

“And who are you, other than a mighty attractive woman?” He touched his hat.

“Callie Rivers.”

“Don’t know the answer to that, Ms. Rivers, except a drop like that probably flattened him out like a prairie pancake—might not have been much to find.”

“So did anyone actually witness the attack?” I asked.

He looked at Manaba for a moment and then turned back to us. “Don’t know that either.” He tipped his hat to her and then to several other women standing nearby before getting behind the wheel, making a U-turn, and driving down the backside of the cliff.

“Why didn’t you tell me this cliff was drivable?”

“Because it’s mostly for jeep tours,” Callie replied.

“Hello, I have a Jeep.” My voice rose.

“Part of the ritual is to climb the face of the rock like the ancestors,” she said as our eyes were simultaneously drawn to the tall, broad-shouldered Manaba, her back to us as she stood overlooking the cliff, watching the SUV drive away.

The wind whipped around her shoulders, her long black hair as captivating as the tail of a wild mustang, her leather trappings billowing away from her body. I had never seen such pride and strength and old world power all in one place. If on top of all that, she was spiritual and cosmic and otherworldly, and Callie was attracted to her, then as the country singer said, I hated her and I’d think of a reason later.

It crossed my mind that I didn’t like Blackstone much either. “The senator gives me the creeps,” I said.

Callie seemed to be only half listening and broke away, striding toward Manaba. With the wind picking up in the opposite direction, I could hear only fragments of the conversation as Callie and Manaba exchanged words that seemed to drift from inquiring and responding to something short of arguing.

“What do you want me to do?” Callie asked her.

“Unearth the truth,” Manaba replied.

Then suddenly the discussion was over, both turning and striding away, the duel aborted, or so it appeared.

The ceremonial dancers dispersed and Callie and I clambered down the steep slope to our car, slipping here and there despite the moonlit night as we clung to each other. She was intense and preoccupied, but I was inexplicably exhilarated by the night air and the dancing. Once inside the car, I was so hot I rolled the windows down and sat in the cool breeze, catching my breath.

"So what deity were they dancing to up there?" I panted as I slumped back against the seat.

"They pray to the earth, the plants, the animals. Their religion is the act of being one with all things—staying in balance with nature and the creator."

"I like that," I said, contemplating the simplicity of seeing the ground and all it grew and supported as holy.

"The Navajo people live amid the four sacred mountains stretching from Colorado to New Mexico and Arizona, and they believe they have always lived here and must never leave."

"Is that what Manaba was telling you?" I asked, knowing it wasn't, but not wanting to come right out and express my jealousy again.

"She believes her ancestors will answer her call for help, but she's also asking me to help her fight a force as powerful as she."

"Sounds like a comic-book plot: us against the forces of evil. Besides, why does someone with her power need yours?"

"She may believe that she's lost hers."

"Looks to me like all her powers are working. How did she learn to stand in the flames like that without burning her ass off?"

"Mind over matter. Believe you're protected and you will be."

"So her mind pulled you into the flames with her?"

"It's only a ritual—joining me with her needs."

"I don't like the way she looks at you. I want to be the only one who looks at you like that. Of course I know I can't control other people's looks—short of killing them—which may be why I'm so—I don't know—insanely jealous."

"I didn't like what I saw between you and Barrett over dinner," she said softly, and there she was again admitting a cosmic wiretap into my evening with Barrett and confessing her jealousy like any ordinary lover laying claim to her territory. I could have sworn she demanded I tell her everything, although the words never came from her lips. Nonetheless, I began confessing like a televangelist with his advertisers pulling out.

"She attacked me," I said, using the dialogue I'd rehearsed with Elmo. My mind wanted to spin it, but Callie meant so much to me—*I can't keep giving her partial truths if we're going to live together*—and before I could stop myself I went venti, in a few tawdry sentences revealing everything from Barrett's touching me to the frightening fish-panty episode and the paramedics' arrival.

Callie was silent. *I* was silent, realizing once again my future with her might be in jeopardy. Trying to maintain some bravado and minimize the impact, I said, "You claimed you saw it anyway so why make me tell it. It was horrible."

"I see images, get feelings, pieces here and there, not everything blow by blow."

And like that time in Vegas when I told Callie's dad I'd rather sleep with her than eat, I'd said too much. "What about you and the smoke dancer?"

But Callie wasn't receptive to a redirection of the conversation, and we rode in silence—so much silence that a black hole would have sounded like a rock concert compared to the lack of sound between us.

As if I could read her mind, I believed she wanted to know why under pressure I delayed the truth, or only partially revealed it, or worse, might think it overrated.

If I thought about it, my cop training valued one-way truth. If I had to lie to get a perp to confess, the truth was I did a good job. If I had to dodge the truth to protect my cop buddies, the truth was I could be trusted. If I was sleeping with two women and neither of them knew about the other, the truth was I was under a lot of pressure and simply behaving like one of the guys. Truth was subjective.

❖

Back home, we moved about the cabin as if the cord between us had been severed irreparably. My truth and Callie's truth were not aligned. Mine consisted of shades of gray, it was truth I could spin, it was an artful truth, while Callie's was naïvely, overtly crystalline, the opposite of black, the prism through which she viewed, perhaps secretly judged, every person, every action, every essence of life.

Before she could head for the bedroom, I blocked her with my body and grabbed her arm to stop her and force a discussion. "Look, I'm sorry if I—"

"It's all energy, Teague. Truth is energy. You have to keep it pure."

"You can't live that purely, Callie, no one can."

"I have to live the truth and only add things to my life that enhance it."

"Then I don't know if you want to add me," I said truthfully and walked into the bedroom feeling hollow. I lay down on the box-spring mattress whose creaking coils now sounded forlorn, like a lone clarinet at the end of a New Orleans funeral after all the mourners have been paid; and I looked up at the ceiling and contemplated this strange crossroads in our relationship, brought on by something as seemingly esoteric as the energy of truth.

Chapter Four

Whoever said the truth hurts had it right. Callie slept on the edge of the bed, our bodies never touching, which took real effort since the old cabin mattress was so narrow. She was up at dawn and moved about the cabin as if I were a shadow, paying little attention to me, and I wasn't quite certain why.

Was she deciding if she could accept me as I was? Was she thinking of ways to tell me good-bye? Or was she simply mad that I'd occasionally been less than truthful with her? I was on the lookout for Callie's discovery that I was short-term fun with no long-term benefit.

I took Elmo for a walk, dog walking I imagined being what every lover on the planet did when she wanted to avoid a fight, or rehearse what she'd say in the inevitable upcoming fight, or pray that maybe the fight, like a pugilistic Passover, would somehow leave her door unmarked.

"I didn't get to check in with you last night," I said to Elmo. "My evening didn't go very well. The whole Burrett thing resurfaced like a dead body on the beach, and Callie was as pissed as any non-psychic woman I've ever dated. I think her feelings are hurt. So how did your night go?"

He walked in total silence, giving me nothing.

"Aw, come on, don't you start. Remember that talk about the aisle? Well, I'm not really aisled yet. She's toyed with me and told me I'm not ready, and said I had a lot to learn, and on and fucking on. And now suddenly at this moment, on this trip, she's decided somewhere back in time I was already totally hers, and that I've fucked up and been unfaithful, and that furthermore I spin the truth and have bad energy, or something close to that."

Elmo gave me a look that could only be described as a glower.

"Fine," I said with sarcasm. "You always take her side. Keep it up and dog biscuits will be a thing of the past."

He suddenly broke loose, ripping the leash from my hand, and raced up the cabin steps and banged into the screen door, reminding me that I could do a lot of things to him, but he would not tolerate threats. Callie opened the door for him and by the time I entered, they had disappeared into the bedroom, apparently allied in their determination to hide from the energy of threats and lies.

I went to the computer and started working on the script, trying to focus on something other than this rift in my relationship with Callie. The thing I loved about writing was its ability to take me to another place when the place I was in was uncomfortable or unavoidable or both. Buried in words I could lose all track of time and forfeit the need for food or companionship. Writing, like lovemaking, was all passion and focus, and that's what I needed right now—and maybe it would even be what Jeremy Jacowitz wanted.

By the time I took a break it was getting dark and I was about seventy-five pages in—not polished pages but first-draft pages—when out of the corner of my eye I noticed Elmo fretting and pacing. Not the kind of pacing that meant he needed a walk, but the kind that said something was wrong. Sounds were emanating from the bedroom, moans and whimpers, and I rushed in to see what was wrong.

Standing in the doorway, I didn't know what to make of what I was seeing. Callie was stretched out on the bed, her body moving as if aroused, as if I were there on top of her, but her face was wrenched in terror. Her hips undulated but her hands pushed off something in the air above her, the hair on her head pulled straight up, electrified, as if someone had hands on it. The room felt like it was filled with sparks, the air ionized as if in an electrical storm. A wind whipped around the room, its source invisible, and I was frozen, frightened, unable to move until Elmo's squeaks set me in motion, and I literally leapt into bed beside her. Then I really felt it—an electricity, a hair-raising sensation on my neck and arms that could only be described as an energy field, a powerful pulsing tide. Caught in the waves with her, I struggled to remain on the bed.

"Callie." I pulled her into my arms and now both of us were being rocked. Then, as if someone shut off the breaker, I sagged into her. Having something substantial to grapple with, rather than the mere air above her head, she pushed me away as if I were the cause of whatever was happening to her and began to cry.

"Stop it. Wake up, Callie. Talk to me!"

Her eyes snapped open and she seemed disoriented. "How long have you been here?"

"I heard you moaning and…"

She sat up in bed and hugged her bent knees in a seated fetal position, looking embarrassed and vulnerable and shook up.

"I need to take a shower," she said suddenly, jumping up and hurrying into the bathroom. Hearing the water running, I waited on the edge of the bed, not knowing what to do and worried something was wrong with Callie that I was now discovering something disturbing.

"Thanks for letting me know," I told Elmo, and he pressed his warm and heavy fur suit against my leg.

Callie was out of the bathroom and into her flannel nightshirt in minutes.

"Were you dreaming? What happened? Your body looked like…like you were making love, but your face looked like you were fighting off a killer."

"It was an attack," she said flatly, sounding almost irritated with me for asking, and I didn't have a clue what to ask next. I must have looked hurt because she put her arms around me. "Someone wanting to steal my energy, suppress and frighten me."

"Someone like a real person?" My head was reeling. Maybe this was why Callie Rivers had parked her sexuality for so many years; maybe this was why she was obsessed with energy.

"Someone with the ability to travel mentally, energetically, out of body," she explained.

"Sorry, but you're going to have to go slower. This is freaking me out. Ghosts were one thing but now a ball of energy?"

"In its simplest form."

I said nothing, trying to think, but I couldn't grasp a traveling, woman-attacking energy.

"There are energy thieves in everyday life, Teague. People who drain you physically and emotionally. An extreme example of that is an attempted rape."

"You were raped?"

"Someone was trying to sexually assault me energetically, which is nothing more than a person without the physical body present. It's hard for someone to shut down my physical form, because I'm so aware. Attacking me on a different plane was another way of trying to take my power, frighten me, when I was asleep and vulnerable."

"Who is it?" I was horrified by the idea and furious someone would attempt to harm her in any way, even ways that seemed crazy to me. "Is it Manaba, because I'll yank the feathers right off her raven head!"

"Never Manaba. She obeys the cosmic laws and would never be part of that kind of imbalance. It's not the Navajo way and it's not in the Navajo heart. She's a spiritual leader."

Something in her tone and protectiveness of Manaba angered me. "I'm not real clear on spiritual leaders. There's one in Rome wearing a dress and fabulous jewelry, some guy in India wearing diapers and sitting on a mountaintop, a guy in China trying to turn himself into a single drop of rain, and then there's your Indian woman who binds her butt in buffalo briefs and dances in the fire."

"Is it the dress code that bothers you?" Callie said in a tone that seemed more reprimand than question.

"No," I replied, defiant and not giving in on this one. "It's a matter of a pure heart and who really has one. I haven't figured that out yet."

Elmo's ears elevated off his head about two inches, and he launched his loose fur suit at gator-speed into the main room and let out a chest-deep bark that made my heart jump. Grabbing the gun and a flashlight from the bedside table, I went out the door, making sure Elmo stayed inside to avoid his putting his nose to the ground and never being found again or killed and eaten by something with a paw print the size of a butter plate.

Taking the porch steps in two jumps, I landed on the ground, pointing my gun with my right hand and shining the light with the left. As if the light had been magnetized to its source, the beam landed directly on the largest fur face I'd ever seen outside of the Discovery Channel. A huge wolf—standing so close the vertical slits in its glistening eyeballs looked like coin slots, its teeth bared, poised to lunge and most likely rip me to pieces—glared at me as the door clicked open behind me. Without looking at Callie or taking my eyes off the wolf, I ordered her back into the cabin.

"Don't kill it!" she warned, running to my side. "Teague, put the gun down." Her hand rested on my forearm and I couldn't believe what she was saying. As if the wolf knew her, it stopped snarling and stood as relaxed as a dog.

I stared into the calm animal's eyes and a chill traversed my arms and across my shoulders and down my thighs. The eyes were human; I would bet my life on it. In fact, by dropping the gun to my side, I had. The soul behind the eyes of this wolf was more human than people I'd known, and I stared, mesmerized.

"Go in peace," Callie murmured, and the animal moved its head in a way that could only be described as acknowledgement. Then, as if mission accomplished, it turned and sauntered back into the woods.

Breath left my body in one relieved and explosive burst. "Holy shit!"

In the clearing to our left, as if beamed in from outer space, Manaba appeared, or had been there all along and we hadn't noticed her. This time, Callie, seemingly nervous, stood close to me as Manaba took two steps toward her, and Callie put her arm around my waist, perhaps for protection.

"She's not doing anything to get herself in any more danger," I interjected.

"Danger exists. We merely walk into its energy field and join it." She addressed me but kept her eyes on Callie.

"You have the more powerful medicine," Callie whispered.

"But it has been unbalanced," she said, not waiting for further discussion, and disappeared as the wolf had.

"You and I need to talk, and that's an understatement," I said, but Callie was already heading up the porch steps. I made one sweep of the area where the wolf had appeared before I followed her inside.

"Okay, you're telling me somebody's energy tried to rape you, then a wolf appears that I believe is going to eat me for dinner and it turns out he knows you and likes you, and then Manaba, who definitely knows you and likes you, comes out of nowhere and demands help. What the hell's going on?"

Callie said nothing and went into the bedroom and lay down on the bed as if meditating.

"Manaba obviously knows about the attempted rape because she showed up right after it happened. How would she know unless she was involved?"

"Intense energy can be felt by those who are sensitive to it."

"Mind if I have a glass of wine?"

I left the bedroom and headed for the kitchen, needing time to think and, frankly, a diversion to allow me to hide my feelings from Callie. *Was she totally fucking bonkers? I'd bought into the astrology, and the animal conversations, and even the ghosts, but now she wanted me to believe that...what? A ball of rape energy was loosed on her?*

"I'm sorry you saw it," she said, appearing suddenly behind me and seeming to understand how this was perhaps one of the hardest elements of her life for me to witness.

I poured a glass for myself and she refused one. I plopped down on the couch, propped my feet up on the coffee table made from a tree stump, and said, "Shoot."

She pulled up an astrological chart on her computer, and my thought process was so overloaded with insane ideas that I welcomed something relatively harmless, like checking out the planets.

"What are you looking for?" I asked, trying to control my internal sarcasm and becoming more respectful of her, which she appreciated because she suddenly put her arm around me as I stood beside her. I melted into her, grateful for her touch.

"I told you when you arrived that this was a dangerous time for women—Mars conjunct Uranus in Aquarius squaring Venus in Scorpio—that we would be under attack. It's in the stars right now. Perhaps this person is trying to drive me away from here because he or she knows Manaba is seeking my help. This attacker is someone very powerful in the psychic world, someone who can attack with more force than anyone could muster in the flesh. I'm grateful you came into the room and disrupted the energy."

"And if I hadn't?"

"It would have left me as violated as if it had been a physical person."

"But what if it happens again, how do I protect you from... energy?"

"Everything is energy, Teague. Accept it, work with it. How you direct energy and redirect it and block it or absorb it is how you move through the world healthy or unhealthy."

When I was in police work, I was accustomed to attempted rapes and animal attacks, but not by people I couldn't see and wild animals who were really people. Callie would say no more about the energy field, but she did seem uncomfortable, as if holding something back. I wasn't in the mood to let anything ride.

"So what's the energy between you and Manaba? Even I can feel that."

"Manaba and I were once very connected spiritually." Pause. "We've had what you might call...a cerebral affair," Callie said, taking my fear and frustration to a higher level.

"A cerebral affair? Is that like you mentally wanted to sleep with her, but you didn't because you were too busy thinking about it?"

"It's more like a very elevated version of a romantic friendship."

"Which is what women had in the 1800s—the hots for each other but fought it for economic reasons."

"Love is intensely aligned energies, and our mental energy was intense...sort of a melding of our minds."

I was getting more pissed and hurt by the minute, and tired of what I considered esoteric bullshit.

"Mind fucking is what I call it. It goes from fucking someone in your mind to, hey, would you mind fucking? So if you're so hot for this, this—" I was searching for the most scathingly negative word I could find because Callie's having a Vulcan mind meld with anyone made me insane, and I started to tear up.

"It's over," Callie said. "And I didn't have to tell you."

"Hey, I always appreciate the truth," I said, giving her a small dig for constantly goading me about truth. "Don't you think I could see it? When she first saw you she was salivating all over her muskrat moccasins."

"I didn't know you then," Callie said, ignoring my fashion barbs.

"I'm referring to now." And I stormed off, mentally analyzing if I'd had virtual sex, cerebral sex, or any other kind of non-touch sex with anyone in my life and concluded I hadn't. *Probably because I tend to have physical sex instead,* I reasoned. *But if I do decide to have cerebral sex I can guarantee it won't be with anyone whose idea of great threads is sinew socks.*

"Is that what was going on in the fire at the ceremonial site," I shouted over my shoulder, "your energy moving together, because it looked like sex to me." There, I'd said what was on my mind.

"What happened in the flames was pure imagery, not sex. Manaba doesn't use her powers like that. Could we call a halt to the jabbing?" she asked and suddenly put her arms around me from behind, stopping my verbal stomping.

Turning to embrace her, I wondered if this is what living together would be like. Right now, I didn't care. Worn out from the energy it took to wage a good sarcastic battle over several hours, I was maxed.

"When I went over to talk to Manaba at the ceremonial site, I asked her for her grandmother's exact time of death, and she told me it was November 21, 1997 at 4:23 p.m. I remembered reading about her grandmother's unexpected transition—the entire community was in mourning over Eyota, meaning 'the great one.' Her time of death at 4:23 adds up to nine. She died on a spiritual number, and of course the number nine signifies distance, a faraway trip. The online accounts said she died of heart trouble, but Manaba thinks her grandmother's passing wasn't accidental."

"So why doesn't Manaba come out and say that in front of me and let's get to it? Too high school for me. If the woman wants help she should speak up or let us alone. Did you ask her for Nizhoni's time of death too?"

Callie perked up, very happy I was speaking her language.

"I did. Manaba didn't know to the minute when she was killed. I could only get within a couple of hours." The computer graphics spun, and numbers appeared and adjusted and reappeared. Then the strange astrological wheel that looked like a blueprint of the cosmos settled in, and Callie studied the computer screen. "I don't see anything at all. Something doesn't feel right. I don't know." Callie shook her head as if trying to sort out the confusing bits of information.

"Maybe you're being blocked from seeing," I said, and Callie looked up at me and gave me a warm smile that seemed like celestial appreciation for my paying attention. "Look up November 21, 1997," I ordered, demonstrating to my lover that all had not been lost on me and surprising myself at how cosmic I could become when a shaman was my competition. Callie began clicking the keys down on the keyboard until the wheel in front of us read 1997 and stared at it silently for a few seconds.

"She lost her grandmother at a time when the Moon in the Fourth House of home was squaring the Sun in the Seventh House of the grandmother of a woman. Venus was in Capricorn in the Ninth House, trapped between Mars, indicating male, and Neptune, indicating disillusionment or deception. Of course, look, Venus was besieged!" She spoke into the computer screen as if my head was in there instead of over her shoulder.

"Run that by me again."

"Besiegement is an old-world astrological aspect that occurs when a planet like Venus is trapped between two heavier planets." Callie pointed to the symbols. "Mars can be many things but certainly, in a negative sense, it means danger or aggression. That's behind her, to the backside of Venus. In front of Venus is Neptune, which negatively could mean disillusionment. With danger at her back, she may have walked forward into deception."

Callie flopped back in the chair as if the energy of discovery had exhausted her. "A woman will save the day, even though the woman is under threat, because Venus, representing women, is trining the Ascendant, which represents the event—her death."

"How's a woman going to save the day? Isn't the day pretty much over, since the grandmother is dead?"

"I'm telling you what I see in the chart. I don't know if it makes sense or not."

I didn't know what it was about Callie studying astrological charts that always made her look so sexy, but it did. Her intense focus away from me allowed me time to examine every part of her without her looking back, and I had a chance to observe her magnificent mane of white-blond hair, short but feminine and full, barely touching the beautiful white sweater she often wore and framing the thick gold necklace that had to be an inch wide.

I didn't ask her where she'd gotten the necklace, afraid perhaps her ex-husband, reportedly of ten minutes, had given it to her, in which case I would have to bite it off with my teeth and melt it down into a dagger with which to stab the sonofabitch. I marveled at how I could still have that much hate for Robert Isaacs.

"What are you thinking? Your energy has gone completely dark." Callie turned to look at me.

"Sorry, I'll wipe those thoughts away," I said, making a windshield-wiper motion in front of my face as Callie had taught me. "Look up November twenty-first in the present."

"So you're becoming an astrologer?" she teased, obviously pleased, and I should have basked in her smile and enjoyed the moment. Instead my thoughts flashed from Robert Isaacs in bed with Callie to Manaba having an affair with Callie, and I became so knotted up inside that I choked on all possible playfulness.

"Right now, Moon, ruler of women, is trapped between Mars and Uranus squaring Venus—so a woman is almost trapping herself. I don't feel the woman is dead," Callie said, shutting down her computer and letting the screen go dark.

"Too cosmic for me. I've got to write a screenplay. I'm on deadline."

Even as I said the word, the irony of it struck me—the line at which we are dead. For me, merely an abstract point in time beyond which I would have no studio deal. For an Indian woman, a literal line at the edge of a cliff beyond which she would have no life.

CHAPTER FIVE

Early the next morning, the phone rang. Checking the caller ID, I picked up to hear Barrett wanting to talk about the e-mail file containing the first seventy-five pages I'd sent her.

"Teague, you ought to spend more time out of the sack and at the computer. Good stuff."

"I'm very glad you like the script, Barrett," I said, intentionally completing full sentences to let Callie know who was on the phone and what we were talking about, and thinking that married people's lives must simply border on hell.

"I like everything about your work..." Barrett's words dangled like a lure at the end of a fishing line—letting "work" encompass the screenplay I'd written for her or the sex I'd once had with her, her tone trying to snag me like a hook passing a hungry fish. I didn't take the bait.

"So I'll continue writing brilliant work and—"

My upbeat tone annoyed her because she abruptly interrupted. "I sent it on to Jacowitz, to let him know you're on it, and he had a couple of comments that I don't think are too off base. Is this a good time?"

That was the Hollywood version of I'm-letting-you-know-I-have-manners-but-I-hold-your-career-in-my-hands.

"Great time, shoot," I said, the last word obviously Freudian.

"You've done wonders with what you've got. I love the interplay between the housewife and the husband, dead-on in its honesty. Makes me believe you're straight." And Barrett laughed so I laughed. "First dialogue between the women, nice. Jacowitz loved it...but he thinks it needs to be a little grittier. Maybe develop a kind of sexy grunge, make it a little more hip, and of course that's going to be hard unless we make a few character tweaks. He was thinking, we make the nun a therapist—"

"A therapist nun…" I repeated, trying to be open-minded. *After all, the novice is studying psychology.*

"Therapist, period. Drop the nun. And the therapist is trying to help this psychologically abused hooker."

"Hooker?" My mind was scrunching into a psychotic ball.

"Don't you love it?" Her voice was gleeful.

"But the abused wife is—"

"Gone. She's the hooker. Who better to know about psychological abuse, to have experienced abuse, than a hooker? So the therapist and the hooker give you that kind of grunge right from the start, and you don't have to deal with the whole church thing and having the movie picketed and all that BS. Now we can get some language in there that's sexier because the hooker can say things like *pussy* and *cunt*, where the housewife wouldn't—"

"Why does she have to say *pussy* and *cunt*?"

"She's a hooker!" Barrett shouted as if she'd written the entire screenplay and I was too dense to get it. I was silently clouding up, the spectrum of my internal energy waffling between corpse gray and hearse black as Barrett rushed her closing remarks. "Think about it. It would make Jacowitz happy to know you're at least listening."

"Look, I'm listening but—"

"I know you're listening." She verbally stroked me. "You listen better than any writer I know, you're the best. It's a small change. You okay with it?"

I sighed. "I wouldn't call it okay—"

"Look, this is your first motion picture with a big-time director. The important thing here is the relationship, right?" Pause. "Right?"

"Right," I repeated at her prodding and then hated myself for it. *Why is the relationship the most important thing? The work is the most important thing.*

"He works with people who get it. You've got to show him you get it."

"Got it," I said, dejected beyond description.

"Got to go to a meeting at the Bev," she said, apparently forgetting I would know why she had a meeting at the Bev—it was her casting couch. "Call me if you have questions and hi to the blonde." She hung up before I could comment further.

Putting my face in my hands, I moaned. "I'm a whore writing about a hooker."

"Don't say that!"

"I'm a fucking Hollywood hamster who jumped back on the wheel of 'love your story, let's do your story, let's change your story, was this *your* story, I thought it was *my* story.'"

"Was she yelling at you?" Callie frowned, having heard Barrett's voice through the phone and seen my dejected expression.

"Yeah, redeveloping my story and then shouting at me because I don't get the plot. By the time this project is over, I won't recognize this as my story, which is good because it will probably be about a psychologically abused aardvark that has sex with a chicken, and there will be enough writers on the credit roll to start a ball team. The entire shape of the story is shifting…subtle at first, a tweak here, a tweak there…and soon it's unrecognizable, like a screenplay suffering from Alzheimer's, the original idea still buried inside there somewhere, struggling to communicate something…but it's forgotten what."

"Your story—subtly shifting like the wolf."

"What?" I glanced over at Callie, wondering why, when I was baring my soul, all she could talk about was the wolf, which as far as I could see had no relevance to my current trauma.

"The Navajo clan in which Manaba was reared." The faraway look on Callie's face was making me squirmy.

"I'm afraid you're about to tell me something that would be very interesting over cocktails in L.A., but in a cabin in the woods might scare the shit out of me."

"For your own protection I have to tell you."

"I hate this part." I winced.

"The wolf could be a shape-shifter or, more aptly put, a shape-shifter has taken the form of a wolf," Callie said, facing me full front and resting her hands on my knees, I presumed, to keep me from running to my car and fleeing into the night. She seemed to weigh my reaction before going further with the explanation.

"I was studying the aspects in the chart and thinking about my time here with Manaba and realizing she once told me about shape-shifters in the tribe. Not everyone can do it, of course. It's a very special talent."

Running my hands through my hair, I fretted. I'd had a terrible review on my script and now this. "When I first met you and you told me about astrology and then psychics and then ghosts, I didn't believe you. Now I believe everything you say, so I have to draw the line here. This is way too voodoo for me. I can't go around looking into the eyes of every animal out there to see if it's really…Ethel."

"I've walked into their energy field, Teague. I've entered their space and gotten involved in someone else's drama. Now he's after me too, as evidenced by the attack on me in the bedroom."

"He who?" I was breathing rapidly, despising that anyone would threaten Callie. "You haven't done anything to show anyone you're involved in whatever's going on here."

"People in tune with this know, the energy knows…the wolf knows."

"The *wolf* knows? I'm sorry but that's insane."

Callie didn't chastise me for my negativity, perhaps knowing I'd reached the limit of my willing suspension of disbelief and, instead, went to the kitchen and brewed me some coffee and let me settle down.

Watching her from behind, the small hips, well-formed shoulders, and the way her gorgeous hair swept back off her features, I sighed. "The one thing I don't want shifting is my relationship with you, unless it's a good shift, however you define *shift*…"

She approached, coffee cup in hand, and we stared at each other for a moment. Then I ducked my head and put it against her chest, and she draped her arms around my neck.

"It's only energy, Teague, don't be afraid. When an athlete stops putting his energy out there and retires, he often gets sick because that outwardly directed energy turns in on him. There's no way to dissipate it. When a woman is repressed and unable to express herself—put her energy out there and say what she feels—that energy goes inside her and she can get diseases of the heart, the mind, the body."

"Do you really believe that?" I flashed on the myriad of women's illnesses and was incredulous that Callie thought merely speaking out could cure them. "I don't think it's fair to say women cause their own diseases by not speaking up."

"Energy flows out of you or it goes in on you." Callie was resolute, and the concept she raised seemed so bizarre I really didn't know where to begin the debate.

"So what does energy have to do with the wolf eyes that were so human?"

"The human used personal energy to travel out of body, taking on another form, and that form was the wolf."

"You mean like a werewolf that's not a wolf but a person." I spoke carefully, as if my words might crack the thin ice of reality and drown me in the dark waters of another realm.

"Many powerful tribal people of both sexes can shape-shift."

"And why would anyone want to do that—leave a perfectly good body having a nice meat-loaf dinner to stalk around in the woods and gnaw on a raw rabbit?"

"To see something, or experience something they might not be able to see in human form."

Elmo suddenly let out a huge sob and crawled under the coffee table, no doubt receiving mental images of people turning into wolves.

"So how do they…shift?" I said, patting Elmo to comfort him.

"A part of the soul leaves the body and goes elsewhere, sometimes with the help of a rhythmic drumbeat. The partial soul can take many forms."

"Is this wolf-person…is that who attacked you energetically in the bedroom?" I said, thinking I sounded like psychic John Edwards and should be locked up.

"I'm almost certain it wasn't. I don't sense real danger from the person who appeared outside our cabin. The other energy had a different vibration."

"So Manaba…is she a shape-shifter?"

"Perhaps. Her grandmother whom I visited once while I was with Manaba—"

"Having an affair." I completed the sentence.

"A cerebral affair," she quickly corrected.

"Which Biblically falls under thinking-it-is-doing-it-so-you're-guilty."

"I don't believe in guilt. I believe in…possibilities."

"It's *possible* you had a cerebral affair with…a wolf, basically."

She paused to weigh that thought and finally shrugged. "Perhaps." True to herself, she refused to view her past as anything but the natural course of events her life was supposed to take, and I had to admit I admired her positive attitude.

"Don't let Jacowitz know or I'll get a call telling me to change the characters to a hooker and a wolf."

"Is a cerebral affair with a beautiful creature like a wolf more or less strange to you than having sex with a woman who has sushi in her slits?"

Callie's remark was quick and struck me unexpectedly, like an animal who, viewed as tame, irritated and hiding the feeling, chose one day to take its revenge with one deadly swipe of its paw. I could have retaliated, but a piece of me knew I deserved it. She was so good, so kind, so ethereal, and I was flippant on my best day, sarcastic on my worst.

But Callie had struck out at me—slapped me as harshly as if she'd physically hit me—and while I could take far worse from anyone else and battle back without missing a beat, I was suddenly devastated by her attack—hurt. My throat grew tight and I teared up. Had I been silly enough to believe that Callie would never say a harsh word to me? *Yes, I believed she never would. And why does this ridiculous remark make me so upset?*

My own ritualistic, threadbare jealousy was too ever-present with its dark strands from which I could not extricate myself. Every new thought, every action led back to a memory that triggered my need to attack Callie for perceived unfaithfulness in the past, the present, or the future. But now she was caught up in the jealous energy swirling around us both, the air full of it.

"We have to stop," I said tearfully.

"Do you see what combined negative energies can do? We're powerful together but we must stay positive," Callie replied softly and put her arms around my neck. Over her shoulder through the window, I spotted a woman striding across the lawn on the backside of the cabin.

I dashed to the door in time to see a heavyset woman with a big flat face in a gray skirt and white blouse, a black sweater too tight to close in front, and wearing clunky black shoes stride up to the cabin. When Callie and I popped out onto the porch, she seemed happy to see us.

"No idea the cabin was full up—sorry, cutting across to the road. Fern Flanagan." She extended one short, flabby arm and gave me a pump-handle handshake as I introduced Callie and myself. "I maintenance the roadside facilities across the way." She nodded toward the two-lane.

"So you clean up the camp areas?" Callie asked in friendly conversational fashion.

"That's me. You can't even think up stuff I've seen. People are dirtier than dirt. Them bathrooms? Looks like cows have been let loose in 'em—pee up every wall!"

Maybe I needed relief but a strange, Shrek-like woman in my front yard talking about peeing up a wall gave me the giggles, which seemed to spur Fern on.

"Honey, I've done it so many years I've put these women into categories. There's sitters, hikers, half squatters, and sprayers. Hikers are one leg up, half squatters hang in the air so they don't touch the seat, and sprayers just let 'er rip from any position. What are you two doin' up here—havin' family for Thanksgiving?"

"A romantic weekend…we're here on a vacation," Callie said, toying unnecessarily with Fern's tolerance level.

What in hell has gotten into Callie? She's outing us to people who haven't even asked, and Fern of the forest is now staring at me.

"Now that's really nice. I had a girlfriend once in school." For a moment Fern's eyes misted up as she stared off into the woods, then promptly snapped back as if to give herself a slap. "But then I ended up marryin' Frankie. He's a little bitty ole fella 'bout the size of you."

She poked Callie in the arm and my mind went to a terrible place—little ole Frankie's pistil in Fern's stamen and how they could ever physically...pollinate. I shook my head to knock that thought out.

"I guess I like their little ole hangy-down parts. Funny how we like one thing or another. Well, you girls have a great weekend." She headed back toward the road and then spun 180 degrees to face us. "Oh, forgot about the bear report. They're on the roam because of the fires up in the hills, so don't leave no food outside your cabin—attracts bears. No food in your car—bear'll rip open yer trunk. And for God's sake don't leave the cabin if you're havin' yer time of the month. Bears can smell blood and it gets 'em excited." She spun again and this time lumbered off into the woods as I suppressed laughter.

Callie suddenly yanked me up against her chest as if we were performing a Latin dance routine and kissed me passionately. Heat surged through my entire body as she dragged me up the porch steps and into the bedroom and pushed me down onto the bed, flinging herself on top of me as if I were her personal trampoline and knocking all the breath out of me.

"You are so cute and sexy when you get the giggles."

"Easy." I giggled as she began tearing my clothes off and kissing me so fervently I felt like this might do it for me and any further arousal might be wasted energy on her part. The heat from inside my body reached inferno levels and ran a race to connect with the heat outside my body, and I broke into an intense sweat and thought if I didn't get packed in ice in the next fifteen seconds, I might blow out through the top of my own head.

"Ahhhh!" I screamed, ripping myself from her grasp, leaping off the bed, and waving my arms around while I tried to pull off my remaining clothes.

Callie's high-pitched laughter continued as she watched me pant and huff and sweat. "You're having a major hot flash."

"No, it's just really hot in here and then you're so hot."

"You didn't tell me you were going through the change."

"I'm not. I'm in my early forties, for God's sake!" I looked at her oddly, wondering where that thought came from.

"I know how old you are, darling." Her voice cuddled me as I crawled back into bed with her, wrapping my entire body around her and kissing her breasts. She slid her hands down my buttocks, and my skin, all of it from head to toe, became damp, clammy, ridiculously hot, like my personal thermostat had been struck by lightning and suffered a meltdown. "You are definitely going through the change, but the good news is you soon won't have to worry about bears," Callie said impishly.

"My God!" I rolled away from her and she picked up a pillow and made an elaborate mock gesture of fanning me, telling me I needed to take something for the hot flashes.

"I'm not taking estrogen—which is made from horse urine—in order to stop sweating like a horse."

"You are inordinately stubborn," she said, no condemnation in her voice. "I'll get you something homeopathic. It's either that or we'll be making love only in our minds…a cerebral affair after all."

I moaned in despair, then asked if she would mind turning on the overhead fan. The cool air whipped across the vast Sahara once known as my body as I refuted the fact that I might be going through the change and Callie educated me on why my symptoms were changelike.

"If you're right," I said despondently, "then God has played a cruel trick on women, making them bleed for decades, then sweat for years, and finally allowing them to go dry. Proving, of course, that God is a man."

"With a warped sense of humor. And the change could make you a little cranky."

"How will we know? I'm cranky by nature. Menopausal could make me postal."

Rocked in her arms, I felt the moisture between our bodies evaporate into one another until our colognes smelled like neither of us and both of us in a mixture of exotic oils and sensual hormones that kept my heart beating fast, even though I had been pulled from the race.

"I wonder what makes a woman decide her life's work is cleaning up roadside-park facilities," I mused, thinking of Fern.

"She seems happy." Callie kissed my shoulder.

"I wonder why I had to be a screenwriter. I would have made a wonderful field general or rodeo cowboy or even a priest… I would have been a great priest."

Callie chuckled, I was certain, over the direction my mind could take when relaxed. "You would have been a terrible priest."

"Not true. It's theater, and I would have packed the house every Sunday. My first official act as a priest would be to get rid of hell as a destination, as in 'Go to hell.' Or 'It was hell on earth,' which sounds like a suburb. I would ask the pope to replace the word *hell* in all religious texts with the word *shopping*, which still has an element of hell to it. If you sinned, you would go to Wal-Mart. Twice, and you would go to Target. If you committed a really evil crime, you would have to go to that huge mall in Minneapolis, lose your car, and never get out."

"I love you," Callie said, smiling at me. "You know more than you know you know."

"When will I know I know it?" I teased her.

"When you open your third eye."

"Don't tell me about that, I can't take it." I put a pillow over my head and could still hear Callie laughing, and soon she began to make love to me, slowly, deliberately, every move making me want her more.

"I don't want to be a priest. I don't think they get to do this," I said, resting my cheek on her pelvis and hugging her hips to me.

"Oh, honey, for an ex-cop, you are so naïve."

Chapter Six

We were curled up on the bed, my arm around Callie's shoulder, cozier than I'd felt in weeks, when I flipped on the ancient black-and-white TV on the rickety table in the corner of the bedroom, mostly curious to see if it could get reception. A recap of the news featured the story about the mall construction site.

A bouncy, young news anchor, with a voice like Minnie Mouse, waxed on about the incredible run of bad luck that the construction company had endured, elaborating on how the Native Americans on the job recognized signs they should not be building the mall on this particular piece of ground because it offended the ancestors. The most recent death of a Native American woman by wolves was cited as further anger from the departed.

"First it was one wolf, now it's wolves. Before it's over she'll have been carried off by ten thousand wolves brandishing spears," Callie said.

"Is this mall going to be built over Indian ceremonial grounds?" the anchor asked the television screen. *"We asked Cy Blackstone, owner of Blackstone Development."*

"Remember up on the ceremonial site when Blackstone told your friend Manaba that as a favor he wanted her to go on TV and settle things down? Looks like he's having to do it himself."

The videotape editor cut to a pre-taped interview with Blackstone, and there he was in all his wiry, old-cowboy glory aw-shucksing the on-the-spot reporter in such a charming way I could almost like him. Easy to see why he was elected to the legislature.

"If it turned out this was Native American ceremonial land, we would be the first to stop excavation and call in the tribal elders and do what's right because this great state is built on our Native American heritage. We in Arizona don't treat our people any way

but with respect and honor. But we've checked that out thoroughly, and we are miles away from anything remotely related to that site." He tipped his hat at the end of the interview, to the cameraman, I supposed. It was a nice touch and apparently his trademark.

Back in the studio, the mouse-voiced anchor said, *"Some of the locals are saying this is reminiscent of Thanksgiving in ninety-seven when concrete wouldn't set up and Native American workers walked off the job due to the unexpected death of one of the elders of the tribe. Well,"* the anchor turned to her starched male co-anchor and bubbled, *"sure hope things get better 'cause us girls like to shop at the mall."* She beamed and he laughed and they both moved on to the next story.

"I don't think that little news clip will get it done if Native Americans are walking off due to their ancestors."

Callie bolted out of bed and dashed to the computer, looking at the astrological chart. "Venus was squaring Saturn in the Venus-besieged chart—another heavy placement showing structural breakdown involving a woman."

"The mall seems to be the only structure causing women to have a breakdown," I quipped, but Callie took me seriously.

"It could be a physical structure, or her grandmother's own structure—her death. Venus is squaring Saturn in the Twelfth House of something behind the scenes. Of course in matters like these something is always going on behind the scenes or we wouldn't be looking at the problem, so I don't know what that means, really."

"So what does 1997 have to do with a woman being killed by a wolf years later?"

"I don't know. The bigger question is who is putting these women under attack, because we know it's not wolves."

"We do? I mean you say that, but I read the accounts and looked at the newspaper photo of the tracks found at the site."

"Close your eyes," she commanded and I obeyed. "Clear your mind, relax, focus on the Native American girl, Nizhoni, who went over the cliff. Say her name in your head again and again and again." I did as she asked. "Drift…think…listen. Now ask the gods if Nizhoni was killed by wolves." Pause. "What do you hear, Teague?"

"I don't hear anything but I think you're right. She wasn't killed by wolves."

"Now ask the gods, ask your inner self, if Nizhoni is dead or alive…dead or alive…dead or alive?"

"She's alive." My eyes popped open and I was startled by what I'd said.

"Yes, she's alive," Callie said firmly and smiled at me, seemingly in appreciation of my newfound ability to know things. "You're tuning in."

"So where is she?" I asked, uncertain what exactly I'd tuned in to.

"I don't know…" Callie said in a tone that seemed to deny what both of us had said.

Having no idea how we might determine if the woman was alive and who had shape-shifted into a wolf, I headed for my laptop to work on the screenplay—*another equally hard-to-explain story,* I thought.

"Do I go ahead and make the nun a therapist and the housewife a hooker?" I asked Callie, sighing as I spoke.

"What happens if you don't?"

"They pay me Writers Guild minimum, thank me, and tell me good-bye. Since they've optioned the story, they can hire someone else to be the writer and—"

"Someone who will happily make the nun a therapist or a wildebeest, for that matter?"

"Yes, so I might as well give it a shot," I said, and Callie shrugged as if that kind of change was infinitesimally important in the scope of things.

Knuckling down, I knocked out ten pages…not the opening ten pages, but the ten pages midway through the screenplay when the two women have their first physical contact. Callie was at her computer when I finally looked up and read what I'd written out loud.

"So the way I've got it worked out is the hooker is lying on the therapist's couch and the therapist is sitting beside her, legs crossed, her notebook in hand…kind of bookish and interesting but professional. And the hooker in the midst of answering the typical therapy questions suddenly says, 'You've got nice legs. You could have been a dancer.'

"The therapist looks down, shy, and starts to speak but the hooker says, 'Or a hooker. Men like nice legs. Long legs that disappear up into the…unknown.' She runs her hand over the therapist's calf and then up her thigh and stops as she says, 'Men like adventure.' She lets her hand drop to the couch and leans back as if she meant nothing by it and is merely ready for the therapist to ask her the next question.

"Of course now the therapist is totally confused and has trouble collecting her thoughts, and she ends the session abruptly, saying 'I think our time is up.'

"The hooker says, 'I have ten more minutes.'

"And the therapist says, 'I'll make it up to you next time.'

"The hooker smiles and says, 'That's what I say to *my* clients.'"

I looked up at Callie. "So what do you think?"

"It's sexy and provocative. You've developed a sophistication beyond what I thought you'd be able to do with it. It's really good, Teague."

"But I didn't have her say cunt or pussy?"

"Why would she?

"Because she's a hooker!" I shouted, imitating Barrett, and Callie laughed. "Jacowitz wants lurid language. Now that I think about it, I remember Barrett telling me about the studio rumor that he's into S&M."

"Jacowitz? The guy I met with the nerdy glasses and the battered briefcase? He looks like Willie Lowman in *Death of a Salesman*."

"Rumor says he likes to get naked and have a woman in spike heels walk across his back and flagellate his buttocks with a riding crop."

"I understand pain and pleasure, but not how one evokes the other."

"Yeah, like having a vasectomy and a lap dance in the same half hour. I'm so glad you like the pages. I'm sending them off to Barrett."

With a ping, the e-mail with the ten pages attached was on its way. “Gone. My dilemma is now sitting on Barrett’s laptop, let’s get back to yours,” I said, referring to the shape-shifter.

“Looking at this chart,” Callie said, “I know the woman is besieged, but I have this calm feeling when I think about her, as if she’s alive but time could be running out.”

“I know, but being alive is a bit tricky when you fall over a canyon ridge into a 2000-foot free fall before you hit the jagged bottom. The vultures almost have enough time to pick you clean before your bones ever bounce off the riverbed.”

“Teague, that sounds terrible!” Even Elmo was sobbing, a sign that my mental imagery had made him need a bathroom break.

“He hates heights,” I said, hooking him up to his lead. “We’ll be right back.” We headed out into the dusky evening, not straying far from the cabin.

I looked left over my shoulder, right over my back, up to the treetops, and down to the ground searching for something, anything that remotely looked like a wolf. Though Callie said the wolf was a human, I still didn’t want to see him or her. Elmo seemed calm and completely unconcerned, so I relaxed and gazed up at the stars, thinking it a beautiful, cold night down by the creek’s wide, frigid waters.

Large flat boulders leaned out from the land, forming beautiful rock sunbathing shelves all along the creek bed, and Elmo and I walked ten feet out onto one and stared into the water below—by day crystal clear, sweeping fish downstream, by night invisible, only sound rushing over the rocks.

On our return, Elmo lifted his short, chubby leg draped with extra fur folds, watered the ferns, and threw some creek sand high up into the air with a few well-placed flicks of his hind feet.

“You’re still a studly, guy,” I said admiringly and we climbed the cabin steps, where I unhooked Elmo’s leash, pushing the door open, and he strutted through it as if he’d accomplished something extraordinary.

The cool air settled in my bones as I walked back down the porch steps and around the side of the cabin to the car, then clicked open the lock to retrieve my windbreaker. Rummaging around on the floor of the Jeep, I found the neatly rolled shirt-jack sack that held my army green windbreaker, yanked it out, extracted the pink one I'd purchased at L.L. Bean for Callie before I left L.A., the only pink item I'd ever seen at L.L. Bean, and slammed the car door. I turned and yelped into the face of the largest wolf I'd ever seen.

The broad, furry face not three feet from mine seemed as large as a ceremonial mask. Frozen in my own footsteps, fearful the wolf would kill me without Callie here, I tried to scream for help, but the sound came out a hoarse squeak. The wolf cowered slightly as if to assure me with its body language that it had more to fear than I, while with hypnotic eyes it seemed to beckon me.

I backed up a few feet, maintaining eye contact. Its face intelligent and focused on me, the wolf carefully turned to walk away, then paused, looking over its shoulder as if to beg me to follow. When I didn't move, it stopped and pivoted to face me, the moonlight slicing down on its thick gray coat, the black-tipped hairs standing up like tiny knives from the field of silver fur.

Through the exquisite white facial markings, flashing eyes stared into mine, and I thought I heard a voice telling me not to be afraid. *Is the wolf talking to me? Is it a voice inside my own head? Is it something I want to hear so I put it into my own head?*

It turned its backside to me again, then glanced over its shoulder and slowly moved ahead as if cajoling me, training me. The wolf couldn't have asked me more plainly to follow if it had spoken fluent English.

Almost involuntarily, I took a step toward it, then another. When I stopped, it stopped and looked over its shoulder and into my eyes again. I was literally dancing with a wolf—following its footsteps. Soon lightheaded and nearly euphoric, I trotted behind the wolf, who had picked up the pace, heading through the woods with me right behind it, almost gleeful like a child, when in the distance I heard Callie shrieking my name.

Her voice was high-pitched, loud, urgent, and terrified, and the wolf's fur twitched across its shoulders as it looked back at me, sensing I was slowing down. The tenuous thread between us stretched thin, near the breaking point, and it hesitated, as if reluctantly making a decision, then turned and ran, seeming to know I would no longer follow—our dance ended. Callie's frightened voice interrupted the enticement, the lure, the longing to tap into something beyond my knowing. My experience with the animal shattered in the night air like pottery on pavers.

Turning back, I headed for the cabin and halfway Callie raced toward me, flinging herself into my arms, her hands cupping my neck, hugging me to her.

"What were you doing?" she asked, breathless, her voice a reprimand and not a question, seeming to know without my telling that I had followed the wolf.

"The wolf—it's human and it—"

"You mustn't follow it! Do you hear me, do not follow that. It's a spirit, Teague, a person who has shape-shifted, but you don't know which person and you don't know its intent."

"But you said it wasn't evil and you didn't feel anything bad around it and that tribal people shape—"

"Swear to me you won't do that again!" Callie's voice came in breathless bursts and sounded more terror stricken than I'd ever heard it.

"Okay, but it wants to tell me something, I know that."

"Yes, it makes you think that. More likely it wants something else. Remember, women have disappeared but bodies are not found and—"

"What women?"

Callie stopped talking, apparently unaware of what she was saying.

"There's only the Native American woman, right?" When Callie didn't answer, I asked, "Are there other women? Talk to me, Callie."

"Someone else was killed…a long time ago. Manaba's high-school friend, Kai, they called her Willow." She seemed to be pulling this information in on some cosmic thread, saying the words slowly so as not to scare them away from her.

"By wolves?"

"No...I don't know." She seemed confused. "Then Manaba's grandmother died. It doesn't make sense, does it?" Callie whispered. "The natives say they found blood and her grandmother's torn clothing, but that could be rumor." Callie's voice had grown soft and reverential.

"Was it her blood or wolf's blood?" Even as I condemned the wolf, I found it hard to believe that something so beautiful—something with soft eyes like a human's—could be the killer.

"The other woman, I feel a strong energy about her," Callie said, and I sensed she wasn't talking about Nizhoni or the grandmother, but about Kai and something that went beyond the present.

"How did you know about her?"

"Manaba dedicated one of her teaching classes to her and said she was killed very young. Everyone thought auto accident or something like that, but one of the women in the class who lives here said she committed suicide."

"You said 'was killed.'"

"I don't know why I said that." Her mind seemed to drift and like a cosmic net encircle fragments of information from the universal consciousness, plucking relevant information for comment. "He knows about the first wolf visitation and he's mimicking it." Callie's tone was quiet.

"He who? Who are you talking about?" I begged.

As if orchestrated by some force beyond our knowing, the wind attacked the pine trees and the needles whistled as if calling forth the dead; air blew up around our bodies with an electrical charge that made my every hair stand up in fear. Powerful centrifugal gusts seized the treetops now, and I expected to see the pine needles part and the devil descend as climax to the electromagnetic anticipation that rolled over me, nearly rendering me immobile.

"Quick, get inside!" Callie ordered, and we jogged back to the cabin as I worried what in hell we'd gotten into and what evil was bearing down on us, borne on the wind.

Chapter Seven

The knock at the door uncoiled me and I sprang for my gun. Taking several long strides across the creaking wooden floors, I slung open the door where Manaba stood smelling of smoke and tobacco and some kind of incense, looking like a centerfold for *Northern Exposure*.

Exotic in leather and feathers, she'd apparently long ago discarded traditional Navajo dress for native-eclectic, taking from her grandmother's culture those things that worked for her and eschewing the rest. She stood in the doorway completely without makeup and showed no sign she owned a hairbrush, her entire presence sensual; yet her dark, knowing eyes seemed troubled.

Callie entered the room and stopped abruptly, as if opposing energy fields kept them at bay like the wrong ends of a magnet.

"I don't want to be involved with this energy," Callie replied to Manaba's unspoken question, and I wondered if she meant the personal energy between the two of them or the energy of whatever was happening around Nizhoni's death. "I cannot unearth the truth when the truth is withheld by those who know it."

I didn't know much about Navajo tradition but I was pretty sure insulting a shaman wasn't a great move, and it sounded like Callie had accused Manaba of withholding information. I also noticed when Callie was around Manaba she started talking like a fortune cookie, and I began to fantasize how bad foreplay would sound with Manaba. *She who takes off her clothes may experience the pleasures of the dancing valley,* or something like that.

There was a long pause.

"Nizhoni," Manaba said, then uttered something in her native tongue that I couldn't understand, much less repeat, but I sensed she spoke Nizhoni's name with love. Callie seemed mildly surprised and finally nodded her acquiescence. Manaba's shoulders noticeably relaxed as if a burden had been removed.

"What's she saying?"

"Nizhoni, the woman she says was recently killed...was Manaba's lover," Callie said, finally revealing the truth Manaba had withheld. Now my mind really took off—the Indian maiden and the shaman in a lesbian affair—wow.

"I do not believe Nizhoni is dead." Callie directed her words to Manaba. "Not like your friend, Kai. This is different, she is alive."

Nervousness in her body, Manaba shifted her weight. "Nizhoni's grave is in the valley vortex, I know that. I need the truth about Kai."

"Ignore the recent death and focus on the old one?" I asked.

"New is but the old revisited," Manaba replied in that circular way she had of answering questions.

Silence ensued as if Callie was trying to make a decision, perhaps a decision about whether what she was thinking was right or wrong. Finally, she said quietly, "We must dig up Nizhoni's grave."

"We do not desecrate the dead!" Manaba's voice showed its first signs of having any range above middle C, and I remembered reading years ago that ancient Navajo culture feared the dead, so maybe Manaba did too. I wasn't so hot on dead people myself, but apparently the Navajos went to a lot of trouble to stay away from their ghosts, and most certainly their graves. Manaba's nervousness was picking up speed as she paced, fretted, and appeared as if merely talking about the dead might suddenly bring the entire cemetery over for a ghost bust. "Proving my young friend was murdered, that is the long-buried truth that must be unearthed, not this fresh grave."

"Do you want my help?" Callie challenged, ready, it appeared, to remove herself from Manaba's drama if she would only say the word.

"Digging up the grave will tell you nothing." Manaba's tone was sharp, perhaps to cover her dread of digging up the person she loved.

"It will tell us if Nizhoni is buried there, if anyone is buried there." Callie seemed to be standing up to Manaba for the first time, as if being drawn into this mystery meant she would somehow take charge.

"I will talk with her family," Manaba said and left the cabin, slipping into the darkness.

"She's not in the grave, I just know that."

"You heard Manaba," I reminded Callie. "She was there, she knows the family, they buried the woman. How are you going to get a grave dug up?"

"You have to help me get permission because I don't think it's on official Indian land. You were a police officer, what do we have to do?"

"Grave digging wasn't my specialty. What makes you so sure the grave is empty?"

"I don't know."

"Good. That will give me lots of ammunition for whoever I have to convince at the Public Works Department or some tribal chief to let us dig up the dead. So the woman we're looking for who's not supposed to be in the grave was her lover, Nizhoni, who was killed after knowing Manaba, like Kai, who most likely was also her lover. Maybe Manaba killed them both—"

Seeing Callie's startled expression, I quickly apologized. "Hey, I barely know Manaba. But it's odd that bad luck strikes twice and she's the common denominator."

I immediately dialed the 918 area code and number for Wade Garner, my old police buddy—the only person I could call from anywhere on the planet and get help. Wade never acted surprised to hear from me and enjoyed exhibiting no reaction to what I told him, even if it sounded outlandish.

"You're in a cabin? Did you get kicked out of your rental house? I want to talk to Callie," he rambled on, filling all the dead air space.

"Listen to me, Wade, I need—"

"Nope, I talk to the blonde or I talk to no one." He'd first met Callie on the Anthony murder case and had liked her then. Now he enjoyed pretending he was closer to her than me, to tick me off.

I handed the phone to Callie, and her sweet voice took on an even more playful tone when she spoke to him. She said everything was fine with us and that I was writing a script and she was visiting friends.

"She *is* a little difficult," Callie said, tossing me a smile to let me know I was the one being referenced.

"I'm not the one who wants to dig up a dead body," I shouted loud enough for Wade to hear. There was apparently a response on his part, and Callie confirmed my statement and then, grinning, thrust the phone into my hand.

"Tell me she's kidding," Wade said.

"Dead people: she sees them, she talks to them, she digs them up."

"Any particular reason, Boris, or are you both just bored?" Wade said.

"Yeah, 'cause the body's not there," I said flatly.

"And the body that's not there, did the family think it was there when they told it good-bye?" Not waiting for my answer, he gave me an exasperated follow-up. "Why would the body not be there?"

"'Cause the woman's not dead."

"And we know that because…" Wade dragged out the words.

"Because…we…do." I grinned at Callie, aware my devotion to her had me not only accepting cosmic craziness but also looking like a nutcase in front of my police buddy. Wade let out a big snort, the kind that always preceded a rude remark, so I stopped him in his derisive tracks.

"If you've got no pull in the human-excavation department, say so and can the comments," I ordered brusquely.

"Hey, Captain Marvel, I was about to say you're going to need someone in that part of the world who can run interference with the local government officials, or the Indians, and fill out the paperwork, and it might even take—hey, was she murdered, because that's a—"

"Attacked by wolves."

"Where the hell *are* you?" Wade's voice rose two octaves.

"Sedona."

"That's right, because I talked to your mom and she said she's brokenhearted you didn't invite her there for Thanksgiving—"

"Okay, cut it out," I said in response to his teasing.

"She said you called her the other night to complain about having to write dirty scenes in a movie, is that true? Are you writing a porno movie?"

"Jeez, Wade, why do you call my mother and have these little talks? Is it to torture me? You know she gets every conversation upside down, and you egg her on. I told her the director I worked for wanted—never mind, I got bigger fish to fry here."

"Okay, okay, I'm making notes. Need contact for digging up Native American woman we don't believe is dead. When in doubt, dig 'em out. You're gonna need an attorney, as much as I hate to say that word. Somebody who can do business in Arizona and knows people. Come to think of it, I might know someone who has a cabin in Sedona and could even be out there for the holidays. I'll check it out and get back to you."

"You're great—once you get to the damned point." I hung up before the snorting began.

❖

The phone rang in the middle of the night, and as I grabbed it I thought it might be Wade. Despite the electronic breakup, I could make out Jeremy Jacowitz's voice. Apologizing profusely, he said he was overseas and could never figure out what time it was. *A famous director should get a clock that tells him, or a secretary who tells him,* I thought but remained politically correct, saying only, "No problem."

"Barrett forwarded your rewrite of the opening scene, the therapist and the hooker, and I think it's brilliantly done. Brilliant!"

I held my breath. There was a day when words like *brilliant* coming from a director would send me into a double backflip and have me high-fiving Elmo. But after years in Hollywood, I understood exaggeration was the norm and, further, that it was sometimes used as a left hook to set me up for the right punch.

"I'm over here in Paris seeing so many avant-garde films—films that take chances, break barriers, change the way people think.

Groundbreaking work and I'm thinking, my God, this film Teague Richfield is writing has that same quality, that potential, and so I wanted to call you while I'm still enthused from my last screening and give you *une petite matière à réflexion.*

He chuckled at turning a cliché like "*food for thought*" into something that sounded a lot sexier. "We're not driving enough young people to the theaters because we're frightened, don't you agree?"

I never thought about young people or theaters, being interested in neither. I only thought about stories: writing them, living them, breathing them, but my breath alone would not resuscitate a screenplay into a motion picture. It was Jacowitz whose creative CPR counted. So I agreed with him and then hated myself for agreeing, because I had no idea what I was agreeing to—to Jeremy Jacowitz, I guessed—agreeing that whatever he wanted me to agree to was fine so long as he liked my first draft. I was no better than any other Hollywood wannabe, and it put me in a bad mood.

"We're afraid to be borderline, we're afraid to say everything is okay, we're afraid to commit in the most fundamental, elemental, raw way. I want us to be fearless, Teague, break open our heads…"

I was getting more irritated as Jeremy Jacowitz led me on a forced march through his mental recesses, a trip short on scenic variety. *Give me the notes. What the hell are you trying to say? I know you're working up to something that undoubtedly involves six-inch heels and a spiked ball.*

"…and so I feel strongly that we go back to the abused wife—"

He'd apparently said several paragraphs between the time I was listening to him and the time I was listening to myself.

"You're right. It has emotional purity," I interjected, feeling myself grow calmer.

"And an alien comes down and has sex with her."

Left hook, right jab, K.O! "An alien?" I said, reeling.

"Aliens represent our primal fears, our alien selves, and this woman represents our inner core as we confront that fear—"

"She's raped by—"

"Attacked at first, but then it's consensual." Jacowitz was serious.

"She has consensual sex with an alien?"

"And because she's been abused and no one has believed the abuse, why would they believe she's had sex with an alien?" he said.

"SHE CAN'T HAVE SEX WITH AN ALIEN!"

"EXACTLY!" He had obviously mistaken my shouting for enthusiasm and was matching it with his own. "So of course they COMMIT HER!" He shouted as triumphantly as if the curtain had rung down on *Gone with the Weird.*

"I should be committed for ever selling you my story. I can't write this screenplay!"

"Don't worry, we can hire a cowriter. I know a great guy—"

"I want out. I quit! My attorney will call your...aliens."

I hung up and turned to Callie, who seemed completely untroubled by my giving a huge motion-picture director the figurative finger. "I'm fucked. I unsold my screenplay."

"You did the right thing."

"How can I prostitute myself any further? It's ridiculous. I don't want to write movies about abused women who have consensual sex with aliens, even if it attracts every date-night teenage boy on the planet."

"What happens now?"

"My attorney calls and yells at me. Barrett Silvers calls and yells at me. People threaten that I'll never work again and I fret."

"Great business." Callie tried to pull me down on the bed and kiss me but I fended her off reflexively, wanting to pace. "Come over here and lie down," she said, wanting, I surmised, to relieve my tension in ways I should have loved but couldn't focus on.

"Sorry," I said as she got up and followed me, trying to be close. "I'm too freaked." We both went back to bed, but this time it was me propped up against the headboard with my arms clutching my legs, chin resting on my knees, wondering how something as great as a green-lighted screenplay could end up a convoluted, corrupted mess.

"I've never seen you this upset," Callie said, making no further attempt to hold me. "You're seething."

"I'm pissed that I continue to walk into the same blind alley again and again. Nothing worth shooting happens through this studio system. It's designed by little boys, for little boys, to play into little boys' fantasies. Because of the boys at the studio, Xena Warrior Princess had to leave Gabrielle and have sex with a guy, and then, she was so confused that in real life she went out and got pregnant."

"I think she got pregnant because she's straight."

"Xena is not straight and don't start spreading that rumor."

"Come here to me." She pulled me into her and I reluctantly gave in this time, but remained in the vertical fetal position up against her.

"I need to get you some herbs. Going through the change makes everything seem bigger."

"Yeah, well, fuck the change," I said, and Callie kissed me and consoled me as she would a fussy child.

❖

We couldn't do much to help Manaba at the moment, at least the way I viewed it. Government buildings, Indian Affairs, and anyone with a brain had closed all offices for the holiday. Nizhoni was dead—seemingly, Kai had died a long time ago, and Manaba's grandmother had been out of the picture for years, so why get hysterical over the historical. No woman was in immediate jeopardy despite whatever planets were trapping Venus and wrestling her to the ground.

Besides, the day before Thanksgiving was supposed to be about celebrating, and I'd surfaced from my funk, never wallowing in self-pity for more than a few hours. Callie and I were in a festive mood despite the death of my screenplay. No one had phoned to chastise me after my director decoupling so I was feeling free and vindicated, looking forward to being snugged in the cabin with Callie and Elmo and cooking our first Thanksgiving turkey together.

We found a fairly large supermarket outside of town, and by noon we were skipping down the aisles literally tossing food into our basket: frozen cranberries, a sack of potatoes, fresh corn, broccoli, and carrots.

"Somebody must be coming," she said.

And I replied that I hoped it would be me, as I picked up the largest turkey I could find.

She giggled over my sexual reference and grabbed my behind as we danced down the aisle in full view of more disciplined and serious shoppers who undoubtedly had relatives coming, in a far more traditional sense—and judging by the sour looks on their faces, relatives they could do without.

At the checkout stand a lanky, mid-twenties boy in a sweat-stained T-shirt, with dirty fingernails and a finger tattoo in place of a ring, began to total our items. Noticing the fresh carrots rang up as $8.90, I stopped him and pointed that out.

He paused to stare at me. "That's what it says." He pointed to the scanner display, which indeed read $8.90.

"But we know that's wrong because carrots don't cost $8.90."

"I have to go by what it says." He shrugged and I could see Callie out of the corner of my eye trying to conceal a smile.

"Well, I don't. Call someone," I demanded.

"No one's here except other checkers and they're busy."

"Well, I'm not paying $8.90 for a bag of fresh carrots."

"So you don't want them?" he asked amicably and cancelled the screen amount.

"I *do* want them but—"

The boy scanned them again and the scanner read $8.90. People behind us were beginning to shift their weight from side to side, the international sign for "Could you move the fuck along."

"We could forget the carrots. I've got other vegetables," Callie said, sensing a war about to break out.

I waved her off, leaned in conspiratorially, and whispered to the boy so the other people couldn't hear and he would be saved the embarrassment of my revelation. "Look, think about it. Do you really believe a small bag of carrots costs $8.90?"

The boy paused to give this inquiry real thought and finally whispered back, "You know, I don't eat carrots, so I don't know."

My body sagged into a worn and weary heap. Callie took the carrots out of my hands, the boy cancelled them from the screen, and the bag boy followed us out to the car.

"How will they ever learn if we give up and let them keep the carrots? He can't figure out the scanner because he's high on something—did you see his eyes?"

"It's a new generation. They go by what's on the screen."

"And what if I go to the hospital for X-rays and the bill pops up 89¢ instead of $889? Will the twenty-year-old technician look at the screen and say, 'Yes, 89¢ for your X-ray. That's what the screen says'?"

"He'll say 89¢. You must have eaten a bag of carrots." Callie chuckled and pushed me into the car. We drove home holding hands and singing along with a young woman insisting "There is no Arizona," and I thought she would have gotten along splendidly with the carrot boy.

Back in our cozy cabin, I spent my time draped over Callie, kissing her soft shoulders, which I reached by different paths up the sleeve of her T-shirt and down the back of her neck as she tried to make me leave her alone while we prepared turkey dressing and cut up vegetables for an appetizer tray, treating ourselves like company, all the while laughing and drinking wine.

"I forget what I've put in the dressing because you are so annoying," she teased.

"Really? Having your lover kiss your neck and slide her hands up the arm of your T-shirt and massage your back…" She dropped the fork she was holding and swooned. "Is that the kind of annoying thing you're referring to…is that the thing that's distracting you?"

She grabbed my arms, playfully pinning them to my sides, and kissed me, her mouth white hot moving to blue flame, an igniting kiss that melted everything below my belt buckle. I kept my lips on hers and slowly walked backward toward the bedroom, happy to desert the dressing for the undressing, and amused that we seemed to only enter the bedroom backward.

The crunch of tires on rock startled us both into awareness that we had company. The sound of feet on the steps made my heart jump, and I signaled Callie to be quiet as I rummaged in a drawer for my gun. Glancing out the bedroom window, which was only a few feet left of the porch steps, I spotted a nicely dressed woman standing on the steps knocking lightly on the door. "Teague Richfield," the voice called.

Callie and I exchanged puzzled looks. A svelte, older woman dressed as if she had left an upscale cocktail party, stood on the porch, in a light gray wool suit and matching cape, her beautiful, thick, silver hair blowing slightly in the wind, something about her familiar but out of context here in the woods. I walked across the living room and opened the door to greet her. My shock was total as the china blue eyes locked with mine.

"Teague, do you remember me? Ramona Mathers?"

Chapter Eight

I was nearly speechless. Ramona, the wickedly enchanting attorney who had worked for Frank Anthony whose murder I'd investigated, the attorney who had hit on me at the Anthony mansion, then again at her estate right in front of Callie, prompting Callie to say Ramona would sleep with anything on the planet that had skin—*that* Ramona was standing in the Sedona woods on our doorstep.

"Ramona!" I swooned effusively the way people in the South do when surprised by someone they don't want to see and are afraid that their internal horror will be externally conveyed in an unguarded facial expression, so they make an exaggerated attempt to exhibit joy to throw the visitor off. "What are you doing here?" I dragged out the words, another sign I was faking it.

"Do I have to stay out on the porch until I fully account for myself, or may I come in out of the cold and have a brandy?"

"Come in. You know Callie."

"Not as intimately as you," she gave us a catlike smile, "but yes."

"Hello, come in." Callie smiled back and took Ramona's cape, heading for the bedroom to lay it on the bed, an odd genteel custom, taking coats from people and making the coats lie down in other rooms when closets were lacking.

"Quite a little love nest you've found here, very chi-chi little nook down by the creek. I love it here. You're looking good, Teague." Ramona eyed me like the last piece of cherry pie on the plate but, like a good guest, left it for the hostess. "Wade Garner called to ask if I could help you, and I laughed when he told me where you were because I'm a mile away." She slid out of her matching gray wool suit jacket and tossed it over the back of the couch, revealing firm breasts and a small waist for a woman of her years. Under one gray cashmered arm she held a stuffed toy in the shape of a basset hound.

"Something for you, Elmo." Ramona handed it to him, smiling up at me as if to say she'd remembered his name and everything else about me. "I couldn't resist this. Everyone needs a girlfriend."

"That's what I was telling him on the way in from L.A.," I said, thanking her and making a mental note that I'd never told Ramona I had a basset hound, much less his name and sex. Elmo examined the stuffed basset toy, a cute twelve-inch fake-fur body, almost a replica of himself wearing a pink bow around its neck. Nudging its plush body, he finally punched it with his nose, dragged it by the leg over to a corner of the room, and settled down to sniff it.

"I think he likes her, he's licking her leg." Ramona smiled. "At least that was always *my* first clue."

"Ramona, a drink?" Callie asked.

"Please. I see you're about to molest a bird." She eyed the turkey in its pan. "Whoever thought of taking a poor bird and sticking its neck up its ass, packing its vagina with bread, and calling it a celebration?" She arched an eyebrow and I laughed in spite of myself.

There was something about Ramona's knowing blue eyes, sly smile, and witty charm that forced me to ignore her chronological age and find her sexy. Something about the way she looked into me and smiled as if she knew a secret she'd like to share if she could only get me alone for a moment.

"So who are you trying to dig up?" Ramona languidly plucked a black olive from a relish tray Callie offered.

"A Native American woman who was reportedly attacked by a wolf and when she tried to escape went over a canyon wall and fell to her death," Callie said.

"They must have recovered the body with a spatula," Ramona said, dangling the word in a way that made me laugh even though I didn't want to, recovery with a spatula appealing to my comic sensibilities—life as cartoon.

"Reportedly tribal people recovered the body and buried her in a cemetery at the base of the vortex plateau," Callie interjected over the chuckling.

"And why do you want to dig up the body?"

"I don't believe she's dead and, therefore, I don't believe she's buried," Callie remarked.

"So the grave holds someone else?" Ramona reached for another olive.

"Or no one," Callie said.

"What does the family say?" Ramona sounded more like an attorney with every passing phrase.

"I've only spoken to Nizhoni's partner. Nizhoni is the woman whose grave we're discussing. The partner is Manaba, who says the family buried Nizhoni."

"And you think otherwise because…" Ramona elongated the words.

I suddenly felt compelled to vouch for Callie. "Because she's a psychic and a good one. She knows things. They may seem like crazy things to you and me, but they turn out to be dead-on…so to speak."

"Spoken like a woman in love," Ramona said and I was suddenly shy. "Well, *dead* is the operative word, it seems. Maybe my old friend Cy Blackstone could lend a hand."

"We met Cy Blackstone at some kind of evilway-payday-hoo-ray ceremony," I said, and Callie looked at me as if she was keeping track of my irreverent remarks, perhaps having some limit in mind, after which she would simply crack me over the head with a ceremonial rock.

"Cy loves being a friend to Native Americans while he develops their land right out from under them," Ramona said.

"How do you know Cy?" I asked.

"Everyone knows Cy Blackstone. He's an old retired politico rumored to have fixed more elections than anyone else in U.S. history," Ramona said. "He has something on everyone and uncanny timing in knowing when to hold it over their heads. Cy and I go way back."

Callie glanced in my direction as if to say I could chalk Cy Blackstone up as another Ramona Mathers conquest—she was seemingly drawn to men of power and money.

"He was on the news talking about the new mall," I said.

"Cy gets press. A lot of people owe him. The mall came about as a result of a debt for which his family took possession of the land in kind."

"Who owed him?" I asked, and Ramona shrugged noncommittally.

"Cy's probably gotten his hands on more land formerly owned by Indians than any white man in Arizona. I represented an Indian fellow who nearly lost his hunting grounds to Blackstone."

"Did you win?" I asked.

A pause while Ramona looked me up and down to make me squirm, I was certain, for asking such a question, but then she smiled benignly. "I always win."

The sound of a car door slamming nearby jarred us all out of our conversation, and Elmo looked up from his stuffed toy and growled. I went to the door without a weapon. We were three women and a slobbering dog, the sight of which should keep the most nefarious out of our living room. Three loud bangs on the outside and I opened the door.

"Barrett!" I said, my mind reeling.

Barrett Silvers stood on the porch looking as if an eruption of some sort was imminent. Judging by her breathing and body tension, I had entirely caused the inconvenience of Barrett having to be on this porch, which in turn had apparently produced enough bile in her belly to sustain her current state of insanity through a glacial thaw.

"What in the goddamned hell do you think you're doing?" she yelled into my face, despite the fact that my face was only two feet from hers.

"Greeting madwomen on my doorstep," I said flatly, taking two steps back to avoid having to share her breathing space.

"Don't get smart with me! Do you realize what this means? Do you realize what this *means*?" she repeated an octave above the first question. "This means…"

"...you'll never work in this town again," I repeated, in sync with Barrett, unable to resist mocking the cliché Hollywood executives couldn't stop themselves from invoking even when, at the moment, they weren't in Hollywood.

"Ahhh!" Barrett threw her arms up in the air as if to hurl my personal being into the stratosphere. Her appearance in a place nearly five hundred miles from L.A. in search of me was a sure sign she believed I'd compromised her reputation with Jeremy Jacowitz, and she apparently had decided beating my lips off would somehow restore it.

"I have driven all the way from L.A. simply to let you know that this is one of the largest fuckups of your entire career. You dumped Jeremy Jacowitz. No one dumps Jeremy Jacowitz!" Barrett was shouting again.

"Come in, Barrett," I offered, realizing I hadn't quite dodged every bullet related to my ankling Jacowitz. Barrett entered the cabin without seeming to know where she was, as if she'd been rehearsing this outburst for seven straight hours on the drive here and now wanted to give it to me unedited at high volume.

"You have made me look like a fool. I told him you were terrific to work with, so professional, so quick, and then you tell him that you quit because he wants to make a few small changes in your fucking screenplay."

That was the flick of the Bic that set my ass on fire. *How dare she suggest they were small changes, and how dare she refer to my work as a fucking screenplay.*

"Not a few small changes in my fucking screenplay. He wanted to change the fucking characters, the fucking plot, and the entire fucking movie!" My vehemence rocked Barrett back, catching her by surprise; however, like all studio executives, immune to battering, she quickly recovered.

"And most likely make it better. He's won an Academy Award, while you on the other hand have not!"

"You and Jacowitz can stick his Academy Award up your collective ass!"

"Yes, well, you've made one of youself!"

"Really, well, as a person who's had her face in every female writer's ass in Hollywood, I guess you would recognize us all!"

"Fuck you, you ungrateful little—"

"Fuck you, back!"

"Alright, enough. I will not have that kind of negativity in this cabin!" Callie shouted, startling me because I'd never heard her raise her voice in anger above my own.

Ramona applauded Callie as if the curtain had rung down on a very exciting play she'd directed.

At the sound of hands clapping, Barrett and I sagged to a stop and both took a deep breath as I turned to Ramona, her rakish grin reminding me I hadn't made introductions. Barrett's gaze must have followed mine and, for a moment, we shared one emotion, seeming embarrassment over having had a brawl in front of a virtual stranger.

"Barrett." My tone was intentionally supercilious. "I would like to introduce you to Ramona Mathers, attorney for…well, actually for your studio, Marathon. Ramona, this is Barrett Silvers, your executive vice president of worldwide talent, who is here to berate me for killing my studio deal."

"You don't have the power to kill a studio deal. I'm here to berate you for killing your career." Barrett flipped me the verbal bird, but her eyes were locked on Ramona's and her larger, visibly stronger hand clasped Ramona's long and slender one. They remained in that tableaux for a full ten seconds until Barrett, of all people, actually ducked her head and backed away in acquiescence of the alpha position.

"I apologize, but this is a deal that is good for the studio and good for Teague if—"

"If I would only prostitute myself along with my character," I interjected.

"Please proceed." Ramona's voice had taken on a deep purr like a well-built engine in a classic chassis, causing me to whip my head around to see what in hell was going on. "It's fascinating to think that you drove all this way to abuse a writer," Ramona said with a wry but velvet twist to her voice.

"I spent a solid year setting her up." Barrett spoke of me as if I'd vanished from the room. "Getting her pitched, finding the right director, and she's here in Sedona to write the screenplay. When Jacowitz called from Paris and gave his notes—"

"They weren't notes. They were his sexual fantasies—aliens raping an abused housewife. Now would either of you two buy a ticket to watch that?" I addressed Callie and Ramona, making them my audience.

"You're very talented, Teague, and you have to write what makes you happy," Callie said, jumping to my rescue, and her support emboldened me and fueled my anger toward Barrett.

"This is what women get caught up in helping men succeed at things that don't benefit women!" I was pumped. "I'd just as soon write a freaking Viagra commercial."

Barrett's expression clearly communicated that she wouldn't lower herself to argue further and dismissed my behavior as childish, so I moved to the kitchen counter to help Callie with the drinks.

Apparently worn out from shouting, Barrett slumped onto an armchair. Her short black Eisenhower jacket open at the chest, the V-neck of her silk blouse falling seductively low, and the gold cuff links twinkling at the edges of the French cuffs, she was a stunning adversary, I thought as Callie and I returned to the living room and gathered in the surrounding chairs.

Barrett's passion for her work, or perhaps the way Barrett looked, apparently stoked a fire in Ramona, whose eyes glistened, and for a split second I thought I saw them travel up and down Barrett's chest performing a breast scan, perhaps as a result of Callie's having made rather stiff drinks.

"Where did a psychic learn to make martinis?" I whispered, taking a sip of mine, amused as she muttered something about not bruising the gin.

"Martinis and high rollers seem to go together," she said, referencing her married life, and as I headed to the kitchen for a tray of cheese and crackers I wondered if I'd ever stop hating her ex-husband Robert Isaacs.

Over my shoulder Barrett, having unleashed all her venom,

was now socially relaxed and inquiring where Ramona was staying. Ramona said only that she lived a mile down the road and had stopped by to visit.

"I met you on the drive to Waterston Evers's estate with Frank Anthony." Ramona's eyes became languid pools of longing as she addressed Barrett. "I made a mental note to contact you after that, and I honestly can't recall why I didn't."

"I suspect you're very busy and move in rather elevated circles," Barrett remarked, and for the first time I realized that Barrett Silvers was admitting she was outranked. Barrett Silvers, who'd had every hot writer and many a starlet, was actually deferring to whom—*a woman who had to be rocketing toward her late sixties? A woman with a shock of silver hair, a trim figure, a funny wit, and okay, great tits, but come on.*

"Not that elevated, I assure you," Ramona said, sipping her martini but keeping her eyes lifted and locked on Barrett. Even I could feel the heat and I made eye contact with Callie, indicating with a nod that she should check out what was going on and perhaps join me in the kitchen and give them some space.

There was a pause as Barrett and Ramona appeared to be analyzing why their earlier meeting hadn't produced the chemistry currently in the air. I mused on that mystery—how a place, a time, an instant coalesces to create a magical, inescapable energy that can be felt across the room, can sear through clothing, can create sleepless nights and lustful longings.

"Do you spend much time in L.A.?" Barrett asked almost softly.

"When it's needed." Ramona's penetrating stare invited Barrett to express a need.

"Good to know," Barrett said and I felt my own heartbeat. *Is Barrett really going to put a move on Ramona? She's not even a writer.*

Ramona must have caught us watching them out of the corner of her eye, because she suddenly turned to include us in the conversation.

"Teague and I are old friends. We met in Tulsa, during the Anthony murder that ultimately had studio ties, as you know. In fact, I recall now that you were heavily involved in that case and were injured and hospitalized."

Barrett said she was, and for the next fifteen minutes they reminisced about Frank Anthony's being shot in the gym by people who wanted to cover up the graft and corruption taking place at the studio. The conversation wasn't about poor dead Frank Anthony at all; it was sexual foreplay as two women who had cruised half the planet let one another know they shared language skills, quick wits, and healthy libidos.

Barrett had pulled her battered leather chair up close to the couch where Ramona lounged like a stately silver cat, her arm, as long as Barrett's, reaching out toward the coffee table in front of her, the quarter-sized diamond on her finger signaling she was a woman accustomed to comfort. She leaned in to grasp the drink glass, never taking her Dresden blue eyes off Barrett, who seemed caught in their experienced net.

"So do you live alone?" Ramona repeated, seeming to survey her present opportunity.

It was the phrase that put a lesbian on the path to a quick close or possible complications. The moment in which, like an archaeologist, she unearthed husbands, live-in girlfriends, underage children, or the fact that the admired lived in her car under a viaduct. Barrett paused, no doubt a tingling sensation rippling from her pelvis to her throat, for the answer was also a moment—one in which she could surrender to her passion or rid herself of an unwanted suitor by pleading anything from herpes to heterosexuality.

A smile played around Barrett's lips. "I live alone."

"We have to make up for that," Ramona said lightly, as if that meant they might meet for lunch sometime as opposed to devour one another across the coffee table. They didn't seem to notice our absence as Callie and I watched from the kitchen, our lesbian children playing in the living room.

Ramona Mathers, whose relaxed and sensual presence clearly indicated she was still interested in anything life had to offer, and her body amazingly offered more than could realistically be expected, was sophisticated sexy, feline sexy, available sexy. When

I overheard Ramona say she once wanted to be a writer and had published several short stories, I smiled at Callie, trying to conceal a snicker.

"This is so going to clinch the deal," I whispered.

Barrett perked up, saying she'd love to read what Ramona had written.

"Is it warm in here or am I getting drunk?" Ramona asked, giving Barrett her entrée, and Barrett quickly suggested they step out on the porch with their drinks.

As the door clicked shut behind them, Callie said, "So, it appears we have a match."

Elmo let out a large bored moan.

"I'm with you, Elmo. Good grief, Ramona is twenty years older than Barrett."

"So what?" Callie smiled. "If she were a man, people would say, 'Good for her.'"

"Well, then—good for her," I said and almost meant it.

❖

Barrett and Ramona stayed outside longer than you would think comfortable in light of the cold night air, and I wondered if they'd gone off into the woods and curled up in a knothole.

Turning the lights off in the cabin, I pulled back the curtain so I could peek onto the porch.

"What are you doing?" Callie giggled.

"I want to know if they're out there porking each other in the pines or what," I whispered. My eyes adjusted and I could see them facing each other, their drinks deserted on the porch railing. Barrett slowly stroked Ramona's long arm and then slid hers around Ramona's waist, pulling her in and gently putting her lips to Ramona's, shifting slightly and then kissing her deeply. *Barrett can't kiss, this is going to ruin the deal,* I thought.

Barrett finally took her lips from Ramona's. A pause. And then Ramona took Barrett's face in her hands lovingly, gently, and slowly kissed her as if she'd discovered something she hadn't known the world contained. Her pelvis lodged against Barrett's generated so much heat I could feel it through the plate glass.

"Omigod, Ramona Mathers must think Barrett can kiss spectacularly and she can't get enough of it," I stage-whispered.

"What are you doing?" Callie asked, shocked, I was certain, over my voyeurism. "Does that bother you?"

"No," I said, somewhat confused over my reaction. "Actually, yes. A couple of days ago I was fending off Barrett, who was practically packing a porpoise in her panties, throwing me on the floor, and talking to me like I was a hooker, and now she's treating old Ramona like she's Cinder-fuckin'-rella. What's up with that?"

"Love, darling." She laughed and singed me with a sensual kiss, her mouth so hot and soft it sucked me into the depths of her, conveying that everything past the surface of her skin was equally wet and warm.

The door opened and our visitors caught the two of us buried in one another, causing Ramona to announce, "The evening is picking up in every corner."

Barrett, like a schoolgirl, held the door for Ramona and guided her toward the couch.

"Sedona is a romantic place," Barrett said as if she really meant it, behaving like a charm-school graduate trying out her newly acquired social graces and causing my mouth to go slack in wonderment.

"Romance is merely energy, transferable—and contagious." Callie smiled at them but her voice held no specific nuance.

The air in the room had shifted the way air does when sex and romance are wafting through it. The pauses were heavy, the unspoken words laced with meaning. The electricity leapt out of the walls and into the room and swirled around us, but this time in the most exhilarating way and, as if to accentuate the obvious, a moan emanated from the corner of the living room where Elmo was engaged. At first glance I refused to believe what I was seeing—the stuffed basset hound wedged under him, Elmo clutching it with his front paws—a bizarre act of pooch porno.

"Elmo!" I shouted in shock, and everyone turned to watch Elmo humping the stuffed toy. "Quit it!"

The four of us couldn't suppress ongoing giggles and I felt a twinge of sadness for Elmo, normally distinguished and well behaved, frozen mid-hump, eyes rolled up at us, caught mashing the girl basset and wondering no doubt why we'd all turned into voyeurs.

"He knows how a nice evening should end." Ramona smiled at Barrett and suddenly Elmo gave it up in one big thrust, falling over exhausted. I was no longer empathetic but simply mortified, having never seen him do anything remotely that obscene and certainly not in public.

"It's the energy, don't blame him." Callie laughed harder.

I glanced over and caught Barrett's eyes lingering on Ramona's cleavage, and then she leaned ever so slightly against her—close enough to make Ramona breathe in noticeably.

"What are you wearing?" Barrett asked, and Ramona must have fielded that question often because she answered without missing a beat.

"Bulgari."

"I don't think I've ever known anyone who wore that." Barrett's voice was nearly sedated.

"You may be wearing some yourself." Her gaze, both intimate and teasing, riveted Barrett, who appeared about to fall to her knees in sexual supplication.

Ramona's tone shifted to business. "Well, I'll look into our little venture regarding the vortex site," she said, speaking in code to Callie and obviously referring to our enlisting her help in the exhumation of Nizhoni's body. "Meanwhile, I think I'll head back to my cabin."

Barrett asked if Ramona had a view of the creek from her cabin and Ramona said she did, and then Barrett launched into an impromptu commercial about how buying her own cabin on Oak Creek was the right investment and offering to let Ramona have a look at the view from hers. I wanted to shout that they were too old for all this toying around and they should go get it on, but love seemed to reduce them to teenage hormone levels. Moments later, both cars pulled out of the driveway, heading in the same direction.

"I can't envision it," I said. "Ramona Mathers humping Barrett."

"They both deserve happiness, don't you think?"

"But they're not…a pair."

"Not by your standards, but we don't want the entire world thinking and behaving like you." She smiled and kissed me, letting me know that despite my obvious faults, she loved me.

"What do I smell?" I sniffed the air like Elmo.

"Turkey. I started cooking it tonight. Tomorrow's Thanksgiving and I thought I'd get it ready ahead of time and then all we'd have to do is…" She reached between my legs. "…warm it up."

I would forever view turkey as an aphrodisiac.

Chapter Nine

Sunlight broke through the slits between the rows of café curtains that hung from tarnished gold metal rods above the battered old wood-frame windows in the cabin's bedroom. I lay across the bed watching the golden slivers crisscross our bodies, finally realizing my dream of Thanksgiving alone with the woman I most loved in all the world. Callie Rivers lying next to me in bed, her body warm and naked and gorgeous, was a lotto win.

Knowing I should be kind enough to let her sleep, I still couldn't resist stroking her shoulders that tapered down to absolutely exquisite hips and, once there, sliding my hand between her legs. She moaned, but it was more in light protest at my waking her.

"Happy Thanksgiving, and I have so much to be thankful for," I said.

She rolled over, causing the bed sheets to rustle, wafting her scent over me as she wrapped her arms around me and graced me with those fabulous blue eyes. "Hello, my darling love," she whispered, and my entire being melted; what more could I ask? Burrowed down in clean sheets and her fragrant breasts, in a Sedona cabin on the creek, the wind wafting the smell of pine through the bedroom windows and across the room, nowhere to go but into one another, nothing to see beyond each other's eyes, nothing to do but make love endlessly, I kissed her passionately…before she rose on an elbow and twisted out of my grasp.

"Oh, I had a dream. It was about the chart. This long thread connected all these women like Maypole ribbons. And this duck had the end of the ribbon in his mouth and was flying from one to the other."

Callie suddenly leapt to her feet, leaving me alone in our bunk feeling stunned that apparently I was the only one having a sexy morning, as she deserted me for her computer.

"I think my dream is trying to tell me that whatever happened to Nizhoni is tied to other women as well."

"By a duck?" But Callie wasn't listening and I would apparently have to wait until she could focus on us again so, meanwhile, I focused on my faithful hound.

"Elmo, as a lover, I must be doing something wrong. Could be I'm moving too slow. I notice when you have success, you kind of sneak up on 'em from behind and jump 'em. I'm thinking that's a good tactic."

Elmo let out a large belch and stretched.

"I agree, far more satisfying." Slipping on a pair of cords, some thick socks under my hiking boots, a black turtleneck, and a short jacket, I took Elmo out for a quick walk. He stretched and yawned and farted in the brisk morning air. I thought about what Callie said last night in regard to Ramona and Barrett being a good match and hoped they too were having a delicious Thanksgiving morning. Feeling good about life in general, I decided maybe I should try to be less judgmental and more helpful—certainly more helpful to Callie, who was always supportive of me.

"Elmo, I'm going to drive Callie over to Oak Creek Canyon and take a look at the spot where Nizhoni went over the cliff. I have a feeling I'll learn something. And Callie needs me on this case. Frankly, I haven't been focused on it. It's the energy thing…too hard to get my hands on."

Elmo's teeth chattered and he looked nervous. A little shiver ran across my own spine, some kind of electricity in the air, like electric eyes sparking around me at a fun house, a sensation that someone was watching me. *What, a squirrel?* I mocked myself and was happy when we entered the cabin, going from crisp cold to the warmth of the snug log-sided room.

I mentioned my idea to Callie, and she seemed genuinely pleased I was finally taking a real interest in Nizhoni's death.

Assuring Elmo we would chow down on turkey when we returned, I gave him a Milk-Bone to tide him over. "Stay in the cabin and don't molest the squirrels."

Elmo rolled his eyes at me.

"Hey, fair comment. Last night you gave stuffed toy a whole new meaning."

Fifteen minutes later, we parked a hundred yards from the edge of the most breathtaking gorge in Sedona, allowing us full view of a vista so deep and broad that eagles soared overhead and dove down hundreds of feet into its basin without coming near any edge, their shrieks echoing across the vastness as they swooped in and out of one of heaven's more massive bowls of air. I imagined how enchanted visitors parked and stared in wonder at this masterpiece of nature twelve miles long and roughly half a mile deep, the bravest of them walking to the edge of the cliffs to envision what it might be like to take flight from this ledge; but this morning, it was beautifully silent and free of other tourists.

We got out of the car marveling at the beauty all around us and headed for what appeared to be the primo view, when suddenly Callie stopped.

"Teague, this is the area where news reports say Nizhoni was attacked by the wolf."

"Where exactly do you think she went over?"

Callie paused for a moment, swinging her body slowly as one would swing a shotgun, moving smoothly from left to center to right and then back again. "Over there."

She pointed decisively and I walked in the direction she indicated. At the edge of the canyon, I crouched like a catcher and ran my hands over the red rock, then swiveled on the balls of my feet, my back to the canyon's edge, and examined a piece of rock directly to my right bearing chalk markings, no doubt the police markings of the accident scene.

"Teague, move away from there!"

I heard Callie's sharp voice as the small red rocks under the ball of my left foot began to give way, sliding like gravel, and my foot slipped out from under me. I managed to get my balance and rise halfway to a standing position when I saw the wolf, fangs bared, charging directly at me, snarling, snapping, the eyes no longer kind, but ferocious, heading for my face. Reflexively I recoiled and went over onto my back, reaching out behind me to catch myself, but found nothing but air. I catapulted in a certain-death backflip off the edge of the cliff, the only sound Callie's prolonged scream.

Airborne, uncoiling, grasping, terrified, weightless, rocks zoom, plants tear, birds scatter, Callie's face, prepare impact!

"Callliiieee!"

Snagged, ripped, slammed, stopped! Alive? Alive! Breathing... panting...breathing... panting.

My trembling body dangled somehow in midair as my mind continued to tumble around in my head, unable to find its bearings.

Near the ground? Will it hold me up, can I hold on? How do I get out of here?

More panicked than I could ever remember being in my life, I felt the pain of something slicing into my armpit. Slowly, I turned my head to see what was holding me.

A rope, so close I could see the fibers in each strand, dirty white, rolled in graceful spirals around one another forming something akin to a seining net. My arm had miraculously hooked through it, and the rest of my weight pulling against it was cutting off my circulation. I turned slightly in the breeze, refusing to look down, and grabbed more of the netting with my unsteady left hand, allowing me to take some pressure off my right arm, but not much, because my left hand was shaking uncontrollably.

Struggling, I tried to hook my feet into the vertical netting that somehow dangled off the side of the cliff, but couldn't snag the bottom portion with my toe. The lightweight net flapped away from me in the wind, and the spaces in the net weren't much larger than the width of my shoe. After resting a minute, I slowly pulled my knees up to my waist, wincing at the rope tearing into my arm. I was grateful I'd kept up my body crunches, because I had the strength to get my feet up closer to a part of the net I could hold steady and slip one shoe in without the net drifting away.

Contorted into a ball, I had both hands and both feet locked in the net where I steadied myself and tried to regulate my breathing. Over time, I could now slowly work my feet and hands up one square of netting at a time and walk myself up…but to where? I couldn't think about that now. Steeling myself, I peered through the netting. The canyon, five or six hundred feet of it, stretched beneath me, as vast as my desperation.

Can you hear me? Callie, I'm alive. Find me! I cried out for her again and again—at first in words and then silently, and finally, I just cried.

Chapter Ten

It took me awhile to pull myself together. I'd experienced plenty of bad things on the force—been chased by every sonofabitch known to man with a gun or a knife and the intent to kill me, been damned near beaten to death and set on fire that night in Oklahoma when I was investigating a murder case, not to mention the number of crazies we'd encountered in Vegas; but I always pitted my wits and my strength against theirs. This was different.

Settle down, I told my terrified self, *and look at the rock wall next to you.* But that advice didn't work because the netting that held me captive swung toward and away from the rock, reminding me I was no better off than a snared bird dangling over the potential place of my death.

A piece of netting hanging vertically along the rock wall would require someone with great skill to hang it here, a purpose for hanging it—and if it has a purpose then someone has to check the net! The last thought gave me a nanosecond of hope. Whether you're catching minnows, animals, or people, you set the trap, and then you check it later. *So someone will come. An Indian,* I thought, in this land of tribal people. An Indian would be nimble enough to find a way down the abyss, although the idea seemed heart-stopping. *Let's hope he checks it daily and not weekly.*

I was starting to shake from the cold air, the fear, and the light wind that whipped through the canyon. *Even if he comes to check the net, how in the world would he ever be able to get me out of here? It would take a rescue helicopter.*

I strained and stretched gently, not knowing if the netting was even meant to hold something as heavy as me, and tried to catch a glimpse overhead to understand what I was tethered to. A sturdy but supple rope seemed to be wound around a large wooden ring, then ascended to a place I could no longer see, too far away for me to bend my head and neck back and look without losing my grip.

God, please get me out of here and teach me something later. And whichever way it goes, please always take care of Callie Rivers and don't let anything bad ever happen to her and please take care of Elmo. Amen.

I don't know how long it had been, or what time it was, but my heart roared into action when I heard the whir of the helicopter blades. *Callie's gotten help,* I thought joyously. And ten minutes later when they whizzed through the center of the canyon, their blades at eye level, I was certain that after one more pass they would see me. They made seven more trips before I realized someone had placed the net precisely in a spot that shielded rescuers from view and, despondent, I wondered if that was intentional.

The sound of the helicopter receding made me tear up and feel sorry for myself. I closed my eyes and tried to meditate, but my hands and arms hurt from holding onto the rope.

Suddenly, my body moved horizontally, jarring me into the realization that I was being towed along like clothes on a wash line headed who knew where, but no matter; it had to be better than here. At some point the towing stopped and I was being hauled up vertically. The sporadic and shaky pulling was nerve-racking, but made me hopeful nonetheless. I thought about calling out, but I didn't want to do anything to stop my being lifted up. It could be a rescue, but if it was, someone would be calling out to me. I had a strange gut feeling this wasn't a rescue, but merely a retrieval of prey. And then as I could see the rocky ledge, the reeling-in stopped.

I hung in stillness, waiting for whoever it was to pull me in, but they didn't. *Can they see who I am? Did they expect a human and not an animal? Do they intend to leave me to die?* My shoulder and arm were half numb, and I tried to readjust without suddenly coming loose from the only thing keeping me alive. Craning my neck to see any sign of life at the top of the cliff, I looked directly overhead and spotted a ledge jutting out maybe twenty feet above me. I had fallen too far down for any rope to rescue me. Someone overhead knew a special path that led to this ledge, and they'd tied the netting to something on that precipice. Maybe that's why the net had jutted out enough for me to fall into.

For a control freak, this is fucking purgatory, I thought. *I can't get out unless someone wants me out. I can't get word to anyone. I can't even pee...unless it's in my own pants.* That thought made me so angry that tears gathered in my eyes again, and I shut them tightly and steeled my jaw, determined not to let my emotions get the best of me.

"If somebody did this to me, I'll kill him as soon as he pulls me up," I said softly, and then I must have dozed off for a few seconds from sheer exhaustion, the wind rocking me in the netting as you would a shivering child.

My eyes slammed open, my heart pounded my chest as if attacking me, and I heard her voice as clearly as if she were beside me.

"Teague."

I looked around quickly, trying to spot her.

"Teague," Callie said, "I will find you."

Certain Callie was with me right now, I started to speak and then realized, of course, there was no way she could be.

Find me. Did she mean find me now or find me in our next lifetime? I hoped it was both. Her voice speaking my name tore my heart out. "I love you, Callie," I whispered, and as if my very words had activated a mechanism to save me, the pulley system began moving me again, only vertically this time.

In another three or four minutes, my feet slammed into the rock and hands grappled with my ankles. Then like a giant marlin hauled in flopping, body banging into the rocks, I was hoisted higher to firm ground.

Face down, I felt the earth—flat and solid beneath the stretched-out length of my body, a mother's warm hug—indescribably comforting and solid and reassuring. Breathing in with undisguised relief, I chose to ignore the fact that a stranger had rolled me like a Cuban cigar and instead focused on my surroundings so I could make my escape: a tree to my left, a smooth canyon wall. Then I realized I was at a lower altitude than the canyon overlook from which I'd fallen.

Must be a ledge or area below where I fell, with a trail leading down to it.

He leaned his dark face with its smiling white teeth into mine and said, "You don't fly too good."

"No, Jesus God, I thought I was dead! How did you find me?"

"Shaman," the man whispered almost inaudibly as he pulled the netting away from my body and packed it like a parachute. "Go back to your cabin," the man said, almost murmuring, and somewhere in the labyrinth of my mind I wondered how this strange man knew to find me, knew I was in a cabin.

But my thoughts gave way to images of Callie running toward me, arms outstretched. I staggered to my feet and caught her, our bodies slamming into one another, unable to hold back our sheer physical joy.

Not saying anything above the tears, but clutching her to me, I realized I didn't care about anything else but Callie Rivers. I'd felt this way once before when she'd been kidnapped during a case we were working on, and I wondered why in between that time and this, I couldn't remember this intense state of adoration when I was arguing with her, or when I was angry with her, or when I felt momentarily trapped.

I held her face and looked into her eyes, experiencing it all now, then pressed her forehead to mine as if to program the intensity of this moment and my love for her through my thick skull and onto the storage disc of my brain.

"My heart left my chest and went over that ridge with you. I thought I'd lost you."

"You mean you couldn't psychically know I would be safe." I tried to tease her.

"I did know, but I didn't believe my knowing because it's too close to my heart."

As we stood locked in each other's arms, she turned, seeming to feel a presence in the air, and I felt it too, a painful energy like the warning tingle you get before touching a hot wire.

"Let's get out of here," Callie said. When she took my arm, I was wobbly and weak and gently complained of her tight grip, predicting I was blue under my shirt from hanging on the rope.

"Wait a second, I want to get a closer look at what I was suspended by—some sort of netting."

Callie protested my wanting to get near the spot where I'd been hauled up and prevented my taking a step in that direction, but I couldn't see any net or sign of my rescue.

"If I wasn't dizzy and all my body parts throbbing, I'd say none of this ever happened. Where did the net and the Indian guy go?"

Not answering, her arm around me, Callie helped me walk back up the treacherous canyon trail to the car, the path so narrow and rough and steep it was slow going. "Did you hear me?" she asked. "The entire time you were down there, I called to you with my mind."

"I heard you tell me you would find me."

"I did and I always will."

"How did you know I was down below the ridge?"

"Manaba told me," she said, and I was too out of breath to quiz her further.

About the time I knew I wasn't up to walking much farther, the parking lot appeared ahead and slightly above us. Leaning against the white Jeep and touching the metal door handle was almost a religious experience. Salvation brought to me by Chrysler. Sitting in the leather seats of my Jeep felt good, solid, warm. Callie drove, taking my hand, and we rode in silence.

"The man who rescued you has to be involved in Nizhoni's disappearance, yet there's no way he could have arranged for you to take a plunge over that edge," she finally said, unable not to discuss in detail the bizarre event that had led to my near death.

Callie momentarily stopped the car, leaned over, and gave me a kiss that was all longing for the present, the future, and always. It seemed that having nearly lost me, she had intensified her desire for me, which I already thought was record breaking. Unable to express how I felt about her without crying, I stuck to the tactical.

"Was a helicopter looking for me?"

"The moment you went over and I couldn't see you or hear you, I phoned the police, the sheriff's department, the park service, and Manaba. I was frantic. I don't think there was time for a helicopter. You were down there for what seemed like a lifetime, but it was really about ninety minutes."

Beginning to shake, my teeth nearly chattering, a habit I had of getting more petrified after a near-death experience than during, I whispered, "Jesus, that was…terrifying."

"How did you happen to fall right where the net was placed? How was a net there…of all the places around the canyon?"

"I wouldn't have gone over if it hadn't been for the wolf." As I said it, goose bumps raced up my legs. "As I was catching my balance the wolf appeared and lunged at me."

"I never saw a wolf." Callie clutched my hand and spoke into the air. "So he sent you over the edge."

"He who?"

"The man whose name I won't speak, the energy I won't evoke. Someone must have sent the Indian man, and he saved you. Was Nizhoni saved by him too?"

I was getting over my fear and getting into being pissed. "I don't know what's going on, but it's getting to be less about Manaba and more about us. Some kind of energy attacked you, and a phantom wolf threw me over a cliff. If Manaba told you where I was, she's in on it along with the Indian man who saved me. Maybe they killed Nizhoni and simply chose to rescue me."

"If they were killers, why rescue you?"

"Maybe because she knows you love me, and she did it as a favor."

"They didn't murder Nizhoni because she's not dead."

"Then your shaman's lying to you."

Callie nodded, for the first time admitting that Manaba was lying.

She dialed the police department and sheriff's department to tell them I was safe—reporting the time I was rescued, my inability to name the rescuer, but describing the location.

I could hear the squawk of male voices over bad radio equipment as they exchanged information, and I thought about how small we are in the world when we search for one another—police merely troops of ants all dressed alike, driving the same cars, fanning out across the unknown to locate one lost ant.

Suddenly I was thinking about life as one giant search party—searching for a house, a job, a mate, the meaning of life, not to mention the search for socks, glasses, and car keys—and before I could search for anything else, I lost consciousness—my mind searching for a nap.

Chapter Eleven

There's something wonderful about bed after a big scare. Soft and warm and comforting, it seemed to embrace me, let me find solace in Callie and fall asleep, leaving the frightening event behind so we could wake up and begin again the next day.

"I've been shown one thing, how very much I want to spend every minute with you," I said, putting my arm across Callie's middle as we sat propped up against the pillows, resting my hand on the inside of her thigh and letting out a deep sigh.

Under the arm that had snagged the net, bad bruises on my ribs led down to discolored areas below them. My arm muscles were excruciatingly sore and my leg muscles only slightly less so.

Callie took body lotion and slowly, carefully massaged my arms and legs, and when I asked if she thought body lotion healed bruising, she said it wasn't about lotion. It was about massage and realigning the energy in my body.

Lying on my back, I closed my eyes as she rubbed the cream up my thighs, over my belly, up my chest, and over my breasts before her hands gripped my shoulders, pausing a moment and then retracing her steps, her hands never losing contact with my skin. Soon the long, relaxing strokes were narrowing their path until she was rubbing a single track between my legs and laid her entire weight on my body, her lips pressed to mine. "Your body took quite a battering," she whispered and laid her head on my chest.

"Happens in life."

"You need to treat yourself better."

"Maybe you could do that on my behalf."

"I will," Callie said, and rolled me over so she could massage my buttocks and slide up and down my back with her naked body, her large breasts brushing my spine, her body getting closer to me with each stroke until her entire voluptuous form was gliding up and down me gently, each pass of her soft skin making me quiver with anticipation. Finally, she lowered herself onto me, refusing to allow me to turn over, and glided one hand under me, stroking me, while fingers of the other slid into me and her body rocked up against me, creating the sensation that she had more hands than was humanly possible and making me break out in a sweat that could have been the change, but who cared.

My body wet, every other part of me hard as she hydroplaned down me, into me with measured rhythm, taking me to the edge of the orgasmic cliff where I hung on, not wanting to fall over, not wanting it to end, holding on as long as I could and then sailing, soaring, explosive, climax. Breathing…panting…breathing…panting.

"Where did you learn that?" I moaned.

She nibbled my ear in response.

"You are so good," I whispered.

As I poured a cup of coffee at the kitchen counter, Callie slung her arms around me, ambushing me from behind. Undeterred by my squeals and the splattering caffeine, she plopped her chin on my shoulder and announced how pleased she was to be driving me sexually insane, admitting it made her love me even more.

"I think of your body as a Mount Everest and myself as a skilled climber who has no trouble making it to the top."

I whirled and grabbed her. "You are so cocky."

Elmo let out a deep bark, startling us both as Ramona Mathers peeked through the plate-glass window, her hand shielding her eyes as if she was trying to focus and see if we were home. I shouted for her to come in. Three clomps on the steps and she was through the doorway.

"What in the world happened yesterday?" she asked without any introductory protocol. Something about your falling off the canyon ridge. Did you?"

"Yes, and was rescued by a Navajo trapper, I'm guessing."

"Why the hell were you standing so near the edge? Do we have to put a harness on you like a three-year-old?"

"My thoughts exactly, and I would have welcomed one as I dangled like a yoyo whipping around in the wind thinking my demise was eminent," I said, my supercilious tone an attempt to cover how seriously frightened I was. "Now I realize someone wanted me to die—like Nizhoni supposedly did."

"Are you saying someone wanted you to fall into the canyon, at the spot where Nizhoni fell, and live to discuss it?"

I made a mental note that Ramona said at the spot where Nizhoni fell. How would she know that?

Callie nodded affirmatively as I added, "I was actually thrown over the cliff by a wolf who wasn't really there."

Ramona paused. "You're obviously not sharing that with anyone?" Although her tone was flippant, I felt she was telling me not to, and why wouldn't she want anyone to know? Because she didn't want people to think I was crazy? Because she didn't want wolves maligned? Because she knew something about Nizhoni's death she wasn't telling?

"Who told you I went over the cliff?"

"The Native American community is abuzz about the rescue by one of their own."

"And you have a hotline to that community?"

"I've had this cabin for thirty-five years and hire Indians to help me occasionally."

"Did you know Nizhoni?"

"One of my clients knew her…I didn't. Speaking of the dead," Ramona intoned, "I've gotten word to a connected friend and had to call in a chit, so I hope this is all worth it in the end. But when the offices open next Monday, if you're still inclined, I can file the necessary documents to get the body exhumed. Jot down the woman's name, date of birth, date of death—"

"Time of death is approximate," Callie said, walking to the kitchen counter and locating a piece of paper with the information on it and handing it to Ramona.

"Nicely done, Sherlock." Ramona's tone was intimate as she held Callie in her gaze.

"Did Barrett go back to L.A.?" I asked to break up any sexual energy Ramona was about to toss Callie's way, marveling that her sexual battery never seemed to go dry. The woman could be turned on faster than a light switch.

"No, actually, she stayed over," she said, her eyes still locked on Callie's, but the words had a playful sound to them as if she was at that moment thinking of Barrett in bed with her. "I like your friend a lot."

"Which one? Because the one you're staring at is taken." I mimicked her playful tone rather than say her gaze was annoying the hell out of me.

"Sweet." Her eyes broke away from Callie to connect with mine and let me know she was merely joking. "I'm meeting Barrett for breakfast, so I have to run. Only came by to see if you were still breathing." Ramona left, looking a little more graceful than I remembered her.

"They're just fucking each other," I said. "And she'd better stay away from you."

"I'm just fucking you too," she said, reaching into my pants suddenly. "But that doesn't mean I'm not mad about you. In fact the two are definitely related."

"I've started buying all my pants loose at the waist." I sighed and allowed her to do with me what she would, which at this moment seemed to be merely fooling around with me enough to make me sexually crazy and keeping me in a state of constant desire.

"I was thinking"...she began and looked deeply into my eyes as I groaned over what great hands she had..."that we should get married." My eyes snapped open wide and all formerly receptive orifices clamped shut. Seeing my startled look she released her hold on me and giggled.

Is my near-death experience coming down to a wedding band? What in the world had prompted a woman who heretofore wouldn't live with me suddenly to want to marry me? My mind locked up as I tried to decide what exactly marriage meant between the two of us, since no one really offered marriage to lesbians in the way I'd come to think of it—two nervous people in monochromatic colors meeting at the end of an aisle alongside a quartet of women all wearing brightly colored clothing—the colors alone telling you who the happy people were.

"Married?" My voice didn't sound like my voice at all, but more like a voice I'd rented from some very nervous person.

"You said you wanted us to live together—"

"I do!" I said, aware I'd uttered the very words that in another context had me freaked out. Lesbians didn't have to get married; that was in fact the beauty of being a lesbian. You could get up any morning and decide this wasn't the bed you wanted to share or the relationship you wanted to wear. Good-bye was no more complicated than tossing your clothes in a bag and computer and books into the Jeep.

Then straight people started muddying the water by denying gay people marriage, and pretty soon perfectly normal gay people were demanding it. If straight people wanted to punish gay people, they should demand they get married. Let them have to hire divorce attorneys and pay alimony and suffer like straights.

"Somehow I don't think you mean that," Callie said, waiting for me to return from my mental machinations.

"I do!" I repeated and wondered why in hell those two words kept coming out of my mouth at every opportunity. "It's simply that we haven't even lived together yet. Don't you think we should live together first? You didn't want to do that and now you want to get married."

"We're living together now in this cabin. Living together isn't a matter of physical location. It's a matter of being physically, mentally, and spiritually in tune."

"You always act like I'm off-key—out of tune," I squeaked.

"You're afraid of being married to me, aren't you?" She leaned back, observing me and smiling slightly.

"Absolutely not!" I said and broke into a sweat. "We got cheated out of our first Thanksgiving—we didn't get to eat the turkey." I changed the subject abruptly.

"We've had the best Thanksgiving ever. Turkey's in the fridge waiting for you."

I went immediately to the fridge as if the wire shelves held the meaning of life and put my head inside to cool off. Admittedly I was having a hot flash and couldn't decide if it was biochemical or matrimonial.

Callie's proposal was startling and I couldn't think about anything else. She didn't mention it again, but it couldn't have been more present for me. I was afraid—she had that right—afraid. *What am I afraid of? I'll tell you what I'm afraid of—the ring. The ring signifies that life as I know it is over. No more private dinners with Barrett Silvers, that's what the ring means. No worrying about anyone showing up bringing Tupper suppers and looking for a quickie. I would be forced to see things differently—to analyze my every move to determine if a particular act could be construed as cheating on her: is that lying to her, would that be disloyal to her? The simplest thing could become a reason for her to take the ring off and throw it across the room at me. That's it, then, the ring is a weapon! It's a marital weapon used as mind control. If my mind strays, look at the ring. Wow! Lord of the Rings has an entirely different...ring to it.*

I glanced over to see if Callie was reading my mind, but she seemed engrossed in her computer screen and not tapping into my thoughts, for which I was grateful.

We dropped matrimony as a general topic for the rest of the day, and by the following afternoon I thought we'd deserted all serious topics in favor of sightseeing, including a trip to a riverbed where Indian artifacts were routinely found. For centuries Native American women had knelt on the rocky soil to fill pots with drinking water, catch fish for the evening meal, or wade into the icy stream where perhaps dirt and worry fell like the leaves from the overhanging trees to drift away on the river's current.

The tranquility of the open spaces took me by surprise, and I sighed deeply, which seemed to release decades of anxiety and bring me into some kind of harmony with the earth. Red clay beneath my feet needed only water to become an earthen vessel or adobe bricks, and perhaps God, when no one was looking, had scooped up the rich red clay into a celestial hand and morphed this beautiful substance into the red people themselves: hard but fragile, faces painted like pottery, fighting until broken.

The bright light on Callie's golden hair held me transfixed as she offered her hand to pull me up from the ground for a climb to the top of a mesa where tribal elders had once offered prayers. Walking hand in hand, we now felt even closer as a couple, seemingly baked together in Sedona's kiln, only poor Elmo fretting over the workout his short legs were getting.

We roamed around in the red dirt for what seemed like hours, then got back in the Jeep, where Elmo promptly passed out and Callie insisted we stop next at a Navajo trading post.

Made of huge unsplit logs, the trading post was rustic and beautiful. Inside, rows of squash-blossom necklaces, lined wood-framed cases, Kachina dolls, and religious icons carved from cottonwood root and painted as mythological figures, some of whom looked like Phyllis Diller on a bad hair day, filled floor-to-ceiling shelves. Hand-tooled belts coiled snakelike in baskets, and beautiful handwoven blankets swung from wooden dowel rods attached at one end to the wall.

Callie strayed over to a glass case full of fine jewelry and pointed to something. A dark-haired, heavy-set woman behind the counter swooshed over in her native dress and unlocked the case. Callie said how elegantly crafted the rings were, then pointed to an unusual pair. "Are these patterned after traditional Navajo wedding bands?"

I bobbed my head up from the Kachina dolls and stared at Callie.

The woman smiled and said they were.

"Come over here, Teague, and try one of these on." Callie looked up at me and gave me the most angelic smile, the light dancing in her eyes.

I couldn't have been more permanently planted to the floor if someone had nailed me there, the mystical experience by the red river momentarily forgotten. Commitment in the abstract always played in my head, but commitment in the now was final, permanent. I panicked. *Callie is looking at wedding bands so the woman behind the counter will know we're thinking of—what: weddings, honeymoons—fucking?*

The woman smiled sweetly at me as if wondering nothing more than my finger size. "If you will come over here, I will measure you," she said and held out the ring sizer.

I glanced at Callie, who hadn't stopped smiling since she'd gone to the jewelry case, and held out my left hand.

"I was thinking we should get matching rings," she said quietly, and the woman looked up, still smiling.

"What a lovely idea," she said, and for an insane moment I thought she and Callie were thinking of getting matching rings. That's what always happened to me when I got freaked—my brain short-circuited and information got jumbled.

"This pair would look lovely on the two of you," the woman said, seemingly untroubled by the idea of two women wearing matching rings.

But hey, it was a sale so maybe money talked louder than prejudice, although this lady didn't look prejudiced; she looked joyful. Flushed, I could feel heat on my earlobes and my chest.

"Do you like this design?" Callie asked me.

"Sure," I said as if I were okaying her purchase for someone else.

"Tell the truth," Callie said.

"I like whatever you like," I whispered, not meaning to whisper, but I'd lost my voice.

"I prefer these with the stones cut at an angle. They say Native American but of the future." Callie took the larger ring and slipped it on the ring finger of my left hand.

A chill raced up my spine and my neck and over my ears as she held her hand there for a moment, and I felt like at this very instant I stood at an altar in front of a priest who was a Native American shopkeeper, taking a vow in full view of whoever else was walking through the store.

"There," Callie said, slowly taking her hand off mine. "You belong to me."

Could she really have said that in public, in front of the priest-shopkeeper, in front of the shopper-parishioners; but the sound of her voice and the ring against my finger felt so good. She carefully lifted the smaller matching ring out of its resting place in the dark blue velvet and slipped it on the identical finger of her left hand, then leaned over and kissed me on the lips.

I laid my hand down next to Callie's, letting my eyes rest for the first time on the two identical rings now side by side. Identical rings. Rings others could spot and in doing so either accept or reject us without even knowing us. *Risk rings,* I thought, my riverbed tranquility all but disintegrated. *Am I mature enough to accept that kind of risk? Why not, life is short. Pleasing strangers isn't nearly as important as pleasing one another.*

"Will that be cash or charge," the priest-keeper asked as I was about to say something, and I thought her remark was no different than a priest's sermon on tithing, directing us to the paper envelope in our pew and offering the ability to put it on our charge card.

Callie suddenly took my hand and slipped the rings off my finger and hers, offering the beautiful gold bands with the dark blue stones and sprinkle of diamonds back to the woman, who locked them up in the case.

"A dress rehearsal," Callie said. "We'll think about whether or not we want to buy them."

I'd tensed up so much in preparing for this event that, suddenly exhausted, I thanked the lady and headed for the car, suggesting to Callie that we go up to the vortex and sit on top of the mountain and watch the sunset at the ceremonial site. I needed to breathe a lot of fresh air and unwind.

"Did we almost get married?" I asked, slightly confused now that the magical feeling of her body near mine was reaching a more sustainable level.

"Let's say we had an opportunity to buy matching wedding bands."

"But we—changed our minds?" I was hoping I hadn't offended her by showing no real support for the idea.

"One of us did." Callie's voice sounded melancholy.

"Are there instances where there are matching wedding bands without marriage?"

Callie laughed. "That would be called two girls who have the same taste in jewelry."

"Nothing wrong with that," I said, more comfortable now. "If you saw us on the street wearing matching rings, what would you think it meant?"

"Anything you want it to mean," she said. "Now if I was one of those people wearing one of the matching wedding rings, for me it would mean you would never fall off a cliff without me, you would never think about another woman but me, and you would always be in my bed."

Elmo let out a moan of deep longing, and we both giggled as I gave Callie a quick kiss. Rounding a bend in the road that would take us to the ceremonial site, I tried to take the conversation to a more philosophical level.

"I think that's all happening now, with or without rings," I said and gave it a few beats. "So tell me more about what wearing matching wedding bands says to you?"

Callie apparently couldn't tolerate my squirming any more. "It means nothing, relax."

Discussion over. I was sad. How ironic. I had chased Callie Rivers across the western half of the United States, begged her to live with me forever, and was determined never to let her go, and now that she'd turned the tables on me, I was moonwalking like Michael Jackson.

"Speaking of being pursued and attacked," I teased, "why did I see the wolf and go over the cliff and you never even saw it. Normally you would look up ten astrological charts on that question, but you haven't even mentioned it."

"I guess I've been having such a great day with you, I wanted to forget all the negatives. They're trying to get to me through you, Teague. He knows I care so much about you. He feels that energy."

"Callie, you have to tell me who this guy is."

Callie looked like a dozen private conversations were taking place in her head. Sometimes I wished I knew everything she was thinking and sometimes I was grateful I didn't. Who in the world did she fear so much that she wouldn't even utter his name?

"A man half Indian."

"Who is he?"

"Luther Drake," she breathed.

A bolt of lightning lit up the sky and flashed above the horizon, a deafening clap of thunder slapped the heavens, and a torrent of rain blasted our windshield and obscured our view. Nature's energy had exploded violently and without warning. I quickly turned on the windshield wipers and shivered at the suddenness of the rainstorm. Neither of us spoke.

CHAPTER TWELVE

The skies were as clear as they had been before the quick deluge, which was now only a passing freak of nature.

"Aren't we climbing up the rock face?" Callie asked.

"Not now that I know about the road on the backside. I'm driving, parking the car, and letting all the tourists on the front side of this rock wonder how I got a car up there." I stepped on the gas and the Jeep shot up the steep cliff, tires spinning and spitting dirt as Callie shouted for me to slow down, perhaps certain I would overshoot the short, flat plateau and take us over the opposite side like Thelma and Louise.

Jamming on the brakes, I staunched her fears and we both hopped out. I took Callie by the hand and together we walked to the ceremonial circle, our arms around each other, breathing in the fresh air that carried the scent of red dirt and cactus and desert flowers and, from somewhere, the smell of mossy creek beds and the down of small animals burrowed in their nests.

Suddenly, I felt as much a part of the earth as any of its other elements, and Callie and I seemed to be alone on top of the world, brushed by the same desert winds that propelled the tumbleweed, swayed by the same celestial breezes that whipped the sagebrush. Forces blowing around us seemed to encourage us to move with the wind, and before I knew it we were whirling in dramatic swirls and turns, dancing in the wind, dust at our heels, the clouds moving around us kitelike as if tied to strings anchored by our hearts.

"It's amazing how we move together so effortlessly," Callie said, smiling up at me, both of us aware that we had never danced together before.

"Even when there's no music."

"I hear music," she said, and we moved in one another's arms as if we were a single being, and perhaps we were. "What do you vow?" she asked me.

"To be yours throughout all time, beyond time, beyond forever. And what do you vow?"

"I vow to be one with you forever," she said, then paused. "How do you know we didn't, at this very moment, get married?"

"You love to mess with my head." I rested my forehead on hers as we spun in circles in the wind, giddy and dizzy.

"Marriage is merely a ceremony where a person says 'I now pronounce you'…so what if the wind and rocks and sand are all whispering 'I now pronounce you.'"

Coyotes howled in the distance and the wind picked up around us. Our conversation muted by nature's sounds, my body too cold to remain still, I ran from the wind and the rocks and the sand and any messages they might be carrying, pretending the cold was forcing us back to the car, holding Callie's hand once we finally climbed inside.

Callie snuggled into me as we drove, and that odd yin-and-yang energy that had cursed my entire life began to whir around me. The energy that guaranteed if something spectacular happened to me, then immediately something of opposite and equal magnitude balanced it out. Yin rear-ended by yang, like winning two thousand dollars only to find out an hour later I needed it for a dental bill. I told Callie about this phenomenon the minute it came to mind.

"Think of it as a blessing preceding the need."

"Sometimes I want random blessings that hang around without a need, but this balancing force seems to dog me, keeps me uncomfortable. It always reminds me that everything changes, and I feel it tonight. Tonight is simply too good to stand on its own."

"Push that negative energy away. Don't accept it. You can, you know."

We rounded a tight bend in the mountain road and suddenly, out of nowhere, a huge animal rushed our vehicle and leaped onto the hood of the car, its claws scraping across the paint on the Jeep's hood, its bared teeth and face smashing into the windshield as we both screamed and I slammed on the brakes.

Elmo's deep growl rose to a sharp squeal as our car careened off the rocky road. I fought to gain control of it, knowing any moment the wolf would slide off, but terrifyingly, its animal face morphed into a diabolical human visage smiling hideously at us through the tempered glass. Callie and I shrieked even louder, like teenagers on a thrill ride, and then the face morphed into that of a corpse and disappeared. The car skidded back onto the road and everything was as it had been, except our nerves were shattered.

"Shit, what the hell was that?" I shouted as Callie and Elmo panted beside me.

"Shape-shifter," Callie breathed, hugging Elmo to her.

"Next time we take a vacation let's stay home. This tribal thing is too intense." My body was shaking, my nerves were jangled, I hated whoever was dogging us, and I wanted revenge.

"The man I told you about—" Callie began.

"The half-Indian?"

"He knows about the wolf visiting us, and he's appearing in similar form to try to trick us. He's the one who showed up at the cabin and tried to entice you into the woods."

"Did you know who he was then?" I asked, and Callie nodded that she did. "That's why you got so upset. And he's the one who showed up in the form of the wolf and sent me over the canyon edge?" Now I knew who the wolf was…and somehow I felt worse and not better. "So where are you, you chicken sonofabitch? I want to meet you in the flesh," I shouted into the windshield.

"You've summoned him. He will show himself now." I could tell from Callie's voice that she was worried, but I was anxious to get everything out in the open—in particular Luther Drake.

❖

Almost as soon as we got back to the cabin, the phone rang. It was Ramona Mathers saying she had been unable on such short notice to get permission to exhume a body; she'd even called Cy Blackstone, who had reminded her that many people weren't back from the holidays and it wasn't going to be possible. I thanked her for giving it a shot and hung up.

"She even asked Cy Blackstone, which was pretty ballsy of her. She's connected, I'll give her that."

"I think she's been warned off," Callie said. "She was so confident and now, before the government offices are even open, she's declaring defeat."

"Should we tell Manaba we can't get it done?"

"She's meeting us late tonight. I knew it would come down to our doing it without anyone's help."

I wanted to ask when she'd contacted Manaba about digging up the grave, but the air in Sedona seemed to carry messages like whispers in the wind. If a woman could dance in the middle of a fire, she most likely could know things without relying on U.S. Cellular.

❖

"Wake up." Callie shook me. It was still pitch-black outside as I yanked on my cords, grabbed a sweater and down vest, and pulled on my mountain boots. I crossed in front of the living room door on my way to the bathroom and halted abruptly.

The figure in the living room only looked up, the face stoic, the outfit the same, Manaba sitting like an invited guest before I'd even heard the front door open.

"Did you let her in?" I said over my shoulder to Callie.

"She let herself in. This is her cabin, remember?"

"Forgot about that. But she might consider knocking when it's rented."

Entering the living room, I greeted her as I crossed to the kitchen to turn on the coffee but saw it was already made, the pot emptied and put away. Manaba offered me a cup she'd apparently saved for me and I took it, grateful to be able to drink and not talk. The cabin brew, always strong and rich, was more bitter than it had been the last time I drank it, as if it too anticipated the thing to be done: an unearthing, a removal of a body from a grave in the middle of the night, an illegal act on sacred ground. I hoped Manaba had said all the right prayers before we left.

Excusing myself, I headed back to the bedroom to see how Callie was doing. "How can Manaba stand the idea of digging up a grave that contains her lover? How can she be okay with that?"

"She's trained to endure many things, some you and I could never even imagine."

I watched as Callie applied her makeup as if she was going to a premiere instead of an exhumation. She caught me staring at her and cocked a questioning eyebrow.

"It's dark-thirty outside. No one will see you, and even Sacajawea in there is without makeup and in her only piece of wardrobe. Why take so much time getting ready? Don't get me wrong. Personally, I think you look fabulous."

"Out of respect." Callie shook her head.

"For Nizhoni? You said she wasn't in the grave."

"For myself."

I realized Callie's principles trickled down into the smallest details of life, and for a moment I saw her as a beautiful warrior applying war paint—preparing to do battle with a form yet unseen.

"I'm not too excited about doing this," I said.

"It's her family's burial place. Nizhoni's uncle is going to help."

"That's even creepier."

When Callie came out of the bedroom, Manaba made eye contact with her for an instant and then went outside, further annoying me with her constant attempts at unspoken conversation with Callie.

As we headed for our car, Manaba was gone. Was there a Manaba-mobile? I didn't know. All I knew for sure was she didn't ride with us and I didn't see another vehicle for her. Perhaps she'd mastered the art of disappearing and reappearing. We'd find out when we got to the cemetery.

❖

"Something's not right," I fretted as Callie navigated, directing me around curves, up hills, and back down the other side. "Manaba's too damned calm." We topped a hill and emerged on a short stretch of two-lane with nothing on either side but sand. "Navajos don't want to see, touch, or talk about the dead because they're afraid the ghosts of the dead will attach to them," I said, turning back toward rockier terrain and thinking that getting lost took on a whole new meaning out here.

"They're very smart. That can happen."

"So why would Manaba and the uncle agree to dig up Nizhoni's grave?"

"I don't care why. I know we have to do it. Could we make it a little warmer in here? You've got the AC so low that snow is coming out of the vents," Callie said and I rolled my eyes at her. "I got you something to take for the hot flashes." Callie pulled a small tin container out of her pocket. "It's all natural." She handed me a capsule and gave me a sip of her Coke to slug it down.

"Where did you get this?"

"It's an Indian remedy."

I noted she didn't answer the question directly, meaning she'd probably gotten it from a local source I wouldn't even visit, much less buy drugs from. "Great," I said, wondering what in hell I'd swallowed.

As the road inclined again, Callie punched a button on her penknife and shone the light on antiquated-looking hand-drawn directions; I was almost certain Manaba had drawn them.

"Left," she instructed as we approached an opening in the road that looked like a goat path. I was grateful for four-wheel drive as she continued with her instructions, pointing this time. "Up that hill with the tree and then down over there."

About two hundred feet in front of the car, a cluster of graves dotted the landscape. Closing the car doors softly, to avoid rattling the spirits, we walked to the dirt graves and knelt down among the modest wooden markers. Beside them, stabbed into the dirt, a few crooked cradle boards that once held babies safely against their mothers' strong backs now marked the end of life, graphically illustrating the phrase "cradle to grave" and creating an even greater sadness about death—that this is what was left.

Manaba appeared out of nowhere. Beside her walked a man—short, muscular, with a piece of cloth across his forehead at a slant concealing his face. Assuming he was Native American from his build and stance, legs slightly arched at the thighs as if he constantly rode horses, I thought tonight he looked sentrylike, as if he should be brandishing a rifle rather than a shovel. Could this be Nizhoni's uncle, here to break open his niece's grave? If so, he was more peaceful than I.

"If I am wrong—" Callie's tentative voice was interrupted by Manaba's loud wail that filled the night air and sent goose bumps roaming across my flesh: a chant of forgiveness perhaps. Never had I heard anyone make those kinds of sounds—of sadness, and longing, and love.

If we're trying to do this in secret, we're screwed, I thought. The volume was making me nervous but the sound was hypnotic. It dawned on me that the chant was one of the most ancient sounds on earth, used by mankind for eons to call people to a common purpose—and now we were called to this most unpleasant of tasks. Despite the gravity of the event, I felt powerful, almost proud, anxious to get this done, certain if anyone showed up I could take them down, and I wondered if the coffee or the Indian estrogen contained an upper.

When Manaba quit chanting, she looked to the sky and offered up what I assumed was a prayer of protection and forgiveness, then signaled the uncle to begin. As I rationalized it would most likely take a lone man with a shovel hours to dig up a grave, the dirt flew and in moments a concave indention formed around the marker. I imagined he was working at triple speed to finish and elude the evil spirits.

Moments later, deeper still into the digging, his speed increased like a video on fast-forward, his adrenaline obviously pumping as he got closer to the body.

Dirt piled up off to one side of the deep hole, the shovel clanked against the top of the box that held the woman killed by the totem that was her protector, and I began to dread seeing what might be left of Nizhoni.

The sides around the grave dug out, an animal howled in the distance, seeming to mourn the dirt's removal, and the hair stood up on the back of my neck. But that cry only foreshadowed the bloodcurdling yell that broke the night's silence—a tortured sound that appeared to emanate from the hollowness of despair and bespoke anger and anguish and raw aggression.

Flint rattled against the bones of a breastplate, fringe slapped the sides of deerskin leggings, a pair of well-worn moccasins stabbed into the earth, and dirt sprayed over the elaborate beading of the intruder's shoes and into the exhumer's face.

I panned up to the angle of the intruder's hips, cut from granite; he was bare-chested and muscled against the wind, a tall man with slick black hair angled at his clavicle, a brow that jutted forward like the red cliffs, and eyes as sunken as the caves buried within them. If the devil materialized, he could take lessons from this man who reeked of death and danger.

Looking first at me, he seemed intentionally to send a ripple of fear across my body, and Callie clutched my arm. He was poised and tense as if ready to kill and appeared to pray for the opportunity. Then as quickly he turned his attention to Manaba.

She glared at him, her eyes ferocious beyond the telling as he jumped down into the dark hole, landed with a loud thud against the packed earth, took the shovel away from the uncle, and used the tip like a crowbar, swiftly prying open the lid at one end, shining a light inside and revealing a piece of bone.

The uncle, apparently having barely managed to keep his apprehension in check while hunkered in the dank dirt, mere seconds from seeing his decayed niece, gasped as if fearful of what he had unearthed, or perhaps unleashed. He cast a terror-stricken glance at the moccasined man, then scrambled squirrel-like out of the hole and ran into the night, leaving us to the intruder.

Staring down into the coffin at the bones, what was left of Nizhoni, the wild-eyed warrior locked eyes with Manaba in an unspoken battle across the grave. They exchanged fierce looks of what appeared to be anger and pain and revenge.

Suddenly he took the shovel and tossed dirt back on the coffin with an alacrity that far outstripped the uncle's efforts.

Manaba waited until the last shovel full of dirt was back in place and then chanted again, this time slowly and with great melancholy. He chanted with her and while I felt his song was unwelcome, their harmonious sounds were undeniably beautiful, as if they'd been trained to chant together and were now bound against their will. Suddenly the chant ended, and he let out an unearthly scream and ran from the grave, disappearing into the night. Callie's eyes met Manaba's as the shaman turned her head away and strode from the gravesite.

Admittedly, I was shook up, and I could see Callie was a little off balance as well. The dead of night, exhumed bodies, bloodcurdling screams from a weird Indian guy—anybody would be looking for a tranquilizer.

"Was that…Luther Drake?" I whispered, and Callie nodded. "No wonder everybody's afraid of him. Nice technique, squealing like a castrated pig when he enters and exits. The hair on my arms is standing up like a whore at a revival."

"That sounds like your father," Callie said absently, her mind obviously elsewhere.

"My father would say someone ought to shoot that fucker and put him out of his misery. So you see I'm an evolutionary step up." I put my arm around her as we walked back to the car.

"How can I be so wrong about the grave being empty?"

"You're not wrong."

"You saw the bone."

"It takes a corpse awhile to look like that. Depends on temperature, embalming method, body size, humidity, and even geography, but bodies buried in boxes in the earth don't turn into bleached bones in less than three weeks, so that can't be Nizhoni's body."

"Then whose body is it?" she whispered to herself.

Chapter Thirteen

At dawn, Callie was in the cabin at her computer pulling up a current astrological chart. "Look at this. Jupiter in the Twelfth House, complete protection in the present. Right now the Moon is trapped, as Venus was back then, between two heavy planets." I had to prod Callie to finish her thought. "Mars and Uranus, male energy, something will happen quickly, bizarrely in the Eighth House of death. A woman is about to be in grave danger."

"Speaking of grave—who was in the one we dug up, if it wasn't Nizhoni?"

But Callie apparently wasn't even aware I was speaking to her or was simply ignoring me.

"Well, Teague," I said, slightly irritated at the silent treatment, "I don't know who's in the coffin. I'll get back to you on that, right after I finish taking my own planetary pulse—"

"Are you making fun of me?" she asked, turning her beautifully sculpted face in my direction and making me feel like a brat.

"I'm just hot and irritable and need to get some fresh air," I said, as my body went nuclear again. As if on cue, Elmo wiggled and jiggled and whined, clearly communicating that the lack of attention I was getting from Callie mirrored the lack of attention he was getting from me.

Hooking him up to his lead, I took him outside; his bladder relief was only perfunctory, his real purpose for our trip apparently to tell me someone was about to arrive. Being with Callie had made me realize Elmo was psychic when it came to visitors. He could lie around all day, then suddenly for no reason sit by the door and whine, which signaled he was picking up images of visitors arriving. At first, it seemed coincidental, but now I knew that Elmo received images of people long before they showed up, and in addition, he had a built-in dog clock that knew what time they would appear. Usually he saw fit to give me a heads-up about fifteen minutes out.

So when Elmo parked his soft, furry derriere in the middle of the driveway and watched the road, I knew somebody was coming.

"Good visitor, bad visitor?" I asked. His deep, short, impatient reply sounded fretful, which I always took to mean he wasn't happy about these particular guests.

Moments later, a white truck pulled into the driveway and the driver's-side door swung open. A tall, sandy-haired young man with a limp—the kind that started at the hip like a tractor had rolled on it—climbed out of the truck cab and strolled across the rocky road and shook my hand.

"Ms. Richfield, right?" he asked, and Callie must have heard the car tires because she suddenly appeared on the porch. Upon seeing her, he tipped his hat not unlike Cy Blackstone. "Ms. Rivers."

"How do you know our names?" I asked.

"Small town. I'm Dwayne Wayne Mucker."

My mind could never store a lot of facts, but a few stuck with me because of their bizarre nature, and one of those popped into my head at this very moment. Over eight hundred and eighty-three accused murderers had the middle name Wayne. Obviously, lots of other middle-name-Waynes were perfectly law-abiding citizens; nonetheless a whole bunch of psychos, killers, and general nut cases had middle-name-Wayne, and now it was possible I could be talking to one.

"Do you all know a lady by the name of…" and he looked down at the small leather book he carried. "I apologize…"

I glanced over at Callie, somehow feeling this guy was screwing with us.

"Mathers." He stopped, letting the upcoming bad news hang. "Missing, from what we can tell, taken off by some Injun." He made it sound like she'd left with a Hemi.

"You a cop or a deputy or what?"

"Self-appointed," he said, and that's when I knew I was staring at Wayne-the-insane-living-up-to-his-name. Wayne's eyes had the look of someone who was self-medicating, with a large pharmacy at his disposal.

"And why do you think she's missing?"

"Neighbor personally told me that around two in the morning another gal…" he checked his notebook again. "…Ms. Silvers left, and that's when the Injun fella must have got her."

"Who's the neighbor?"

"Confidential. There's an element up here, ma'am, is why I'm believin' Ms. Mathers is in trouble. Now don't get me wrong. I'm for red people exceptin' a few. But when this Mathers woman went for permission to dig up a grave on Injun land, I knew that'd put her in the crosshairs of that element."

Part of me wanted to write this guy off and believe that Ramona was fine, but why would this nutcase take the time to come to our cabin unless someone had her—maybe even him.

"How did you know she asked permission to dig up a grave?"

He gave me a big grin. "This is a little ole one-horse town out in the desert. By the way, permission denied, right?"

"Sounds to me, Dwayne-Wayne, like the song says, you got friends in low places."

"You're friends with the shaman lady, ain't ya? You see the news today? Rumor that she was standin' next to the girl before she went off the cliff…and the shaman had the killer wolf with her. Right beside her, like it was a trained attack dog or somethin'. Makes you wonder, dudn't it—is she siccin' the wolf on people? Anyway, if Ms. Mathers shows up, do me a favor and leave word for me at Cy Blackstone's office."

"How do you know Cy Blackstone?" I thought an awful lot of people, including Ramona, claimed a connection with Blackstone.

"Do some work for his family." He handed Callie a card. "If we find her, might lead us to the Injun." He tipped his hat like a Blackstone wannabe and got in his truck.

Not waiting for Dwayne-Wayne's tires to clear the driveway, Callie and I headed for Ramona's cabin, dialing Wade Garner from the road.

"Yeah, he wasn't a cop of any kind, and he was obviously

looking for Ramona under the guise of helping to find her. So what do you make of that?" I asked Wade.

"I'm catching the first flight out. Ramona's helped me out on a couple of occasions and I owe it to her," he said flatly, anger in his voice, devoid now of all horsing around.

"Stay put. If it looks like there's been trouble I'll let you know. I thought since you talked to her before she came to our place maybe she mentioned going somewhere else."

"She's always on some Indian's legal case when she's out there—a real bleeding heart. A do-gooder liberal." Wade snorted but I could hear affection for her beneath the derisive sound. Having been a cop alongside Wade, I knew his soft side and, despite who Ramona might take to dinner, to bed, or to court, he'd never mistake her mansion for her morals.

Wade seemed worried a little too quickly for a cop. As I ended the call an alarm was already going off in my head that said Wade knew something he wasn't telling me, and something Ramona knew had gotten her into trouble.

We pulled up in front of the cabin Ramona had described the evening she'd visited and saw her black Mercedes parked in the driveway, which made me feel somewhat more relaxed. I bounded up the steps and knocked on the door, but no one answered. The interior lights were off, the cabin dark. I circled it once but saw nothing unusual.

"Do I break in?" I asked Callie, looking around.

"Yes," she said nervously.

Careful to keep my fingerprints off the doorknob, I took out a credit card and popped the lock that apparently our cabin's locksmith had installed with equal haste and waste, since it was useless as protection. I flipped on the lights and we looked around: everything tidy, no signs of struggle, nothing that indicated she'd left hastily.

In her bedroom, the down comforter was tossed back as if she'd gotten up and decided not to make the bed. It crossed my mind that she and Barrett had probably warmed those sheets. The kitchen had a few orange and yellow Fiestaware plates with leftover toast and eggs stuck to them, communicating only that she wasn't the quickest to tidy up. Feeling awkward now that we were definitely breaking and entering, I suggested we leave and lock up.

"Doesn't look like anything weird. What if she simply went shopping?"

"Maybe give Barrett a call and see if they're together," Callie said.

After ringing Barrett and getting no answer, I left a message for her to stop by our cabin or call us the moment she got this. Then we drove by her cabin to see if she was there with her cell phone off. Her car was gone, and we decided it was possible she'd picked Ramona up and they'd gone off for the day.

Relaxing a little, I decided that maybe Dwayne-Wayne was some local guy who was mentally two bricks short of a load.

"I mean, what was all that stuff about Manaba having the wolf with her like a trained attack dog? The whole wolf thing's got me baffled anyway," I said. "The wolf is a woman with really nice eyes, next thing you know the wolf is Luther Drake, now the wolf is the shaman's attack dog, then he's the phantom that sent me over the cliff—hell, this is the busiest damned wolf in the woods. So do you think this Luther is—"

"Don't keep saying his name."

"Why?" I was a little irritated, the hocus-pocus level having about pegged out on my fun meter.

"If you say a name, you give it energy. You communicate with it."

I rolled my eyes so far up in my head they were in danger of getting stuck there.

"If you say, 'I wish my mom would call' and then suddenly she calls, you say, 'I was thinking about you.' That seems normal. You said her name and drew her to you. Why is it abnormal if I don't want to say the name of someone because I don't want to draw him to us?"

I didn't have an answer and drove back to the cabin.

❖

Stepping out of the car, I saw movement by the creek and quietly approached the pine trees as a figure came out of the woods a few feet from us. I spun and grabbed it by the arm, and the scream was instantaneous and high-pitched. I let go immediately, having attacked Fern Flanagan.

"Jeez, Fern, I'm sorry."

"You almost blew out my pacemaker!" Fern panted.

"Are you okay?" Callie asked.

"Do you have a pacemaker?" I asked, worried.

"No. All my body parts are real. I got no inflated boobs, hair plugs, bacteria in my lips, fat outta my hips, no Botox, fake cocks… only what the good Lord gave me and I'm usin' it up at a great rate." She loped over and plopped down on the steps. I glanced at the tightly rolled pink fabric in her hand.

"Came to give you this, my boy found it down by the creek." I recognized it as the L.L. Bean shirt jack I'd bought Callie.

"Thanks, Fern. Must have fallen out of the car and something carried it off. Tell your son thanks, too."

"Aw, he's workin' today at the grocery." She laughed good-naturedly and the sun picked up a glint of red in her graying hair.

"Is your son redheaded? I think he was our checker the other day." I left out the part about him being so damned dumb he couldn't ring up carrots, because from the light in Fern's eyes, I could tell she thought her son was the Second Coming.

"Yeah, I work a few extra hours each week to help him out, till he gets on his feet," Fern said proudly, and I wondered what the hell it was about grown boys that kept a mother happily in bondage her entire life.

"Well, I'm betting your son will grow up to make you real proud, Fern. It'll all be worth it." I made myself say it, wanting Fern to feel like her life was rewarding.

I caught Callie looking at me sweetly as Fern said, "Well, thank you. Better get a move on." She hoisted her frame off the porch steps, caught her balance, and bounded off into the woods after wishing us a good day.

"I love you, Teague Richfield," Callie said.

"Because I occasionally proffer the kind lie?"

"Maybe," she said as I handed her the slightly battered pink jacket.

"It's a great color. And I even like the teeth marks."

I snatched it away from her to see if the wolf had touched the jacket.

"Only kidding." She giggled and this time I threw the jacket at her playfully.

❖

An hour later, in response to my call, Barrett Silvers burst into the cabin, talking as she hit the door and not giving me a moment to tell her why we were searching for her.

"I'm glad you've come to your senses. I was going to phone you as soon as I got dressed—slept in due to a very late night because Jacowitz rang me at two fucking a.m. and wanted to go over his thoughts on your damned pages. That conversation lasted until nearly four so I'm a little sleep deprived, and excuse me if that comes out as pissed off with you.

"A note you might want to jot in your diary—I put my personal life on hold at two a.m. in order to go locate your e-mail with the pages you sent to Jacowitz and proceed to sweep up your crumbling career, and here's all the man is asking. He likes your writing, he likes your style, he likes you. Give him ten pages on the alien sex scene with the housewife. Ten fucking pages. Would it kill you to try it?"

"We can talk about that later—"

"No, we talk about it now." Her tone dropped an octave and she shifted into a soft, seductive approach, since yelling was obviously not working. "Nun sex, hooker sex, alien sex, who-gives-a-flying-fuck sex. Write the scene between any two people you like, make it sexy, then change one of the names to Alien. I don't care. What I care about is that you complete this movie and get your picture on the screen, and I know what you're going to say. You're going to say you don't want a movie on the screen if it sucks. Well, sucking is at least a sound. Right now your career is silent."

She flopped onto the couch and finally took a breath.

"Barrett," Callie said softly, "a man named Dwayne, some guy we've never met, was here and said Ramona is missing and that it happened right after you left her cabin this morning."

It was clear from Barrett's expression that her brain had stripped its gears; she couldn't get from Jacowitz and aliens, to Ramona and missing, in that short time frame. We watched her as she sat silent, blinking, her mind seeming to leave her body as if time traveling to the last place she'd seen Ramona. She got to her feet, and for a minute I thought she was hyperventilating.

"Why did I leave? Why didn't I stay over?" She paced, clasping her hands, rubbing her palms together in a masculine wringing of them.

"Obviously you left to help me with Jacowitz," I said, but she wasn't listening. "And we don't even know for sure she's missing."

"We have to find her." Barrett looked genuinely distressed.

For the first time since I'd known Barrett, I saw a vulnerability, a chink in her business armor, a spot that the older, more sophisticated, more elegant Ramona Mathers had apparently penetrated, among other spots, I was almost certain.

"I'm hiring a PI," Barrett said and executed a one-eighty, leaving the cabin in an over-the-top reaction typical of stressed studio executives.

"A private eye? How about you call her cell phone first before you marshal an army?" I shouted after her.

"I've been calling her cell phone all day, and I drove by several times. I thought she might be…blowing me off." *So, after a night of sex with Ramona, Barrett is hooked and worried that Ramona isn't and, worse, that Ramona is avoiding her.*

Barrett jumped into her car and peeled out of the gravel drive.

"What next?" I asked Callie

"I think we should meditate together. Combined energy has great power."

I didn't know about that, but I never turned down an opportunity to get into bed with Callie, especially for mutual vibration.

We lay flat on our backs next to each other, our arms touching, and she told me to close my eyes and ask our guides to tell us what they wanted us to know. I did it kind of halfheartedly and then, tired, found myself drifting off. In a twilight sleep it hit me—I was falling backward off the ravine, weightless and terrified, spinning, falling, grasping, about to smash into the floor of the riverbed when suddenly—I sat up in bed and gasped for air.

"What did you see?" Callie asked as I tried to breathe but could only pant like a nervous pup and then shake my head as if that would knock all the fearful images out of my brain.

"I keep having that falling-off-a-cliff sensation." I clutched at my heart. "Feels like I'm suffering from post-traumatic stress syndrome or something. If I'm meditating and asking for answers and I'm getting that horrible image, then what does that mean?"

"That the message is about the fall. We need to find the Indian man who pulled you out. I think he's involved with Ramona, and other people are looking for both of them."

"Why do you think that?" I drank water from the bedside table.

"Dwayne-Wayne—he doesn't care about Ramona. He wants the Indian man but he knows we'll want Ramona. So by engaging us in the search for her, we'll help him locate the poor Indian guy he's after."

"I wouldn't want to be wanted by Dwayne-the-insane," I said. "Why do I have the feeling that Manaba's not coming clean with us?"

Callie didn't defend her, seeming to know I was right. The shaman's truth serum was obviously a quart low.

❖

First we drove the short distance down to Ramona's cabin, which still looked calm, quiet, and vacant. But in the melancholy light of late afternoon, it looked less like Ramona had merely made a trip to the grocery store and more as if she'd left permanently.

Callie suggested we find Manaba and see what she could tell us, and I sensed that my needling about Manaba's on-and-off truthfulness was in the back of her mind. I turned the car toward the cemetery and headed northwest of the goat path, where the sunlight cast lengthening shadows on the scrub brush.

Finally, Callie said we should park the car and walk. I wasn't so hot on leaving my Jeep in the middle of a sand dune and traipsing out over the desert, but Callie was already walking ahead so I locked it and jogged to catch up with her.

"Where the hell are we?" I asked, annoyed at the sand and grit seeping into my shoes as my feet sank in the soft ground.

"It's the place where Manaba's grandmother raised her. No one ever comes out here."

"Yeah, not a great time-share. So are we one thorn tree and two iguanas from where we're going?"

Before I could come up with another smart remark, I glanced up from the sandy soil and right in front of us was a small, but beautiful, oasis, as if the LPGA had decided to underwrite an incredible putting green in the middle of nowhere.

A gnarly old tree bent over the small pool of water, the grass was thick and green, and rocks that were obviously used as chairs could not have been more artistically arranged if Hermann Miller had stopped by and placed them himself. Embers burned in a tiny rock circle, and something was steaming in a pot outside the dome-shaped earth-and-bark hogan, supported by four posts representing the Navajos' four sacred mountains.

"It was her grandmother's. The hogan is never deserted." Callie walked ahead of me making a slight clicking sound. Moments later Manaba stepped out of the hogan.

She said something to us in her native language, which could have been a greeting or simply Navajo for "What the hell are you doing here on the ninth hole?"

Callie asked how she had been, and Manaba replied she had been participating in a healing ceremony at the hogan to help her deal with danger and restore balance. She looked a little more settled to me—maybe that meant balanced.

"A guy named Dwayne came to see us," I said. "He claims that Ramona Mathers, a friend of ours, is missing."

Manaba nodded to her right and Callie seemed to know that meant "take a rock," so we sat down. Manaba produced two wooden cups that looked like they were carved out of half a croquet ball, but were lightweight. She dipped them into the liquid in the pot and handed one to each of us.

I had no intention of drinking from a dripping bowl, particularly since I couldn't see what was in it, but Manaba indicated I should drink, and somehow I felt rejecting the offer would be a personal insult. Taking a sip, I had to make myself swallow, imagining this bitter brew that looked like green tea and tasted like pond scum was good for me.

Callie didn't drink any of it and was signaling me not to, but it was too late—my Midwestern manners had overridden my common sense. I'd slurped some of the scum to avoid offending my hostess, and for a moment I wondered why not offending someone was more important than my own safety. My upbringing could have conceivably killed me, Midwesterners preferring death to social disgrace.

"She is alive," Manaba said, and as I wondered if she knew for certain that Ramona was alive, she gave me a signal that meant drink up.

The second sip of the tea wasn't as bad, perhaps dread being the bitter taste and the tea only a drink. Manaba stoked the fire with large pieces of wood, then lit a long pipe and blew smoke into the sky. I was beginning to relax and nearly forgot why we were here.

"What do you believe happened to her?" Callie asked.

"With a man who knows her," Manaba said and looked deeply into Callie's eyes.

"Okay," I said, drunk enough not to care, "I'm tired of you looking at Callie as if she belongs to you when in fact she belongs to me." *There*, I thought, *the truth will out.*

Manaba looked at me without expression. "I look deeply into her and see what she is thinking and who she is. You look only at her surface. If you believe her heart and mind are yours, then perhaps you will travel there more often."

The truth of her words stung me as my head spun and I lay down, looking up at the sky, which had become a backdrop for the stars that slashed across the dusky darkness. Then pulsing lights and flickering images burst across its vastness: women of long ago in native costumes dancing across the land, quick-cut images of a white man, a struggle, the rape of a young woman, the moaning of an old Indian woman clutching her heart, dissolving to a powerful dark-haired young Navajo girl pressing her body to Manaba's, deriving pleasure from the earth that breathed beneath them, breasts touching, souls igniting, transporting Manaba to places even a shaman cannot go alone, the energy around them whirling like a prairie fire.

The dark-haired young woman swung her head in my direction as an animal would upon hearing a twig break behind it in the forest. And when her eyes met mine, I gasped, a chill ricocheting back and forth across my body. It was the wolf-woman, then the diabolical face of the man who hit our windshield. As I tried to see more, I blacked out. Or perhaps I was already out and the images merely went black.

Chapter Fourteen

When I woke up, I was lying beside Callie, who was sitting on a rock facing east as the light came over the hills. Manaba had disappeared. Callie had a small fire burning in front of her, that I imagined Manaba had set, and a lightweight Navajo blanket draped around her shoulders. Apparently Manaba had placed a blanket on the ground for me as well, but now it was wadded up in an unrecognizable shape, thrashed and pummeled in the night as I must have attempted to ward off crazy images dancing through my head.

Staggering to my feet, I knocked the sand off my pants. Callie tilted her head to kiss me when I approached and handed me a cup.

I eyed it suspiciously, staring into it. "What was I slurping in the croquet ball?

"Peyote juice—from the cactus—induces hallucinations." When I refused the coffee she assured me she'd made it herself. "And don't ever drink something you haven't examined. Not that I think Manaba would ever hurt you."

"Speaking of our hostess, where is she?"

"I don't know," Callie replied, her mind elsewhere. "Did you dream?"

"If you can call it that. I remember something about the land, and then Manaba was boffing this great-looking Indian girl. I hope the boffing part is true because it means she's got someone on her mind other than you. What did you dream?" I turned the question on her.

"The same."

"What do you mean, the same?"

"The images were made available to us simultaneously. This spot is very powerful so they came through for anyone here. We may have seen a few things differently but we had the same vision. Yours was helped by the drink. I needed only to open my mind."

"Which would imply that not only do you think we had the same dream, but you know what I dreamed, so what was the white guy doing in my dream?"

"He raped a woman—an Indian woman."

I stumbled as she said it. *Can people really have the same dream, like a simulcast?*

"It's all out there, you merely tune in," Callie said, reading my mind. "Words or sounds exist forever, floating in the universe. Scientific instruments can pick up those frequencies in the atmosphere and rebroadcast what was said over forty years ago. Images are out there too."

"We need an image of where Ramona is," I said, changing the subject, not ready to go down the pictures-are-forever rabbit hole.

"She wasn't in the dream."

We wandered away from the strange lush scenery as one would a desert soundstage after the production is over, and I slipped my arm around Callie and held her close as we walked to the car. Inside, I turned on the heater and warmed the car up for her, mulling over what Manaba had said.

"She said I only look at your surface."

Callie smiled at my being troubled by the accusation.

"Life's so crazy, there's no time to sit and stare deeply into your eyes, but I would like to. However, I have no idea why I'm defending myself."

"We're all evolving."

"That wolf that flew onto our windshield and then morphed into a tortured face—I think that's the white man I saw in the dream."

"Who is he?" Callie asked.

"You know who it is. The man whose name we don't mention." And this time I wasn't making fun of the energy of names. This time I truly didn't want to conjure him up.

I backed up, then sped across the sand, heading for the goat path to retrace our drive home.

"I liked the shaman boffing the good-looking maiden—best part about the dream."

"You seem to have that on your mind. Remember that a snapshot of any two people in the position of the shaman and the young Indian girl could have many interpretations: were they making love, or is one giving the other CPR, or is one attacking the other?"

I almost thought Callie didn't want to see Manaba with someone. "Looked like a midnight rodeo to me."

"It could be none of those things or all of those things."

"All? That would be interesting—being attacked, revived, and made love to all by the same woman. Too rough a night for me."

Callie was ignoring me now, which she often did when she felt I was bantering with her. "There's something we're not getting. I feel Manaba is blocking my energy because there's a piece of this she doesn't want me to know. Maybe Ramona's not missing. Maybe she left of her own accord."

"What if she *is* missing and Manaba killed her too?" At Callie's look, I quickly added, "Every mass murderer in the U.S. always has a neighbor who says he's the nicest guy they ever met—mowed their lawn, babysat their kids. All I'm saying is that you may not know Manaba like you think you do."

❖

We drove back to the cabin, the light a panoply of colors across the distant red rocks, as if God's own lighting director had determined this was the stage against which life should be played. I wondered why I happened to be here on this stage at this time with this gorgeous woman beside me. Perhaps life was a lottery and I had merely drawn the lucky numbers.

"You're overthinking things again," Callie said without even looking at me, and before I could deny it she added, "The world is full of mysteries we don't yet understand, but that doesn't mean in the scope of things they don't make perfect sense."

"Like murder makes sense?"

"It's part of...the plot," she said in an attempt to explain something in my vernacular.

"So God is a writer?"

Callie let that thought dangle, taking my hand instead and kissing the palm.

❖

When we pulled into the driveway, Elmo was beside himself, having been given no heads-up about our being away so long, and I apologized profusely.

"Mom drank pond scum, Elmo, and passed out, and that's why I'm late taking you out."

He licked his lips in a gesture of empathy, no doubt recalling occasions when he had drunk from a toilet. Quickly watering the nearest bush, he headed back inside where Callie helped him up on the couch and hand-fed him bites of leftover turkey. He had his paws on her leg and tiny slobber marks on her pants.

"Sorry," I said about the drool and she shook her head slightly, letting me know it was of no consequence. After finding a small space to snug in on the couch next to them, I put my arm around her.

"You put yourself in too much danger, Callie. I mean, if I weren't around, I know you'd go right ahead and drive into danger in the middle of the night, go to remote locations without letting someone know where you are. I feel like I have to keep an eye on you all the time to make sure you're safe. Is that a sign I'm insane or in love?"

"You're a protector...and you may be passionately in love." Callie snuggled up in my arms and I kissed the top of her head as she ran her hands up under my shirt, massaging my breasts.

I asked Elmo to give us a little room on the couch and had begun kissing Callie and unbuttoning her blouse when there was a knock at the door. I got up to answer it, and Barrett Silvers, looking worn and worried, slumped into the room to report that she'd gone to the police station and personally taken an officer over to Ramona's cabin and searched her belongings for a note or information that might tell them if she'd left voluntarily.

After a few attempts at calming her, reassuring her Ramona would be found, we were absolutely out of conversation.

Barrett began to fill the dead air with strange musings. "She's a painter, did you know that?"

I stared at Barrett, thinking her voice had a soft lilt I didn't know it possessed.

"No, we don't know much about her," Callie said.

"Well, she paints beautiful landscapes of the plains with the oil derricks and cattle. She said she's going to paint one for me..."

Barrett sagged down into a chair with her head in her hands and I looked over at Callie, having no idea what to say or do. This was a new Barrett, a lovesick woman.

"You gotta cut this out," I demanded gruffly. "I like the cocky, arrogant, oversexed, studio shark. This lovesick thing is not attractive."

"Go fuck yourself," she whispered.

"That's starting to look like an option, since distraught dykes have been repeatedly appearing on my doorstep and derailing my love life."

"What did you find in the cabin?" Callie asked, as if she knew Barrett was concealing something.

"Nothing, really..." Sheepishly she added, "Something I took off her dresser." Barrett fished deep in her pocket and pulled out a small green slate arrowhead, obviously a trinket and not an artifact.

Callie took the item from Barrett and rolled it around in her fingers. "Did she buy this somewhere recently?"

"I don't know." Barrett seemed too upset to think clearly.

"I've seen these somewhere...Teague?"

I looked at the arrowhead about the size of my thumb, and the image of a small wicker basket full of children's arrowheads popped into my head. "Trading post."

"Yes," Callie said, grabbing her coat. "We know Ramona most likely didn't carry this around with her in Oklahoma and she'd only been here a short while, so she either bought it at a store, or her kidnapper did, and maybe she left it on the dresser as a clue."

"Unlikely there would be time for that if someone dragged her away," I said quietly, not wanting to take away all hope but wanting to be realistic nonetheless.

"Maybe the kidnapper left it," Callie said.

"Why would a kidnapper be that careless?" I asked.

"Maybe he left it there on purpose to help us find her." Callie smiled, quite proud of her theory.

"Why do you kidnap someone and then ask to be caught?" Barrett stared at us.

"Maybe the kidnapper was working against his will, or maybe he knew it would be us who would find it," Callie said. "Things can look one way and be something entirely different. Come on."

And like a battalion commander, Callie herded us both toward the door, leaving Elmo on the couch in a turkey-induced tryptophanic trance.

CHAPTER FIFTEEN

We were only ten minutes from the jewelry store, and I smiled nervously at Callie as we walked up the wooden steps and entered the rustic building made expansive with its tree-sized logs that acted as beams and room dividers to separate rugs from jewelry and trinkets.

"Over here." Callie quickly located the basket of green arrowheads and compared them to the one in her hand.

"Identical," I said, picking up a few of them.

The beautiful Indian woman in the pleated dress and elaborate turquoise jewelry greeted us. "You're here to make your ring purchase?" she asked me with a broad teasing smile on her wide, open face.

"Still getting comfortable with the idea," I said, and tried to seem casual.

Barrett listened to the exchange and glanced down at the rings in the case for the first time. "Are you getting married?" She looked at me quizzically but without her usual tone of condemnation or even the slightest hint of jealousy.

I couldn't formulate a sentence so Callie stepped in. "I asked her to marry me but she thought I was joking." Callie turned her attention to the shopkeeper, leaving me to my own demons and to Barrett's stare. "We're looking for someone who bought an arrowhead like these green ones you sell…she bought it no more than a few days ago."

"It's a very common keepsake for people who want to put it in their pocket as a remembrance of their trip or as a good-luck charm. They're under a dollar," the shopkeeper said and set the ring tray out as if I'd made a silent request to see the rings again. I fingered the matching pair.

"A tall, elegant, silver-haired woman—are you sure she didn't come in? Her nails are long and tapered and she wears a pale silver polish on them and her watch is a Cartier gold band..." Barrett asked, and the shopkeeper paused.

"I don't remember anyone like that."

We stood around for a moment, not knowing what to do next. Then the shopkeeper broke the silence. "She will most likely return, I believe."

"Directions would be more helpful than beliefs," I muttered.

"Little Horse," the shopkeeper said quickly. "The man who buys the most of these is the trapper-trader who has the mule-team trail rides. Everybody calls him Little Horse. He buys them by the boxful because he gives them to everybody who goes on the trail ride. He also has a guide service. He'll take you on foot into remote areas, or by canoe down the river, or to a sweat lodge, stuff like that."

"Where is he?" Barrett's words leapt from her lips. Barrett, who had bedded every woman in Hollywood, was obsessed now with finding a silver-haired, bisexual studio executive twenty years her senior.

The shopkeeper laughed. "Well, that's the big trick. He doesn't have a cell phone or pager. He shows up to buy groceries and goes back to his camp."

"Where's his camp?" Callie asked.

"Way up in the hills, you would need a guide," the shopkeeper said.

"Where does he buy groceries?" I asked.

"Little Mojo's Corner." She pointed toward the front of her shop and south up a hill.

"We'll find her." I turned to address Barrett but she was already headed for the door. For all her butch elegance, her sophisticated not-caring, her chic it's-all-about-me attitude, she was beyond merely upset, and it flashed through my mind that Ramona Mathers must not have been popular with oilmen for nothing—she was obviously a good lay. After all, Barrett had known her for only a couple of days—hell, a couple of hours really—and most likely only slept with her once. I asked myself if I was sorry I'd passed on the opportunity to find out how good a lay, but looked over at Callie with pride as she said, "I know exactly what you're thinking."

I didn't know how to block energy, but I gave it my best, thinking of a giant brick wall separating my mind from Callie's.

"You could have slept with Ramona."

"Wrong. I was thinking it would be fun to know how good in bed Ramona was, if one didn't have to sleep with her to find out."

Callie raised an eyebrow. Honesty had its hazards.

❖

In only minutes we were headed for Little Mojo's Corner to find out if Little Horse came there often and when they'd last seen him. The store was a small former gas station sitting back off the two streets that crossed in front of it. Barrett went inside to question the clerk, who apparently described Little Horse as a short, stocky man who was only slightly bowlegged, or enough to comment on, while Callie and I tried to organize our thoughts.

"So let's do a little Indian update," I proposed. "Kai, high-school friend of Manaba, dies mysteriously. We don't know why. In 1997 Manaba's grandmother dies. We don't know why. Nizhoni may be dead. We don't know why. Are you getting the pattern here?"

"We do know that the grandmother's land was special to women of the tribe. They came by the hundreds from the surrounding hills and danced all night by the campfires to honor the female spirit. With the grandmother gone, the land was somehow deeded over to Blackstone Construction. The transaction might not have been filed at the courthouse until recently, when they wanted to develop the land." Callie paused to study me intently. "It's the besiegement the chart indicated. In 1997 women were being attacked, their power under siege. This land mass is female and has large energy connecting those attacks to the present ones and until the energy is redirected—"

"You lost me on the big female land mass."

"Women, hundreds, perhaps thousands have danced in the dust

and sand of this sacred place—many moccasins. The sound of their voices, the energy of their hearts, the prayers emanating from their spirits…all of that is still here and people feel it. The construction crews feel it as they cut into her soul, and the energy of the violated land frightens them, and they run, quitting their jobs."

"Wow, Callie, the way you see things—"

"Disturbs you, I know."

"No. It's so…well, it makes me feel better. Like there's beauty and sense to the world and you're its cheerleader." I realized I was choking emotionally on the words.

She paused. "I love you, Teague." She kissed me, her mouth warm like the ocean on a cold night.

"So what does women's energy have to do with the missing and dead?" I murmured.

"I don't know."

"Do you ever worry that maybe there is no connection, that maybe we're trying to tie things together that make no sense?"

At that moment, we saw them—Manaba and Cy Blackstone across the street in the shadows of the trading post. Their bodies close in conversation.

Without waiting, I towed Callie across the street, dodging traffic, and got within earshot of the two, their conversation barely audible.

"He knows," Manaba said.

"How?" Blackstone shifted his weight and glanced over his shoulder.

"We exhumed the grave," Manaba said.

A pause while Blackstone breathed. "So he knows."

Manaba said nothing in reply, turned, and hurried away.

"I thought those two were mortal enemies," I said. "That night at the ceremony they looked like it to me. Let's follow him." We raced back across the street and jumped in our car.

"What about Barrett?" Callie reminded me as we squealed out of the driveway, tailing Blackstone in his black pickup truck roughly an eighth of a mile behind him.

"Can't help that, she'll have to find her own way home. I don't want to lose Blackstone."

We were headed back toward the Indian reservation near the area where the cemetery was located. The land was wide-open and cars easy to spot, so I had to drop back even farther to avoid Blackstone's seeing me.

About five miles up into hillier country a white pickup, perched on a side road like a marauder in an old-fashioned train robbery, bolted from the intersection, spraying sand across the horizon. It headed down the incline onto the roadway, throwing more dust into the air and blocking Blackstone's path. When he tried to cut a sharp left and get around the truck, it veered even more sharply, blocking him. He swerved right and the white truck roared into reverse and charged left, blocking him again, sagebrush sacrificed under skidding tires, flying like confetti.

Two metal cutting horses, they swung and blocked and spun until Blackstone whirled a full three-sixty to spray sand in his opponent's windshield and, while he had him blinded, plowed forward. But the white vehicle was in his path and he crashed into the truck bed. The driver jumped out and slung open Blackstone's pickup door and threw him on the ground in a stranglehold. Blackstone lay still. Suddenly the attacker spotted us, and in a split second he was off the ground, limping to his truck and fleeing across the sand in a grinding of tires.

"That's the Dwayne-Wayne guy," I shouted as we pulled up to the scene, having recognized the limp. I rang the police department to say we needed an officer and an ambulance right away, and described our location outside of town.

"He said he knew Blackstone," I told Callie as I hung up the phone.

"Apparently he does." Callie knelt beside Blackstone, assuring him an ambulance was on the way.

I couldn't see if his head had hit the steering wheel or Wayne had pulverized his nose with his fists. Whichever, the guy was pretty smashed up.

Callie looked up at me. "He's breathing, but he's bleeding from the mouth and his eyes are rolled back."

"I've got a lot of questions I'd like to ask him, but I don't think he's going to have answers any time soon."

Chapter Sixteen

The ambulance and the police officer arrived almost simultaneously, so while Blackstone was being strapped on a stretcher the officer asked me what we knew about the mugging. Not wanting to admit we were following Blackstone, I lied, making a mental distinction between telling Callie the truth and coming clean with Officer Tumbleweed.

I said we were taking a ride to see the surrounding countryside and stumbled on the two guys trying to kill one another.

The officer, whose name tag pinned to his shirt said Sgt. Striker, wrote as I spoke, never taking off his dark wraparound sunglasses. His crisply pressed shirt and his military demeanor told me he was one of those cops who took himself seriously.

"So why are you in Sedona?"

"We're here on a combined writing project and vacation," I said. "We've seen this guy in the white truck before. His name is Dwayne-Wayne and he showed up at our cabin—"

"Dwayne or Wayne?" the officer interrupted, to let me know that he controlled the interview, not me. He stopped writing and raised an eyebrow at me for no apparent reason other than perhaps he'd seen the expression on a cop show. I would have bet money he stood in the bathroom mirror for hours practicing getting that eyebrow to arch up that high over the top of his sunglasses.

"First name Dwayne, middle name Wayne, and he's the same guy who came to our cabin to tell us that a friend of ours, Ramona Mathers, is missing."

"We know about the Mathers report," Sergeant Striker said, this time letting me know he'd "let me know" if he wanted more discussion about the Mathers case. "Why do you say he's the same guy?"

"Because I got a look at him and he has a distinctive limp. Can't be too many guys around here who limp at the hip."

"Slows 'em down, which is good." Striker's lips pulled back from his teeth in a nearly mechanical grin.

A fat black bug about the size of a quarter lit on his neatly ironed shirt, and he flicked it off and onto the squad car. Without pause, he pressed his left thumb down punitively on the beetlelike creature, exploding its guts onto the hood of the car, then with a manicured fingernail sent the empty shell sailing out into the wind. While I contemplated the ease with which he'd unnecessarily dispatched the insect, he jotted our cell numbers down.

"You women know the victim?"

When I said we didn't, he asked the question again and I repeated that we didn't know him.

"You're not lyin' to me now, are ya?" He spoke in the patronizing tone I suspected he reserved for scatterbrained women.

"If we were lying, would we tell you we were lying?" A smart remark, but his smirking questions annoyed me.

"Step over there." His voice was sharp as he pointed his short baton at my midsection to keep distance between us. "Right over there against the car!"

A voice in my head said that Officer Tumbleweed had hair-trigger hatred for women who spoke up, and he could be dangerous, and this was the desert, and I didn't want the shifting sands slowly covering our dead bodies. I moved in the direction he pointed.

"Now, I'm gonna ask you politely again. Are you lying to me?" He spat out the words.

"I'm a former member of the Tulsa Police Department, an officer myself, Officer Striker, and if you need to verify that, I can give you a number to call—"

"I don't recall asking for your work history. I asked you a simple question."

"Where I come from, there are consequences for intimidation, for the sake of intimidation." I held my breath as Officer Striker's anger played across his jaw muscles.

"May we go, Officer—please."

Callie's polite "please" seemed to break up the angry energy and help him save face. He swung his baton toward our car muttering, "Go."

Hearing the ambulance doors slam shut, we pulled out right behind the vehicle.

"That is one scary damned dude. The only difference between Sergeant Striker and Dwayne-Wayne is the starch in his shirt."

"You shouldn't have gotten in his face."

Pausing to think about that, I finally agreed.

"Was Dwayne-Wayne following Blackstone and lying in wait for him?" she asked.

"I don't know, but I'd love to shoot the jackass for whaling on a guy forty years older than him, even if it was Blackstone." I rechanneled my anger over Striker.

"Notice how everything ends up with you wanting to shoot someone?"

"Which says I'm only a pressed shirt away from being kin to Dwayne-Wayne or Officer Bug Squash, but you have to admit my killing plan does solve recidivism. If you shoot 'em, they don't do the same shit again."

Callie laughed at me and I enjoyed making her laugh.

"By the way, have you noticed I'm punching out fewer people than I used to—I must be evolving."

Callie said nothing in reply, but graced me with a wry smile.

"We need to locate your friend Manaba and find out what's going on. She and Blackstone looked pretty friendly and then he goes off and gets bumped. Did she set him up?"

"Manaba's a healer—she's too trained, too honorable."

"Must be the cop in me but I've seen priests, daycare workers, and doctors do despicable things, yet I've watched hookers do some fairly decent ones. So for me, it's not the profession, it's the person. She's a healer. Good for her. She'll have to prove to me she's not a bad one."

"Barrett!" Callie said.

"Damn, I completely forgot about her."

"Under other circumstances I would consider that a win."

Callie smiled at me and I decided not to remind her that jealousy wasn't supposed to enter her cosmic consciousness, all the while happy my lover felt a little jealous. It was a sign she was paying attention.

I drove up to the Little Mojo Grocery and hopped out, walking quickly through the store to see if Barrett was around. She wasn't so I dialed her cell phone.

"Hi, we came back for you. I'm at the Mojo."

"Thanks a hell of a lot, Galahad. But you've been gone two fucking hours. Did you expect me to be sitting there chowing down on a can of pork 'n beans?"

"Sorry, but we had to follow Blackstone, who was attacked by Dwayne-Wayne—"

"What kind of bubba name is Dwayne-Wayne?"

"A guy who's nuts and drives a white truck—but not as nuts as Officer Striker who—"

"I got a lead on Little Horse's place," she interrupted, obviously not interested in my desert sagas. "So I called a cab and got back to my car, and I'm on my way out there now."

I had to hand it to Barrett for sheer butch bravado. "Listen, don't go way out of town by yourself," I pleaded.

"Oh, thanks for caring, you who left me at the Mojave-mart," Barrett snapped.

"Listen, which direction are you headed?"

"Signal's breaking up. I'm heading toward the reservation. I've got to find Ramona." And before I could answer, the line went dead.

"I don't feel good about this," Callie said.

I hated it when Callie and I had the same bad vibrations.

"Can we get a cappuccino?" I asked, maxed out. "And we've got to get back and walk Elmo."

"I think we should go after Barrett. She could be in trouble."

"She's fine. Caught in a skip zone. I'll ring her again later." I didn't know if she was caught in a skip zone or not. I wanted to skip looking for her right now.

"We should find her."

"My entire screenwriting hiatus in Sedona is a debacle and my love life isn't much better, thanks to Barrett. She fucked up my screenplay, fucked the attorney, and now she's trying to fuck my day."

At Callie's reprimanding look, I spun the car around and headed back toward the reservation to search for Barrett, saying nothing to Callie as we drove the next thirty miles and I continued to call.

As the vast landscape opened up around us with its spotty dwellings and side roads, Callie spoke first. "This isn't getting us anywhere. We have no idea which way she went. Even when I concentrate on her, I get nothing."

"Well, if you're getting nothing, I'm sure not driving around in the sand any longer, because I started getting nothing hours ago." Using a side road to spin the car a hundred and eighty degrees, I headed for civilization. "I need coffee."

✣

Thirty minutes later, we pulled up on a cliff flanked with chic adobe shops, parked in the back near the store entrances, and went inside where the view included not only merchandise, but beautiful valley vistas through the plate glass.

I ordered a triple grande non-fat cappuccino, two sugars stirred in, and Callie ordered a tall caramel frappuccino.

"I wonder how many adjectives we can list preceding our drink before we become suburbanite assholes?"

"Don't say that," Callie warned.

"I'm at three: triple, grande, and non-fat, if you don't count the sugars. I'm damned near there. I think if I ever add 'with whipped cream and a mocha topping,' someone should shoot me."

"There you go with the shooting thing again. Energy draws energy."

"Obviously, because I've got you drinking tall caramel fraps. Remember when you used to order a Coke? See how simple that sounds. I'll have a Coke."

"Are you feeling stressed? I notice when you're stressed you start overanalyzing things and you get sarcastic."

"I don't think it's overanalyzing. I think it's knowing at exactly what point in my purchasing habits I become a shallow jackass. I'm on the lookout for that."

"Take it off your list, darling. I'll let you know if you ever get there. *I'll* look out for it." She reached over and held my hand, and I figured maybe it was these kinds of moments that being married might be like—having someone who pledged to look out for me. Keep me from becoming shallow. What more could I ask from matrimony?

❖

We took our drinks back to the car and proceeded to the cabin, where Elmo greeted us with one open eye, not offering to raise his jowls off the floor, apparently bored with our having to go out even more than he did. Callie took her cell phone and disappeared into the bedroom.

I tried Barrett's cell again, but apparently wherever she was required smoke signals and that irritated me even more, as if it were Barrett's fault that cell towers weren't readily available.

That's when it dawned on me that I owed Wade a call, and as I dialed, our last conversation replayed in my head. Wade answered immediately.

"What's up with Ramona?"

"Missing," I said, and intentionally went quiet. He breathed. "Okay, it's obvious you and Ramona are buds because otherwise how would she have known I had a basset hound and that it was a he? I never told her that. So you two must chat each other up." Silence ensued and it crossed my mind that Wade could have slept with Ramona, but I quickly pushed that thought away. "So are you gonna tell me what you know about her disappearance, or do you just want me to flounder around in the sand out here?"

"She has a client in Sedona, an Indian guy she helped on some deal about his hunting ground. He called her up and said he was in trouble and needed her help. She called me that night she was supposedly kidnapped to say she was going off to meet him, and she swore me to secrecy for his safety. I didn't get the damned name." Wade's voice clearly said he was beating himself up.

"So it's possible she's on a business trip and she's okay?"

Both of us were silent this time, not believing it.

Through the window, I saw Manaba approaching and I finished up with Wade, telling him I'd be back in touch, as Callie jumped up and greeted her at the door.

"Twenty years ago..." Callie said softly, and it amazed me the way Callie and Manaba began conversations in the middle with no preamble.

Manaba bowed her head as if praying or contemplating or perhaps ignoring us. Finally, she said, "We were seventeen, and I was in love with her. He hated her for that, and when she died he was accused of her death but acquitted."

"But he did it?" Callie asked, and Manaba didn't answer.

"Why does Luther have such a hold on you?" I asked, and his name seemed to propel Manaba across the floor as if she was running from him right now. It was obvious she was hiding the truth and, unable to exit through her mouth, it was finding its way out through her incessant body movements.

"If truth is your own personal territory, maybe you will visit it more often." I paraphrased her admonishment to me. She looked at me in that dead-stop stare she always gave Callie, the look that went into me and through me, and seemed to decide perhaps I was more than she had seen on her first cursory visit.

"My grandmother had two daughters: my mother, who was raised by my grandmother in the tradition and gave birth to me, and my mother's sister, who had a child—the child of a white man. My mother's sister died in childbirth." Manaba spoke in a formal way about her aunt. "My grandmother raised the baby, named him Yiska, meaning 'the night has passed,' and treated him as a Navajo child in the old ways. Grandmother insisted Yiska would be Indian, even though Yiska's birth caused her daughter's death."

Manaba sat quietly awaiting our questions, but out of respect neither of us said anything.

Finally, she spoke again. "He wanted to be me, following in my grandmother's footsteps, but he is a man and not fully of the blood. He has powerful anger and his anger brings his power."

"Did he kill Nizhoni?" I asked.

"No," she said emphatically, and as if the wall had opened up and let him in, Luther Drake appeared, frightening us all with his stealth and cunning.

"Are you telling the story of our growing up?" His voice dripped with revulsion as he pulled up a chair and straddled it, resting his arms on the back of it, his forearm revealing a long, recent scar as if slashed by the teeth of a wild animal. Placing his chin on his hands, his dark eyes fathomless caverns, black holes, he said, "You ignored me in school for her, then you ignored me again for the next one. But Nizhoni is not dead at all, is she, Manaba? I might not have known, had it not been for your newest one." He indicated Callie with pursed lips, in what seemed a mockery of old Navajo ways.

My thoughts raced back to the day we dug up the grave and how Luther was the man who had jumped into the pit and pried open the lid where the bones lay. *Whose bones were those*? My mind no sooner registered that question than the answer flew from his lips.

"You and I know the bones of animals."

"She went over the cliff when the wolf attacked her. You know that, you were there," Manaba said flatly, and I looked at Callie, questioning if she knew Luther had been at the death scene.

"And you threw your cape across her and hurled her over the cliff. So you murdered your lover when she wouldn't leave you alone, as you murdered your lover Kai, and you wanted everyone to believe I did it, when all the while it was you!" He thrust a finger at her in a violent gesture. "Evil cannot be suppressed forever, and your evil lies are the source of my anger!"

He stood up, knocking the chair over, and whirled out the back door, the air in the space he occupied inverting on itself, sucking all oxygen into a small vortex that seemed to pull the breath from my own chest. A small black crow feather fluttered to the floor.

When I looked at Callie, I saw something even more frightening. She was clutching her throat and gasping. Jumping up to perform the

Heimlich maneuver, not knowing what she might have swallowed, I was held back by Manaba, who leaned in quickly and grappled with something unseen at Callie's throat, blocking it in the air with her forearms and wrestling it away. Callie took her hands from her throat and sucked in air.

"Are you alright?" I asked and hugged her to me.

"He's trying to frighten you," Manaba said.

"What are you talking about?" I asked, but Manaba ignored me.

"Is what he said true? Did you hurl her off the cliff?" Callie asked.

"Yes," Manaba replied quietly, and then she too turned and walked out of the cabin.

I shivered. "What the hell happened to your throat?" She rested her cheek against my chest, her small arms pulled in tightly, her fists balled up and tucked between us as if she wanted to be shielded by as much of me as she could.

"An attack," Callie said, and I knew she was referring to the same kind of attack that had occurred while she was sleeping. "He believes Manaba loves me."

"He and I are on the same page when it comes to that."

"She admitted to killing Nizhoni," I said, but Callie softly refuted Manaba's confession, saying she had only admitted to hurling the girl off the cliff.

"'Hurled' is pretty final. She's lying to you," I said without malice.

"Maybe she did throw her off the cliff but didn't kill her, Teague. The net. Maybe she intentionally threw her into the net." Callie pulled back from me.

"Why? And do you know what kind of shot she'd have to be? She'd have to be the Michael Jordan of the Sonora. The odds of my catching that net were a million to one. I don't think it could happen twice."

"Maybe she threw her off the cliff to save her."

"Like Vietnam: we destroyed the village to save it?"

"I'm trying to figure it out, that's all."

"You won't give up on her. God, she and Luther are really a pair."

"That's what I'm getting—that they're a pair," Callie said. "He's in love with her. Perhaps lovers in another lifetime. Whatever it is, they're locked in a struggle that goes beyond this one, and his jealousy of everyone and everything is making him insane."

"Can we go home to L.A.? This whole thing is taking place in a dimension I wasn't trained for. I think we should just get the hell out."

Callie turned her focus entirely on me. "It's not what you think, Teague. It's not sexual desire. It's a power struggle at a very high level, and the loser could die."

"I believe that, Callie, and I'm not going to let it be you. He thinks you're the competition now—like he thought Kai was and Nizhoni was."

Suddenly, her mind seemed to be transported to another place as she whispered, "The dream I had—the duck with the ribbons tying everything together—a male duck is a drake…tying the three deaths together."

My flesh rippled in response to her words.

"You're getting chills," she said. "That's a sign of affirmation."

Chapter Seventeen

I vehemently punched the End Call button on my cell phone as if it were personally responsible for my inability to reach Barrett after hours of trying. "No answer. I think we need to get a guide who can lead us to Little Horse."

"Even Manaba doesn't know where he is," Callie said.

Glancing out the window I spotted a tall, scrawny boy leaping across the lawn toward the cabin. He banged on the door before I could get to it, and standing before me was the kid from the grocery store. He looked shy and made no eye contact as he talked.

"Hi, uh…my mom said you guys were looking for Little Horse."

I asked him to come in, but he scuffed his beaten-up tennies on the porch steps and insisted his feet were muddy from being down at the creek.

"My day off. I work tonight," he said. "Uh…I can, uh…tell you how to get up there. I worked his mules for him up at the trail ride one summer."

I couldn't believe our good luck. Fern's kid knew where Little Horse was.

"I could draw it…but it's kinda complicated. I got a guide map back at my place and I'll loan it to you." I thanked him and he promised to bring it before dark.

"Carrot boy saves the day," I said. "He's got a map!"

"You see, you thought he was useless and stupid," Callie reminded me.

"I did. So did I misjudge him or did he become useful and bright because I told his mom he was going to turn out that way, or is he really only useful and bright on this singular occasion—"

"Or are things what you name them?" Callie kissed me. "You're very sexy."

"Let it be so." I grinned. "Let's go to the hospital and find out why Dwayne was trying to kill Blackstone and why Blackstone was whispering in dark corners with Manaba. Is he covering up for her or did she send him out into the desert and set him up?"

Grabbing my jacket, I tossed Callie hers and patted Elmo on the head, then doubled back and tossed him the plush basset hound toy. "Live it up. We're all too busy chasing crazies to get any ourselves."

Callie punched me in the arm playfully and I kissed her.

As we drove toward the hospital in silence, I tried to put together the elements I knew to be true.

"The Indian rescued me from that net. If your theory is right, he had to be in on the plan."

"But who is he and how will we find him?"

❖

At the small hospital, we stood patiently in line at the reception desk, waiting behind the Sunday visitors to ask where we could find Cy Blackstone's room. The receptionist hit a few computer keys, then announced that Mr. Blackstone was in intensive care and could not have visitors.

We took the elevator upstairs and got the same answer from a floor nurse. After quizzing her, then informing her I could get permission if necessary to talk to Senator Blackstone, I watched the tired woman give a maternal shrug. "Dear, you can get permission from Jesus Christ, and I'll let you go in and talk his head off, but you won't be getting any answers, because Senator Blackstone is comatose."

"He could have the nursing staff say he's in a coma to keep people away from him," Callie whispered.

"Got an idea." I began walking to the elevators. Callie followed, and once inside I punched a button that took us to the chapel level. Getting off the elevator and sinking into the plush mauve carpet and heading toward the polished pews had Callie twitching and demanding to know what we were doing here.

"Stealing," I replied, and entered the chapel as Callie gave me a questioning look. Scanning the room, I didn't find exactly what I was searching for, so I had to make do. I picked up a Bible from the back of one of the pews, crossed the room to a shelf where the brochures were stacked and lifted a small six-inch crucifix from the wall above the literature, then checked out the area near the pulpit.

"I hope you're not doing what I think you're doing," Callie said.

Ignoring her, I approached the stole hanging over the pulpit behind the altar rail. It was white with gold crosses above the gold fringe at each end. "Have you got a safety pin?"

When she shook her head no, I said it would have to work regardless of length. I draped the scarf around my neck and let the fringe fall down in front on both sides, hitting me slightly above the knees, then tucked the Bible under my arm and clutched the cross in my other hand. "How do I look?"

"No comment," she said as she followed me out of the sanctuary.

"I'll bring it back."

Getting on the elevator again, I altered my demeanor to a reflective silence, and even Callie was impressed, I could tell. When the doors opened, we were on the intensive-care floor, and I went to the nurses' station to say Senator Blackstone's family had asked me to look in on him. The nurse at the desk pointed to the cubicle in the corner, and I walked quietly in, leaving Callie behind. The ICU nurse was checking his chart and stepped out of the room to let me talk to the senator, who had his eyes closed but seemed to be moving a bit.

"How are you, Senator?" I asked, touching his arm. When he didn't respond I bowed my head. "Dear Lord, heal this man, make him whole in mind and body, relieve him of this pain, in Christ's name we pray."

I didn't see my words as blasphemy, since prayer was anyone's prerogative and basically beneficial, so in fact I'd performed a service for a guy who probably wasn't the all-time best citizen on God's planet.

"What happened to you, Cy?"

He opened one eye enough, I suspected, to see the cross in my hand and the Bible open before me. Then he turned his head away, refusing to speak or perhaps unable to, and I figured with my luck Cy Blackstone was an atheist and wanted me to leave him the hell alone. For all I knew, he could be dying, and I certainly didn't want to torment the guy.

That's another reason I'd made a lousy cop—I couldn't torture the near-dead into confessing. It seemed to me at the point a perp was checking out, he ought to have special dispensation to cross the River Styx without somebody on this side jerking him around and demanding answers.

Logically, I should get him to confess with his last worldly gasp, but practically speaking, I couldn't do it. I turned to go as Blackstone looked like he was about to board the boat for the Beyond. *Rest in peace, Cy Blackstone*, I thought.

He made a gurgling sound, which compelled me to turn back, and I caught him looking at me, his head back slightly and one arm raised weakly.

"Something to say…" he whispered hoarsely, and I realized that was probably a variation on "Would you take my confession?"

I glanced up at the nurse, who was about to enter, and asked for a moment longer. She nodded and turned away out of earshot.

"Alright," I said.

Thinking no doubt that he was about to die and not wanting to fly from this earth weighed down by guilt, he let everything tumble out in his hoarse whisper—what he'd done the night Nizhoni was to be killed. I suggested we pray together and we said the Lord's Prayer in unison. After the amen, he added out of the blue, "I double-crossed my son."

"Your son…?"

"Luther."

So much blood rushed to my head I felt dizzy. Cy Blackstone was Luther's dad! Blackstone, by Ramona's admission, had the scoop on everything and everybody; therefore, his son must too. And the social power of a white political family would outweigh the spiritual power of a Native American shaman's. It also meant that Dwayne could be a friend of Luther and indeed might know Cy Blackstone's family. So why was Dwayne trying to kill Luther's father?

Trying to keep my questions calm and priestlike, I took a breath and prepared to ask Blackstone to explain what had happened, when he closed his eyes and journeyed back into the unconscious.

"Damnation!" I uttered at not getting my questions answered, as the nurse walked in and stared at me. Glancing down at the cross on my scarf I added, "Damnation can be overcome with prayer. Thank you, nurse. Bless you." I made a hasty exit to the waiting area where Callie jumped up to join me.

Slightly out of my body, as if putting the pulpit scarf around my neck and carrying a Bible had afforded me entrance into a private place I shouldn't have visited—allowed me to become a voyeur into someone's soul—I managed to whisper, "He confessed, not knowing who I was. His son is Luther Drake."

I paused to let Callie take that in.

"Blackstone was headed out to kill Nizhoni on Luther's behalf—well, a fake killing by Cy Blackstone—but before he could, the shaman threw her over the ledge. Apparently, you're right that Nizhoni isn't dead, or they didn't mean for her to die. Anyway, the way I see it, Blackstone and Manaba double-crossed Luther, so his friend Dwayne-Wayne took Blackstone to the woodshed."

"He told you all that simply because you walked into his room carrying a cross?" Callie seemed to marvel at that. "Do you see what 'double-crossed' can mean?"

"Yeah, I guess so," I said as we dashed back to the chapel and I replaced the priestly props and privately said a prayer of contrition.

"Why would Blackstone cover up the murder of a schoolgirl years ago or take part in a staged murder today?"

"For the love of his son?"

"No. I don't see that. I would say threats—the kind of threats maybe that got Eyota, the grandmother, to sign over her land."

"Want to go to the newspaper office and see if they've got archives, because it's a cinch their old copies aren't online."

Callie nodded and minutes later we were in front of a tiny red-brick building with the word *Publishers* carved in stone over the front entrance.

"Closed. I forgot it's Sunday." We'd turned to leave when a pair of eyes peered through the shutters in the front window. I waved in a friendly fashion, hoping whoever it was would come to the door. Perhaps an employee was working on a Sunday.

Moments later, an elderly Native American woman opened the door for us, almost as if she'd been told we were coming, listened to a description of what we were looking for, and offered us a chair at a small table in the back of a room filled with boxes and rusty filing cabinets. We scanned hundreds of old articles, but it seemed that over the decades this fledgling newspaper had either struggled to fully report the news or the newspaper owners had only reported what suited them, because controversy was kept to a minimum.

It was near dark when she came back to find us, tired and discouraged, hunkered down over the piles of articles from twenty years ago. Without a word, she set a file down in front of me—an old, tattered, dog-eared 8 1/2 x 11 manila folder—and flipped open its bent cover. The article placed on top said, "Young Aide, Luther Drake, Worked on Senatorial Campaign—Says Election Not Rigged."

"So the campaign was rigged and Luther knew it, and he had Blackstone by the balls?" I whispered.

Without speaking, she flipped to a second, much older article, and I raised my eyes to look into hers, then lowered them to the page where her tan finger pointed.

The headline read INDIAN WOMAN ACCUSES CITY COUNSELOR OF RAPE. The photo caption said "Beleaguered Counselor Cy Blackstone denies ever knowing the Navajo woman."

"She was a friend," the Native American woman said, and the simplicity of her statement struck an emotional chord as I watched her retrieve the folder and turn to go. I wondered how long she'd saved it, what she'd thought as she clipped each of those articles, and where she'd hidden it, hoping someday someone would care to ask.

"Thank you," I said to her broad, tired back. "Thank you for caring enough about your friend to save this."

But she had already gone into another room as Callie and I walked out of the building and into the night.

"So Luther and Cy Blackstone share a long and sordid history," I said as we climbed into the car and headed back to the cabin.

"More than we know," Callie said. "Their secrets are old and dark and exist even to this day."

"What more could there possibly be between them?" I mused.

"A son who covers for his father's rigged election in exchange for the father covering for the son when he's accused of a teenage girl's death—conspirators who protect each other yet hate each other. There's more. That much I know."

Elmo was ecstatic to see us, perhaps feeling bad about his previous low-key greetings, and I led him down the porch steps for a potty break and bumped into Manaba, who nearly scared me into the next millennium, her deerskin-clad arm in my face as she tried to calm me.

"Manaba, it would be spectacular if you could approach the cabin like a normal person instead of like a freaking apparition. Terrific that you have that ability but—"

Ignoring me, she walked past and up the steps, as I glanced around to see if she'd been tailed. Then I followed her inside where she paced, refusing water or food or conversation, and Callie and I resigned ourselves to the fact we'd have to wait until she could get the words out.

"How did she know we wanted to talk to her? Did you call her with your mind?"

"No, with my cell phone," Callie said dryly.

I had never associated Manaba with a cell phone and wondered if she had a kangaroo pouch built into her hides so she could keep her phone with her. Glancing over at Callie, I could see her resoluteness.

She was focused on Manaba and I had a feeling, having gotten that look myself on occasion, that Manaba was in for it.

"Luther Drake is Blackstone's son. You knew all along and you didn't share that with me. You knew Nizhoni wasn't dead and you let me dig up that grave. What else do you know that you're not telling?" Callie said, and her voice was stone.

Manaba didn't even attempt to avoid it or spin it or refute it. At least she was smart enough to know when she'd been checkmated.

"I didn't know that he'd made plans to kill her, but Blackstone knew, and his conscience forced him to come to me. On that night, Luther Drake drove Blackstone to the ridge to meet Nizhoni. Blackstone and I arranged the net below, strung like a hammock then, and a rope around her waist hidden under her clothing, so in case she missed the net, she would still not fall below. Luther thought I had killed her, which put an end to his jealousy."

"Long way to go to dump a personal problem," I said.

"He is not an ordinary man," Manaba said. "He was happy when Nizhoni was gone. I had proved to him that he was more important than she. Blackstone gave her over to an Indian man to keep her hidden until I could prove Luther Drake was a murderer. Then you exhumed the grave—"

"How did Luther know to show up at the gravesite?" I asked.

"The wind carries the message."

"How did you keep this from Nizhoni's parents? They would know animal bones," Callie said.

"Distraught, they left it to Little Horse, Nizhoni's uncle. He has known all along."

Hearing the name reminded me that carrot boy was due back with a map to Little Horse's place. I dashed out on the porch to see if he'd been here and sure enough, stuck under the doormat, was the map he'd promised. Her back to me, Fern was about to disappear into the woods when I shouted her name.

"Didn't want to disturb you. My boy said you wanted that map." She pointed to the paper I'd retrieved on the doorstep, and I realized Fern was taking on her son's commitments.

"I'm sorry you had to make the trip."

"Love walkin' the woods." She dismissed my apology. "You and your girlfriend havin' a good time?"

"We are," I said, and smiled.

"You know, I was thinkin' if you find one person in this lifetime you can't stand to be without, then you're the luckiest person alive and you better grab ahold and hang on. Well, I got to get back to work."

Fern gave me a little wave before hiking off into the underbrush, and for a moment I felt like I'd been visited by an oversized angel in sensible shoes. I stood still, taking in what she'd said. Callie was that person for me, the one-in-a-lifetime I couldn't do without.

Absently, I unfolded the map and sagged against the porch post, seeing a series of intersecting scrawled lines with no markers of any kind. *Completely useless.* I started to toss the paper back into the trees from which it came but thought of Fern picking up after everybody, and I crumpled it up and jammed it into my jeans' pocket.

Returning to the living room, I heard Manaba tell Callie she would not let Nizhoni be killed, even if she had to kill Luther Drake. The words were cataclysmic; no Navajo and certainly no shaman would ever take a life.

"Ramona Mathers has disappeared. An arrowhead was found on her dresser at her cabin, and now a business associate, Barrett Silvers, has gone to find her," I interjected.

"You mean the studio woman who searches for her new lover," Manaba said. Her mind seemed to drift and then it appeared that she went into a trance, the kind of leaving her body that Callie did, only worse. Her body looked almost corpselike, she was so out of it. I sat quietly with Callie, waiting for her spirit to return. Minutes later, she stirred, rolled her eyes back down out of her head, and seemed to find it somewhat startling to be in a room with us. "Two are together. The other is lost."

That phrasing jolted me. Did she mean that her lover and Ramona were together and Barrett was lost, or perhaps Barrett and Ramona were together and her lover was lost? And what did "lost" mean: missing, dead, unsaved by the blood of the lamb?

"What do you mean?" I finally asked.

"I don't know what I say or see," Manaba replied. "I do not allow myself to recognize the location, only the feeling and the voices and the information."

Great, she takes trips and doesn't know where the hell she's been, I thought.

A whirring sound ensued outside the cabin, like a wind had picked up in the few trees along the creek bed and was blowing tales of evildoings around us. Manaba looked up at the ceiling, as if contemplating something unseen, then said she had stayed too long and left immediately. I had a feeling that staying too long had less to do with guest courtesy and more to do with her safety.

"What in hell was that about? Now she tells us Luther Drake killed her first lover and would kill this one if he could get his hands on her, and she threw her lover over the cliff in a mock murder to muddy the trail. On top of everything else, Nizhoni's nice uncle took Ramona, but God knows where." I stopped my tirade long enough to try Barrett's number again, then tossed my phone onto the couch.

"I talked to Wade. He says Ramona knew the Indian man she went off with. So does that mean she knows Nizhoni's uncle or is it a different Indian guy?"

While Callie contemplated these scenarios, I added, "I got the map from carrot-kid—well, Fern, actually." I pulled it out of my pocket and Callie stared, rotating it ninety degrees and cocking her head to look at it. "I know, absolutely useless. And what's-his-name's feathers are falling out," I said, picking up the crow feather Luther had left on the floor.

"Throw it outside," Callie said.

When I asked her why, she was suddenly upset. She would only say that birds can mean death, and sometimes their feathers portend a similar end. Tossing the feather out the door, I didn't respond, unwilling to allow every errant feather to become a death knell. Life was complicated enough.

❖

In the dark, we burrowed into the downy comforter and soft sheets, and I put my arms around Callie's soft middle and whispered, "I want to make love but I'm exhausted. Maybe this is the time I should learn to have a cerebral affair."

"Maybe," Callie said, snuggling into me but not taking the bait.

"Okay, teach me how to do it."

"It's not like that, you evolve into it."

"Evolve over the course of the evening, over the course of dating—"

"Over centuries."

"It took centuries for you and she-who-has-one-dress to have a cerebral affair? So that means I'm not evolved or—"

Callie suddenly placed her forehead against mine and closed her eyes, pressing her weight against me. It calmed and quieted me. My eyes immediately closed and I was silent, feeling an energy buzz that ran through my head, then trickled down my extremities the way children describe an egg breaking over their heads. The connection was electrical and spiritual…and sexual, the rippling sensation moving up my legs and inside them. Then Callie's hand followed that energy between my legs and I kissed her.

"This last part doesn't feel like a cerebral affair," I murmured.

"None of this is a cerebral affair. It's a way, as the song says, to get you to shut up and kiss me."

❖

I awoke from a love-sated nap to Callie's warm hip and leg pressed up against my still-sleepy form and the sound of her fingers clicking on the keyboard as she sat in bed beside me, making me grateful for battery-powered laptops and wireless. She glanced over as I stirred and then patted me through the covers.

"Hi, honey," she said, and I swooned upon hearing her words. I would always get to hear them as long as I could keep her loving me. She belonged to me now, and it was hard to believe this fabulous creature had chosen me.

"Do you think you own me now?" she said without looking up, and I could see her reading glasses propped up on her thin, angular nose that looked so beautifully Greek.

"I do," I said, and she smiled absently about the matrimonial phrase that continued to come out of my mouth by accident.

Feet scraped across the cabin porch and Elmo let out a large bark. So far this trip had been anything but relaxing for the nervous basset, and now we had more uninvited guests.

Chapter Eighteen

Barrett Silvers staggered onto the porch looking tired and gaunt, saving us the trouble of hunting her. We helped her inside and she sagged into a chair, her *Esquire* good looks only slightly less elegant than when she left, her shirt loose but still bearing her trademark cuff links. I was amazed at the way she managed to look good regardless—it had to be her tall, trim figure that overpowered any inelegance.

Callie brought her a glass of water, and Barrett asked for a Bloody Mary instead. For a non-drinker, Callie was a good bartender, and Barrett was soon stirring her drink with a celery stick and describing how she had driven through hell trying to find anyone who knew Little Horse's whereabouts.

"I don't think there is a fucking Little Horse, or if there is, then his friends have warned him I'm looking for him and he's laying low."

"Little Horse is Nizhoni's uncle," Callie said.

"Who's Nizhoni?" Barrett seemed weary.

"Nizhoni is the girl who went over the cliff," Callie said.

"So why would Little Horse kidnap Ramona?" Barrett asked.

"Callie thinks Ramona went voluntarily, and my police buddy Wade Garner said before you ever met Ramona she had dealings with a Navajo man. He'd asked her to come and see him because he was in trouble. So maybe she's on a business trip."

"That's insane," Barrett said, and I could see she was in no condition to absorb information. The plot wasn't going the way she'd expected so she was rejecting the script.

"We tried to call you but there was no reception," I said.

"I tried to call Ramona the entire time I was driving—nothing. Either her cell phone's dead or it's not on her or…I don't know."

"The military locates people. Hell, there's a company that collects data on everyone's cell-phone location and creates a detailed view of their life patterns—when they're working, sleeping, traveling, and of course who they're doing," I said. "All that based on phone calls. We might be in the middle of nowhere, but there has to be a way to find Ramona through her cell phone."

"But the phone you're zeroing in on has to be turned on. Her battery's got to be long gone," Barrett said.

I slumped on the couch and leaned my head back and stared at the ceiling, thinking how technology could pinpoint a lunar landing but couldn't track a cell phone. The ice cubes clinked in Barrett's glass as she took another slug and said, "Are you in some kind of cosmic trance too or is your neck broken?"

It was obvious she was feeling better.

"Lat long," I said.

"And you're speaking in tongues?" Barrett remarked.

I stood up, excited now. "Latitude and longitude. We simply pinpoint her via satellite through her cell-phone signal and get a lat long on her."

Barrett stared at me, obviously giving my suggestion some credence. "Still requires a working cell phone."

Grabbing mine, I rang Wade Garner in Tulsa. Neither of us offered to spar with the other, both of us worried about Ramona. When I hit Wade with my idea he said he had a friend at a company back East that did cell-phone signal tracks and he'd give him a call.

"Hey, if you were techno-cop, you'd connect your laptop to a mobile fax, enter your NASA code, scan the surrounds with a GPS, pull up a database, and tell *me* where she is."

"You're wasting time," I said, and he hung up.

An hour later, Wade called back to say he'd set it up and now he needed Ramona's cell-phone number. Barrett had it memorized. Armed with that, Wade said he'd be back in touch. We all looked at each other and began to smile, pleased that hope might be on the way.

Night fell and all businesses back East were long closed so we hit the sack, talking Barrett into sleeping on the couch. It was strange to have the woman I'd once slept with sleeping in the living room and the one I was sleeping with now in the bedroom...but then this was a strange trip and it had been an incredibly long day.

❖

At eight a.m. Pacific time the phone rang and Wade said they had her location in their crosshairs. He'd Googled the lat-long map and entered the degrees and zoomed in on the terrain. He said basically she was at a point several miles southeast of our current location.

Barrett was so excited she kept shouting for us to hurry up and throw on our clothes...we needed to get out there. Even Elmo insisted on going, ducking out of the door at the last minute and standing by the car. Callie let him jump in, saying he'd saved us twice so he'd earned a seat. Barrett looked less certain but didn't argue, most likely not wanting to create any delays.

❖

We drove south out of the city over the winding highway, curving around the red rocks and into flatter land. I pushed the trip-meter on my dash to be able to calculate the exact mileage as Wade had described it to me. The sun blinding us with its intensity, I turned left off 179 onto a road that was more a path than anything else, and I realized we were southeast of the spot where we'd had the infamous campout with Manaba. Sand kicked up around the car, creating a mist of dirt, filtering the sunlight and making the morning appear surreal, leaving a sand signal visible from miles away if anyone was interested.

Barrett was leaning over the front seat checking the odometer. "We're here," she said, and we all looked around, clear on one thing: here was nowhere and we were in the middle of it. Elmo, his nose pressed to the glass, sobbed.

"You're right about that, Elmo," I said, not attempting to get out of the car. "We have no clue where to look." At Elmo's insistence,

I finally conceded, got out, hooked him up, and we walked around among the sand burrs. He relieved himself and stood with his ears slightly elevated, staring across the desert.

"Barrett, ring her cell phone," Callie said quietly.

"You're right. We're tracking her cell phone, it might not be on her body," I said.

Barrett dialed the number she knew better than her own, then waited for it to ring. A light wind rustled across the sand and nothing but silence followed.

"Shit," I said, and turned to get back in the car, but Elmo dug in and refused to go. His ears were alert, his body poised, and I remembered he had better hearing than any of us. "Dial it again, Barrett."

Barrett rang Ramona's cell phone one more time, and Elmo strained to pull me in a direction away from the car. "Again," I shouted, and Elmo pulled me farther away. "Again!" I shouted to be heard over the expanse of sand, but this time Barrett and Callie were running to us, and Elmo was pulling me faster. Head down, he stopped where I could hear a faint sound.

Barrett had caught up with us, and she fell to her knees and dug into the gritty earth until the silver case of the small cell phone caught a glint of sunlight. She fumbled with the phone, for an instant stroking its slick silver casing as if it were the sleek silver hair of Ramona.

"It's Mona's," Barrett said. Hearing the glacially wicked Ramona Mathers referred to with such endearment and by her apparent nickname made me suddenly sad that occasionally we have to see someone through another's eyes to understand them.

There on her knees in the dirt in the sunlight, holding the last item that might ever be found of Ramona Mathers, Barrett made me feel as if I'd interrupted a church service. Callie and I looked away to give her a moment to collect herself.

"So if Little Horse is such a good guy, why is her phone out here, buried?" I whispered to Callie, who shook her head as if she wondered that too. "Okay, she left her cell phone on, which means she's trying to help us find her and she hasn't been gone very long from here, because it's still got juice," I said, trying to change the mood. Sobbing over Ramona wasn't going to help anyone.

"Look," Callie nearly whispered, and pointed to a faint plume of smoke maybe half a mile from us if we proceeded in the southeasterly direction we were already headed. "That could be them. They might not have gotten very far."

We jogged back to the car, and I helped Elmo into the backseat. "You're a smart dog, Elmo," I said to him, not caring if Barrett heard me talking to my dog. "Other dogs might not have realized the importance of that sound, but you hung in there, and I'm proud you're my hound or, better said, that you've allowed me to be your owner."

I waited for any smart remarks from Barrett and glanced in the rearview mirror to see the expression on her face, but she was staring out of the car window intent on the plume of smoke, her long, languid arm draped over Elmo, snuggled up against her side. I took Callie's hand, wondering if she had opened me up to greater possibilities in people.

Driving slowly, trying to kick up as little dust as possible, I pulled the car about two hundred feet from the fire. We got out, this time leaving Elmo inside with the windows cracked. His feet were rough from the stickers and the hot ground, and he was sagging physically. Like most hounds he was good in short bursts and after that he needed a nap.

"Don't let anybody in the car. We'll be back."

We closed the car doors quietly. We must have all intuitively known whatever was on the other side of that fire was a turning point.

Checking to see that I had my gun with me, tucked into my jacket pocket, I led the way across the sand. On the backside of a tiny rise of sagebrush and shrubbery a small fire burned, and seated next to it, her back to us, was Manaba. My body, geared for confrontation, relaxed, and my mind was disappointed.

"She's not here," Manaba said to us without looking around to see who "us" was.

"Where is she?" Callie asked.

"With the man whose whereabouts I do not know."

"We found her cell phone so she *was* here," Barrett said.

"We are all here." Manaba's voice held a tinge of ennui. "The end is spoken of in the ashes of the fire."

"And the beginning is found in the flames of desire." The voice above us spoke evenly, startling me and I assumed everyone, except Manaba, who seemed to be expecting Luther Drake.

"Our grandmother used to say that." His voice was quiet like thunder in the distance, rumbling low before it bursts upon you in deafening booms.

"She used to say many knowing things, Yiska." Manaba sounded almost wistful.

"She taught them to us both."

It was as if they didn't know we were there or that our presence was insignificant in this drama.

"Great teachers give the message to all. The student is transformed by the knowledge according to his own desire," Manaba replied.

"My desire was to be with you," he said.

"Your desire was to own my power."

And those were the words that ignited Luther Drake like an incendiary device. He leapt from his perch above our heads and seemed to fly across the small expanse of sand, landing within inches of her. She never flinched but looked up into his eyes as he yanked her to her feet.

"I know where Little Horse is. Therefore, I know where she is, and I am going there now to finish what you could not. No one comes between us. We were raised together. We are of one mind, one understanding, one knowledge, and one power."

"We are none of those things. You broke that power when you killed Kai. You made everyone believe she killed herself because she was jealous of my love for you, when it was you who were jealous of my love for her. You will not kill again."

Luther Drake's smile was diabolic and his low laugh like the sound of tectonic plates grinding together before the earth's upheaval, and like the suddenness of a quake, Luther Drake grabbed Manaba by her hair with his powerful left hand.

"*My* desires will be fulfilled!"

I aimed my gun at his leg, the only place I could get a clean shot, and was seconds from pulling the trigger when he flung his right arm toward me and let out a high-pitched scream, a duplicate of his graveside visit. The mere gesture knocked the gun from my hand, nearly breaking my wrist, his hand not even near mine.

I clutched my wrist and moaned, wondering how he'd managed to get in such an intense blow with a single non-contact shot.

Summoning strength beyond anything I'd imagined she possessed, Callie shouted, "Luther Drake, the universe severs the bond that binds you to this woman!" She swung her arm up over her head and down with the force of an ax onto his wrist, and Luther winced and weakened his grip on Manaba.

He spun and glared at Callie. Infuriated by her words, he slammed his forearm into her chest.

I screamed as she sagged to the ground, fearful a blow of that magnitude could have altered her heart rhythm, or at the very least have broken her ribs. Despite the attack, she appeared to be breathing steadily, and dragging her to safety wasn't an option because Luther had regained his composure. He flung Manaba to her knees, apparently prepared to kill her.

My gun gone and my wrist seemingly paralyzed, I jumped him and clamped my teeth onto his ear in a Tyson-like move designed to rip it from his head, and my onslaught produced a deafening howl. Suddenly, I was writhing on the ground as if I'd been run over by an eighteen-wheeler, and Callie rolled over and clutched me to her. Out of the corner of my eye, I saw Barrett backhanded by a blow from Luther, who was bleeding from the side of his head, the result of his murderous attempts.

Manaba, seeming to resurrect, rocket-launched herself on Luther and grabbed him by the throat, making me believe that very powerful spiritual battles begin close to where the Word emanates. Luther whirled and clamped both of his large hands around her neck, and I feared it was over for her. Although large for a woman, she came nowhere close to the kind of drug-induced strength he exhibited.

"Luther, putrid seed of a rapist…defiler of Indian women!" She croaked the words as if they would be her last.

My mind was awash in words and images—*Cy Blackstone raped Manaba's aunt and Luther was the result?*

Luther's hands tightened on her neck until she appeared lifeless. I staggered to my feet and threw myself at him at about the same time that Callie and Barrett joined me, all of us screaming for him to let Manaba go.

Instantly, a windstorm blew in out of nowhere and swirled what seemed like dump-truck loads of sand around us, and Luther Drake began to choke along with the rest of us, who covered our mouths and retreated. Angry over the unexpected force of nature, he seemed about to explode out of his body.

The air crackled, electricity flew above our heads, and while I was trying to determine the cause of the fireworks, flames flared above us. Then, as if caught up in the seething storm, Luther and Manaba bent and twisted and coiled around each other, flashing hotter from red to white, then flew apart and back together.

"Get away!" Callie warned, towing both Barrett and me farther from the fight as the air filled with electricity and the two adversaries sagged to the ground, still gripping one another's throat. Then suddenly they fell over, as if they were both dead.

"Good God," Barrett yelled as earth scorched next to her. We watched, mouths agape, trembling, and I occasionally glanced down at the two apparently dead people whose fighting had started an unnatural attack.

"Earth, wind, fire, and now water," Callie said, loud enough for me to hear. Thunder rolled across the sky, lightning cracked, and a torrential rain forced us to take cover or drown.

"Stay away from the metal vehicle!" As I spoke, I dragged Callie and Barrett back up onto the hillside where Luther Drake had first appeared.

A roar unlike any I'd ever heard began up in the hills, and while I was trying to decide what was approaching, a river of water barreled our way, a desert flash flood, a torrent washing past us and then over the bodies below. The edges of the newly formed stream lapped alongside Manaba, covering the right half her body. But the water engulfed Luther Drake and, as it intensified, flopped him over facedown and swept him along the desert floor like a maniacal Moses.

Callie ran to Manaba and held her head in her hands, telling her to wake up, she was alive. Manaba's eyes rolled into awareness.

"Luther?" Manaba asked.

"You thought earth but water claimed him," Callie said.

Callie asked me to get her some water from the Jeep so I jogged over and grabbed a bottle out of the backseat, quickly filling Elmo in.

"I don't know what the hell's going on, but I can assure you that you're in the best spot." Elmo whined, letting me know he was still nervous.

On the jog back, I rang Wade. Reception was poor, but I managed to get in that we'd found Ramona's phone but she wasn't there. Wade said she had to have turned it off to preserve the signal strength, which meant she'd gone with the Indian willingly and then gotten in trouble later and turned the phone back on. I wasn't sure I agreed with that theory, but told him I'd call him as soon as I knew anything.

I dashed back to Callie, where she and Barrett were making Manaba comfortable while Barrett grilled her, trying to find out what she knew of Ramona's whereabouts. However, Manaba insisted she knew nothing.

Distraught that we had obtained the latitude and longitude of Ramona's cell phone but hadn't found her, Barrett stroked the silver phone and sat silent.

Callie watched, her mind seeming to wander, then said, "Barrett, see if there's enough juice left to check her messages."

Barrett glanced at Callie and a moment of hope crossed her face. She flipped open the case, then quickly put it down. "I don't know her code so there's no way for me to pick up her message, even if she left one."

Callie was silent for a moment. "Does she have text messaging, or notepad, or a draft file?"

Barrett clicked through the options and found the message. *Find me S. shadow lodge pines clearing. Man armed.* The sender ID was blocked.

"Let's go!" Barrett was on her feet along with the rest of us. Manaba, too weak to travel, insisted we leave her there and she would follow.

"Will she be alright?" I asked Callie, then remembered Manaba's war with Luther. "What am I thinking, she'll be fine."

Back in the car, Elmo took up his post next to Barrett. I asked how Callie had ever thought about checking Ramona's own cell phone for messages.

"Uranus in the chart indicated technology. But when we discovered her phone, it told us nothing and I kept wondering why, thinking the answer was in there, but we didn't know it. She's smart and she knew someone might find the phone, so she left a text message for them."

We backtracked up to the main road, where I pulled a GPS out of my glove box and plugged it into the cigarette lighter.

"You have a navigation system?" Callie was stunned.

Self-conscious, I admitted I had bought one.

"But you take directions from no one, you check nothing out and you're constantly lost, and all the while you have a nav system in your glove box?"

"For emergencies. Put in Shadow Lodge. Please."

Twenty miles later the woman on the GPS, whose voice sounded as if she'd happily had a lobotomy, informed me I should turn left in one-quarter mile, then right, and proceed up the hill. Callie watched me as I obeyed the robot-woman and stared at me as if trying to decide how she'd missed this little piece of my personality.

"What?" I asked as I continued to follow directions.

"It must be her dispassionate tone."

"No. I trust she knows where she's taking me."

"Although she's a disembodied voice in a box."

"You two are meant for each other." Barrett spoke for the first time. "You go back and forth like you've been married for fifty years."

"Makes you glad you're unattached?" I asked.

"No," Barrett said, and I detected a loneliness that made me feel bad for having joked about it.

A visitors' parking area fanned out below the spot where tourists climbed up a few steps to experience the view from the ledge overlooking the canyon.

We jumped out of the car, leaving Elmo safely inside, and went to the edge of the ridge to try to find the area described. Nothing surrounding this tourist attraction seemed to match the text message Ramona had left us.

Checking the backside of the hills behind the parking lot, I saw a patch of scrub pines and rocks near an open expanse of land. I waved my arms to signal the others to join me, and we walked without talking down the slight slope toward the forest. I felt for my gun, a habit that hadn't done me any good during the most recent battle, but I was counting on it now. Little Horse, good guy or bad, had to be more mortal than the people I'd encountered.

"Stay with me." I took Callie by the hand and could feel that Barrett was sticking right behind us. We moved through the pines that ringed the expanse of barren land, careful to stay away from open spaces, and I hoped Elmo would be okay as we went farther away from him, and we would be okay as we went closer to something we couldn't name.

I pointed toward a single fallen log that looked almost petrified. Barrett nodded, understanding there could be something behind it. Tense and nervous, I motioned them to stay back and crouched down, half crawling around the outer edge of the log so I could see what was there. After a quick peek around it, I jumped back out of gunshot range, but I'd already glimpsed something—a body in a blanket lying up against the log.

"Over here," I whispered, and Barrett and Callie ran to help me.

"Oh, no," I heard Barrett gasp as we rolled the body over, not knowing what to expect.

Chapter Nineteen

The blanket was slightly wet. The contents' stillness and weight suggested that if someone had been alive in there, they were now long gone.

We rolled the blanket toward us and peeled back the edge, catching sight of a bound ankle, and I could tell by the way Barrett recoiled that we had to be unveiling Ramona Mathers. As we continued to work the blanket loose, we heard a stifled moan. Barrett dug in now, ripping at the blanket as if it were Christmas.

"She's alive." Barrett's voice cracked and I too recognized the moan as Ramona's. Pulling out a pocketknife, I sawed away on the rope bindings around her wrists and ankles as Barrett pulled the tape off her mouth. It looked like a bad episode of *Miami CSI*. We all asked the standard questions in rapid fire: Was she okay? Who had done this to her? Did she know where Nizhoni was?

She said Little Horse had come to the cabin to ask her help after Luther saw the animal bones, because he knew Luther would be looking for Nizhoni again to kill her. Little Horse asked Ramona to come talk to Nizhoni to see what she could do to help him find her a place out of state and to prosecute Luther. On their trek, a man intercepted them and tried to kill him.

"This man who attacked us wanted the girl and became furious when Little Horse led him in circles, so he bound me and left me for dead, not wanting the burden of dragging me around, then told Little Horse to take him to the girl or he would kill him on the spot. Law enforcement here obviously has its issues," she said dryly, exhibiting her first sign of humor.

I asked Ramona if the man who attacked them had a limp, and she confirmed the description of Dwayne-Wayne. Luther had apparently enlisted Dwayne to expedite the killing of Nizhoni, and more than likely that's why Dwayne had attacked Cy Blackstone—in an attempt to get him to reveal where Nizhoni was.

"Did you get my text message?" Ramona asked.

"Yes, you're brilliant!" Barrett hugged her. "I'm going to find the man who did this to you and kill him."

"Delighted that you're going to take up the gauntlet to protect me." Ramona tried to sound jaunty, and she put her arm around Barrett, who held her up lovingly. "The night was so cold, I had to think of everyone I'd ever slept with to stay warm. You kept me the warmest."

Barrett kissed her gently and rubbed Ramona's wrists and ankles to restore circulation, then got her coat and put it around Ramona. The coat, a rugged corduroy garment with leather piping, hung jauntily over the beleaguered Ramona's shoulders. As she draped it around her, Barrett's arms followed, holding the tall, slender Ramona who, even with her hair awry and no makeup, had a fascinating elegance. Like a great silver heron, she bowed her head, her body still stiffly at attention, and rested her forehead on Barrett's shoulder.

"You two stay here. Callie and I will get the Jeep and pick her up. I don't think she can walk."

"I'm perfectly capable—" Ramona began.

"We're picking you up because we want to, not because we need to," Callie said, and we left them alone in the moonlight and walked back to the car.

I assimilated the pieces like a crime-mosaic. "Sounds like Little Horse was pulverized by Dwayne-Wayne, who in addition to being Luther's friend could be his dealer."

"What makes you think so?" Callie asked.

"Watching Luther, I'm thinking he's on PCP—horse tranquilizer—makes the druggies nuts. When I was on the force and we got a call to deal with some guy on PCP, it took six grown men to bring him down."

"I went to get your menopausal herbs and saw a man picking up something, and it dawned on me it probably wasn't for hot flashes."

"That would explain a lot of Luther's power."

"But not all," Callie said.

I rang Wade and told him the good news about Ramona. He felt relieved enough to take credit for the entire operation, and I was relieved enough to let him.

When our car came into view I pulled my keys out of my pocket and clicked the automatic door lock. The cab light came on and I froze. Seated behind the steering wheel was a large, perfectly still figure. My first thought was that whoever it was had come to kill us, and my second thought was for Elmo's safety.

I pounced on the car and yanked the door open. Manaba was slumped in the front seat unconscious. Elmo was sound asleep in the backseat, and my next thought was how in hell she got into my locked car. But she stood in fire, so Chrysler engineering was probably nothing to her.

Both began to stir when they heard my voice. Manaba offered an apology, saying she hadn't meant to startle us. She and the dog, as she termed Elmo, were fine. Apparently Elmo didn't buck spiritual leaders even if they invaded his space. He was smarter than me in that way.

We told her what had been going on and that Dwayne had forced Little Horse to take him to Nizhoni somewhere up in the canyon. I refrained from telling her that most likely Dwayne-Wayne had killed them both. Manaba remained quiet.

"Can you travel and look for them?" Callie asked, and I had the feeling she meant by mind, not Mazda.

"I'm very weak, but I'll try," Manaba said, clearly stating her condition as fact, not a source of sympathy.

As we drove back to get Barrett and Ramona, Manaba seemed to be out of her body again and I was silent, thinking about that particular skill set. Why couldn't people travel out of their bodies without people like me thinking they were nuts? If we'd been riding around on horseback in the 1700s and suddenly told our companions that one day they could walk on the moon, they'd have made fun of us. So maybe these tribal people were way ahead of us.

"I like what you're thinking." Callie took my hand.

"I like that you always know what I'm thinking. It saves a lot of time." I glanced down at the zipper on her small jeans. "What am I thinking now?"

"The thing you never stop thinking," she whispered and rested her hand in my lap. Electrical current rushed through my body, exciting every cell.

❖

I would have expected Barrett and Ramona to be sitting on the first red rock with their thumbs out, anxious to get out of the middle of nowhere, so I was surprised to find them out of the general view, pretty much where we'd left them, huddled in each other's arms.

But I didn't expect to see them sucking each other's lips off, their sexual fervor evidenced in the tight body grip, mouths welded, Ramona's blouse open and her bra askew. Her skirt was hiked seductively, Barrett's arm under it locked around her hip and, guessing from the way Ramona shifted and moaned, beneath her panties, in exploration of the entire topography of her sexual landscape.

The woman who had hit on me and struck out and the woman who'd hit on me and scored were now only interested in one another, and in an inexplicable way, I was happy for them. I took a moment to watch them in a deep, sensual embrace, Barrett now tenderly kissing Ramona and not so tenderly reaching inside her clothing to stroke her body. I wanted to shout, "Give the woman a break, she's been bound and gagged," but Ramona Mathers didn't look like she wanted a break.

"Curfew, kids," I said, and the two of them broke apart sheepishly and followed me back to the car, where I dug into my pocket and gave Callie the hand-drawn map.

The five of us and Elmo were pretty packed into the Jeep. Callie put him in the front seat with her and he sat on the floorboard, his paws up in her lap facing her. She stroked his head and talked to him and explained why his transport suddenly looked like a city bus.

"I think Little Horse had Nizhoni at his place. If we could read this map, we could get there," I said.

Callie handed the map to Manaba, who only glanced at it for a second, then said, "Straight ahead and cross the goat path running diagonally southwest to northeast. Then leave the car and we will proceed on foot."

"How could she read that chicken scratching?" I said.

"She went there as a bird and the map was a reminder," Callie said.

"You travel as a bird?" Ramona asked Manaba, reviving enough for a slightly caustic side to resurface.

"She shape-shifts like her grandmother, who taught her," I said flatly, realizing as the words came out of my mouth that I'd joined the ranks of the incurably insane. "If everything on earth is made of protons and neutrons, whether it's a table or a human, and we can put a table in a molecular chamber and raise the vibrational level up so high the object actually disappears, then humans can obviously vibrate at a level that would make their bodies disappear, leaving their spirits free to roam, and if the spirit was talented enough to enhance and harness that energy, then it could basically…do stuff the rest of us can't." I stopped for breath.

"Very good," Callie breathed.

"Had to be able to sort of justify it in my mind," I said.

"Beats pledging a sorority," Ramona quipped, and Barrett grinned widely, obviously believing everything she said was witty. I was reminded that love makes fools of even the most sophisticated.

Ahead a small adobe dwelling, smoke coming from the fireplace, rose in the sand. We pulled up and cut the motor, slipping out of the car as quietly as possible. Having had all the stalking around in the sand I could take for one day, I attacked the small wooden door of the adobe house as if this were a drug bust: kicking first with my foot, jumping back against the wall, then shooting down into the lock and blowing off the doorknob. When I slammed my shoulder into the door and entered, the Indian man facing me looked completely dazed and fearful.

"You Little Horse?" I asked, and he nodded yes. Eyeing the four women who came in behind me, he must have thought he'd been busted by women's bridge night.

In the corner on a small cot, a dark-haired woman lay in the shadows. Manaba moved quickly to the tattered bed, knelt down, and felt the woman's forehead. She took something out of a leather bag at her waist and forced it between the woman's pale lips.

As Little Horse moved closer to the lamplight, I shouted, "You're the guy who rescued me and the one who dug up Nizhoni's grave." I wanted to find out every detail of what happened below that cliff—how he caught me and why, but he seemed terrified that I knew him and grasped a sheaf of gray stalks, set it aflame, and let the pungent smoke fill the room, then moved from one corner of the room to the next as he swung the sage through the air, apparently too paralyzed with fear to speak and now only able to chant for protection.

"Where's the guy who kidnapped you?" I persisted in addressing Little Horse. "Look, Ramona vouched for you and said another guy kidnapped you." But Little Horse was mute and, if not terrified, at least preoccupied with driving away evil.

Manaba, ignoring all else, talked softly to the woman on the cot, telling her we would be taking her out of here. A sound at the door and Barrett made a quick move to put a chair up against it, but the door was blown open from the other side. Standing before us was Dwayne, his frame filling the doorway, and I realized what had Little Horse so nervous.

"Gotcha all in one spot. Good."

Dwayne-Wayne might have been nuts, but he was no match for three women with PMS. He reached for his gun as Barrett picked up a chair and swung it at his midsection and Callie brought both arms down full force on his forearm in the same move she'd used on Luther, which momentarily threw Dwayne off balance. He took a second to recover before making a staggering attempt to aim at her. I was waiting for him and yanked him inside the cabin and slapped him over the head with the butt of my gun, which put him on his knees and split his head open.

"Anybody got a belt I can borrow?" I asked the room at large and Barrett removed hers. Glancing at it before tying Dwayne up, I realized this was the most expensive rope ever used on anyone, but Barrett probably wouldn't need it. Gathering from her glances at Ramona, she'd have her pants off at the earliest convenience.

"We may have to tie you to the hood of the car like a deer, since we're flat out of seats," I told Dwayne.

Manaba seemed oblivious to the commotion as she helped her lover to her feet and began walking her to the door, Manaba's inner strength visibly overcoming her outward fatigue. Callie reached for the door and I noted that Little Horse was shaking so badly the smoke was almost making rings.

No time to digest that thought before the door exploded open again and nearly splintered off its hinges. A huge, ominous, raging energy mass filled the room, the blast followed by Luther Drake. He stood in the cold night air, bare breasted, face painted, a black crow feather in his hair, his dichotomous grin a warning he could smile while ripping the skin off your face.

Manaba never flinched, but I personally was one large goose bump, having thought the sonofabitch was dead. Hell, for all I knew, maybe he was dead and this was more weird energy returning to haunt us. Callie grabbed me by the arm and pulled me away from the door.

"Surely you didn't think I had drowned?" he asked Manaba.

She handed Nizhoni to me, and I felt as if I had been deemed guardian by a parent who knew she was about to die and was entrusting me to care for her child. I shook that feeling off and helped Nizhoni to her bed, then returned to guard Callie. Ramona and Barrett retreated to the corner as if observing a horror movie and Callie stepped forward, afraid of nothing in the spiritual realm.

"The grandmother spirit asks that you release your hold on this woman, Nizhoni, and let her live," Manaba said.

"The grandmother spirit wants the land back." Luther leered and mocked her.

"You threatened and tricked her into signing, telling her the developers were coming for the land and you would fight them."

"The grandmother wants your lover to live, wants me to give up my power, but the grandmother spirit is dead, and her granddaughter does not honor what I know and bring. I am the same as you."

He swung his fist down on Manaba's head and blood spewed from her scalp, the blow smashing her to the ground. The sound of her body hitting the floor seemed to be the downbeat for an orchestral symphony of sights and sounds. The wind picked up exactly as it had before, but this time it blew papers around the room and people's hair back and the lights out as if we were in a cyclonic wind tunnel. Light bounced around the room, its source unknown, illuminating the room sporadically and allowing us to see the whites of Luther's eyes and the gleam of his teeth.

Barrett yelled as a lamp missed her head and she covered Ramona with her body, and Callie stood amid it all, tall and unafraid and dealing with whatever was happening as calmly as if we were merely in a small argument. In the dim light, I realized Luther was choking the life out of Manaba, who was too exhausted to overpower his energy again.

"He's killing her!" I screamed and dove on him. Callie picked up an andiron and smashed it into his head, but it was as if she'd merely tapped him with a plastic pipe; his strength shocked me. He bled but he didn't weaken, and his rage increased tenfold. He seemed to grow twice as tall and lunged at us, this time physically connecting with me and then Callie, hurling us across the room.

I landed, momentarily too injured to walk, then crawled to Callie to see if she was alright. Then he grabbed me, and I realized I was only in the path of where he was really headed, which was Nizhoni and then Manaba, intent on killing them. Fighting him and shouting for Callie to get out of the way, I felt myself losing, crushed by some super strength beyond my comprehension.

That's when I heard the cry, a long wailing supplication from Manaba. "Shimasaniiiiii."

I cringed, thinking maybe the head wound had claimed her life.

My mind was racing, trying to figure out how we could overpower him, when in the partial dark, the wind kicked up around our feet, the power of it nearly lifting us off the ground, sending chills across my body, a wind I'd felt only in severe thunderstorms, but now somehow it was in this cabin. The air was alive, charged with electrical current that pulsed around us in waves of energy that seemingly controlled the rhythm of my beating heart. Then I heard the growl, a visceral, guttural grinding of innards. My mind flashed on Elmo, but I had never heard him sound like that.

Then the leap, the flash of fur, bared teeth, ripping and tearing and flailing and screaming and blood—*it must be blood*—a liquid substance splashing through the air, and then a loud groan as if the devil had relinquished its hold on something—the battle over, ended, silence.

Callie managed to reach a table lamp and turn it on. The partial light revealed Luther Drake dead on the floor—this time dead for sure, blood dripping from his mouth, his heart torn out of his chest. Beside him a huge wolf stood, tired and bloodied, breathing... panting...breathing...panting.

It turned and surveyed the room, seeming to make eye contact with each of us, then walked quietly out of the cabin and into the woods. From the looks of the faces in the room, we were all in shock.

"What did Manaba scream?" I whispered to Callie, somehow knowing Manaba's shrill cry was tied to the appearance of the wolf.

"The Navajo word for grandmother."

And for my money, it appeared her grandmother had answered the call, perhaps removing the man from this world who had removed her—if one believed in that kind of energy transfer.

"Anybody got a working cell phone?" Barrett asked. "I'll call the police."

"Let me have your cell phone," I said to Dwayne, then realized he was dead. "What the hell happened to him, not a mark on him?"

"Heart attack," Manaba said authoritatively, and I believed it was the same kind of heart attack her grandmother had suffered.

I got a signal on Dwayne-Wayne's cell phone. Calling the police from his phone was justice.

I threw a blanket over Luther Drake, not wanting to look at the condition of this particular dead guy and the mess made of his corporeal self.

Thirty minutes later, Sedona's answer to crime fighting showed up in the form of Sergeant Striker, sporting his perfectly pressed uniform and, despite the low light, aviator sunglasses. He planted himself in the doorway, legs apart, gun drawn, the Atlas of law enforcement.

"What's goin' on here?" he barked at the room in general, and before I could answer, he flipped the blanket back and caught sight of Luther Drake's body. Striker bent over for a closer look, gagged, and spewed vomit like squashed bug guts. "He's had his heart ripped out," Striker said, trying to explain his weak stomach.

"Slows 'em down, which is good," I said, mimicking his remarks to me and reminding him we'd met before.

He listened as I told him Dwayne-Wayne had attacked us, followed by Luther Drake, and while they were threatening us, a wolf came through the door and killed one and gave the other a heart attack.

I skipped the part about the wolf being the grandmother; I didn't think it mattered. None of us could have inflicted the claw marks or bites on Luther Drake's body. He was clearly done in by a wolf. A wolf in what dimension was something we'd have to sort out among ourselves.

Chapter Twenty

The ride back to town in the Jeep was quiet. We were all tired and exceedingly lucky and, ironically, we were in pairs. Three couples. Manaba and Nizhoni, Barrett and Ramona, Callie and me, and of course Elmo, who was still in search of basset love. There could not be three odder couples, I thought as I glanced in the rearview mirror to see Nizhoni and Manaba asleep on one another.

"We drop Manaba off at any particular tree stump?" I murmured so only Callie could hear me.

"She wants her cabin back, now that she has Nizhoni."

"She rented us her cabin."

"And now her need is greater," Callie said calmly.

"My need is pretty great—"

Picking up on the conversation, Barrett leaned over and patted me on the shoulder. "You'll stay at my cabin. I'm staying with Mona."

"Maybe Ramona would like to stay at carrot-boy's cabin, and then we could stay with Squash Blossom the jeweler's—"

"Change in her environment makes her sarcastic," Callie said, taking my hand.

"My poodle is like that," Ramona commented in a lovesick, lazy voice that made me swivel my head around to see if it was really her. "By the way, very butch entrance into the cabin, blowing the door handle off, very exciting," Ramona said, then suddenly pulled Barrett in for a sizzling kiss and I decided, like Barrett, damned near anything could turn her on.

An hour later, we'd dropped Ramona and Barrett off and pulled up in front of our cabin, now Manaba's.

"It's the right thing to do. They've both been traumatized and haven't seen each other in weeks," Callie whispered and patted my leg.

"Are they going to sleep on our sheets?" I nearly mimed so they couldn't hear me in the backseat.

"I'll wash the sheets," Callie said.

"Because I don't want bear grease in my bed. That's all I've got to say on the subject."

I jumped out of the car and dashed inside the cabin and gathered up toothbrushes, nightshirts, makeup, Elmo's dog bowl, and our laptops, not planning on being displaced by Manaba for more than one night or I would move us to the comfort of a hotel.

When I returned to the Jeep, Manaba, her head bandaged, stood by the passenger side of the car with Nizhoni, both of them talking to Callie in what looked like a strained and awkward conversation.

When I approached, Nizhoni smiled and said, "Thank you. Balance is restored." The first words I had ever heard her speak and I wondered how Manaba had ever put the move on a woman like Nizhoni. It must have taken a really long time, since conversation didn't exactly flow from either of them.

"Truth is restored." Manaba spoke and I thought she might have added a bit more in light of the fact that she'd nearly gotten both of us killed.

Callie nodded, saying nothing else, and Manaba and Nizhoni departed as Callie got back in the car.

"Not big talkers, these Indian friends of yours."

"They say all there is to say."

"So I guess in their eyes, I'm a babbler," I said, and she took my hand.

"Say only positive things about yourself, Teague. The soul remembers every negative word."

"There's a positive word for babbling?"

"You're...expressive," she said and kissed me to keep me from expressing any other thoughts.

❖

Inside Barrett's abode, I felt like a break-and-enter. All her stuff was lying around—slacks over the backs of chairs, cuff links on the dresser, leftover dinner in a plate on the sink. Barrett Silvers, pressed and perfect, coiffed and quintessential butch, was sloppy around the house. "I guess she didn't know we were coming," I said, clearing a path to the bedroom. "In L.A. she has a maid. Now I know why."

Callie pulled back the covers. "I'm not sleeping on these sheets."

I rummaged through the cedar closet and found another single sheet, stripped off the old one in favor of tucking in this loose but clean one, and crawled into bed, tugging Callie in beside me.

Neither of us spoke, and I knew she was squirming. "Hard to sleep on someone else's sheets," I said. Without further conversation we got up, dragging a blanket with us, and went out to the couch where we lay so close together the circulation in my arm almost stopped, but I felt so good I didn't care.

"I want to stay in bed, or 'in couch,' with you forever and do nothing…and I guess that's possible since I blew my whole scriptwriting gig." I laughed at the thought—the whole blowup with Jacowitz.

"You didn't read me your alien pages." Callie's fingers made lazy circles up my leg.

I clicked open my laptop on the table but had trouble focusing on pulling up the screen due to Callie's toying with me.

"Am I disturbing you?"

"I like being disturbed by you. In fact, your look, feel, and taste are constantly disturbing to every molecule of my body." I sat up and suddenly pulled her onto my lap. "Hmm, reminds me of chair sex. One of the first times I tried to make love to you in L.A., you were sitting on my lap."

"Yes, and it caused an earthquake." Callie grinned mischievously. "Read me what you wrote?" She trapped my hands.

"So the way I've got it worked out is that it's Halloween and the married gal is attending a costume party and she goes off to the library of this big home to keep from crying in public over her husband's infidelity, and an alien, who she believes is a costumed guest, enters the room. The alien—face oddly attractive, body androgynous—moves a little closer to her. The woman is a bit twittery, aware that something is odd about this person, but it's hard for her to be suspicious of a person in a blue costume.

"The alien, incredibly strong for its size, lifts her easily into its arms and carries her over to a couch as she protests, giggling. Whipping its head toward the door, it spies the bolt, and with that look the door locks. The woman is unable to make a sound. Lifting her hips to its mouth, the alien watches with great interest as she finds enormous pleasure in this sex act—and then it morphs into a beautiful woman from another dimension.

"Let me act it out for you," I said, and slid my hand between her legs, playfully, pretending that if the manuscript didn't satisfy her, I might.

"It's…actually—"

"Terrible. And Jacowitz knows it. He sent me a personal note bypassing Barrett to say he didn't appreciate my turning his suggestions into a farce. How can my writing this scene be any more of a farce than his suggesting it?"

Callie slid off my lap, excited now about something other than my close proximity to her body. "The characters in your story have been everybody in the world from nuns to hookers to therapists. Why can't the two lead characters be an older woman with power and position who has been around the block and a younger woman who has slept with everyone but never found love—"

"Who are they? What brings them together?"

"One is on the board of a motion-picture studio and one is a development executive."

"You want me to write the story as if it's Barrett and Ramona? How prostituting is that?"

"A thought," she said with a shrug.

"But they're characters Barrett will fight for, stand up for against Jacowitz because she has a personal stake in them. Pretty smart."

"Trying to be helpful." She kissed me and I realized that might be what a mate does…comes up with ways to fix things for you.

I emailed a quick note to Barrett suggesting the new plot outline and sent it to her in an instant ping. "You've now become my own personal plotmeister."

"Do you realize it all turned out exactly as the chart said?" Callie changed the subject, never overly interested in screenwriting. "Venus was besieged, women under attack: Nizhoni, Manaba, you and me, and really all the Native American women who wanted that land back but didn't get it. Eyota, Manaba's grandmother, was tricked into signing over her land, like the chart said, with Mars, a man, at her back threatening her, and Neptune's disillusionment, the loss of her land, ahead of her. It said Nizhoni wasn't dead and she wasn't."

"And it said a woman would save the day and I would say that's you."

"And you," she said, kissing me.

"So when we were fighting off Luther, you were pretty damned strong. Where did that come from?"

"I'm a lot stronger than you think. Besides, it's all in my chart. Speaking of charts." She pulled up an astrological wheel with today's date at the top. I recognized the grouping of planets and panicked.

"Don't tell me we're heading into another besiegement."

"We are. But there are two kinds: malefic, as old-world astrology calls it, and benefic. We've been through the malefic one, and I thought it might interest you to see a benefic one. Mercury bounded by Venus and the Sun." At my look she elaborated. "Mercury, or communication, sitting between woman or lover and the Sun's ardor and vitality."

"I want to communicate my ardor with vitality." I tackled her and she laughed.

"Is that the only thing you ever have on your mind?"

"No. It's the only thing I have on my mind when I look at you."

❖

The following Saturday, the sun broke over the red cliffs, preparing to highlight the mall groundbreaking and surrendering the ancestral ceremonial site on which it had shone for so many centuries to the developers, poised with heavy equipment and television cameras for this, the first day of construction. Callie and I gathered with crowds of people waiting to see the ribbon cutting and wishing along with many others that this sacred earth could remain untouched.

Cy Blackstone, alive and ready for the news conference, was decked out in his black pants, white cowboy-cut shirt, and black bolo, holding his black hat in his hands and looking rugged, if not a few pounds thinner after his hospital stay.

Ramona had gone to see him and told him she'd be happy to help him halt the construction of the mall. He said that even with Luther gone, he had to press on. It would make him look bad in the community, and everyone would lose money.

Nizhoni and Manaba both spoke to him and begged him, but he wouldn't give in. Despite his blaming so much on Luther, now that he had the chance to release the land to the Indians, he wouldn't do it.

"Senator, could I see you for a moment?" Ramona Mathers extricated herself from Barrett Silvers long enough to sidle up to the senator and say something very coquettish in his ear. When she pulled back, Blackstone reared up as if he might get angry, but her large, bejeweled hand gripped his arm.

The heavy yellow dozers, skid loaders, and earth-moving equipment were taking their positions, strategically placed for the cameras to get a shot of the massive construction about to begin.

The young TV announcer addressed the camera, saying this was the big day—the moment for which all parties had waited, as they determined if the mall would or would not happen on this disputed site.

As she spoke, women began appearing over the hillside, at first dozens, then hundreds, and finally what appeared to be a thousand. So many women that the video engineer in the truck could be heard through the open door asking what the hell was going on and shouting for a wide shot.

The camera pulled back and captured the hillside teeming with women in native dress. Finally, even Cy Blackstone looked back over his shoulder and did a double take.

When the announcer asked Cy what was going on, he looked stunned and didn't say a word, so Ramona took the microphone and said, "As friend and attorney for Senator Blackstone, I want to share with you that the senator is overwhelmed by the wonderful outpouring of Native American women wanting to keep this ceremonial site as their home. He has decided to donate this land to them and use this earth-moving equipment on land south of here, but not here—not where so many women have danced and prayed and sung."

The onlookers broke into wild applause as Ramona handed the microphone to Cy, who paused only a moment to assess the political landscape, then said he was happy to restore this land to the Indians because he'd always been an advocate for Native American women.

After that, Manaba took the microphone and, ignoring Blackstone, said a blessing over the land and all the grandmothers who had danced upon it. Nizhoni stood by her side, the two of them looking strong and happy.

The newspeople were so excited they forgot to be cynical, reveling in getting this scoop live.

By the time the cameras had cut and wrapped, and Cy had privately cussed Ramona, and the women had disappeared back over the hill, Callie and I were staring at each other in disbelief.

"What did you say to Blackstone?" I asked Ramona as she strolled back over to Barrett, who stood beside us.

"I told him I had gotten word from a friend of mine that Luther Drake was Cy's son, the product of his having raped an Indian woman thirty-five years ago, and that restitution for that crime looked like the mall was going somewhere else."

I smiled. "Surprised Blackstone took your word for it."

"Men have always taken my word for it," Ramona said slyly. I had no doubt her elegant charm had made men from every walk of life do her bidding, and now Barrett Silvers was in line. "Anyway, Cy's a dyed-in-the-wool politician so he knows when to retreat and regroup." Ramona leaned on Barrett, who held her as if she were the most delicate, priceless prize on the planet.

"I can't believe how many Native American women showed up. My God, where did they all come from?" I asked.

"Extras—the studio will be getting the bill," Barrett warned Ramona, who merely laughed. And I realized that Barrett, knowing Ramona was going to do a little soft blackmail on Cy, had turned the entire event into a production worthy of television cameras and had actually hired extras, which made me laugh too.

Barrett walked past me, never more than a foot away from Ramona, and whispered, "Got your new story idea—love it. I'll call Jacowitz. It's a much better twist than the alien, and moviegoers adore Hollywood. Two strong women executives…Sigourney, maybe."

Callie giggled when Barrett was out of earshot. "I knew she'd love it. You can call it *Narcissus*."

"Looks like we could be shooting in New York after all." I high-fived Callie when Barrett wasn't looking.

The morning's activities drawing to a close, I offered to buy Callie lunch, telling her we'd stop at a deli and get a small basket of sandwiches and drinks. We hopped into the Jeep with Elmo in tow and collected our repast from a local gourmet shop, then headed up to the ceremonial site for one last look over the gorgeous land that was Sedona.

"Do Native Americans believe in astrology?" I asked as we drove.

Callie said there were books on Native American astrology. "By their chart, I'm born a woodpecker," she said, grinning at me, and I bit my lip to avoid making jokes about her occasional hammering on me. "Do you know what you are?" When I looked blank she said, "The wolf."

"You're kidding!"

"Nope, and it might interest you to know that Woodpecker and Wolf together have perfect harmony of heart and soul."

"What about Woodpecker, Wolf, and Hound?"

"Magical," Callie said as I parked the car, patted Elmo, and whispered for him to keep an eye out for intruders. Then I took the blanket and a picnic basket and walked up the last fifty yards, invigorated by all that had been accomplished.

Callie stood on the edge of the plateau, her arm around me, and we let the soft breeze blow over and through and around us.

"I have something for you." I squeezed her waist.

"And would that be—wine or cheese?"

Reaching in my pocket I pulled out a small box and flipped it open. Inside were the matching Indian wedding rings we had tried on together in the store. Callie looked down at the rings and then up at me. I could tell the rings were unexpected.

"When did you buy these?"

"When you weren't looking."

"What does this mean?" she asked, smiling.

"Whatever you want it to mean," I said, lightly mocking the way she always talked to me.

"Are you proposing?"

"I'm proposing we wear matching wedding bands."

"Even though we don't live together yet."

"Our hearts live inside one another, our souls were mated eons ago, and our minds are one." I took the smaller ring and slid it onto the fourth finger of her left hand, then handed her the larger ring, extending my hand. She slipped the ring on my finger, and the sensation was one of strength and protection and love. We placed our hands side by side like two wings of a small bird, and the sunlight glinted off the gold and reflected into our eyes and our hearts.

Callie tilted her head up and kissed me, her arms tightening around my neck, and I grew weak: wet from love, dry from the winds, enveloped in desire. I pulled her down on the blanket I'd arranged, anchored with stones from the ceremonial circle. *What could be more fitting than my lover's bed being anchored by ceremonial rocks?*

"You can't make love to me here on the ground," she whispered.

"It's been done for centuries," I said, lying on my side facing her.

"And what if someone comes up here?"

"Elmo's positioned to watch the trail, and you know he always gives a fifteen-minute warning for approaching visitors. So there's no getting out of this. What better honeymoon than being naked on a Sedona ceremonial plateau high above the gorgeous Native American land? Love is energy, beautiful energy. You either believe it or you don't, so let's see some energy," I teased.

And with that, Callie Rivers stood up and yanked her clothes off, in seconds standing naked in the wind. I had never seen her look so magnificent, majestic, powerful, as if carved from the great rocks that formed this valley, and I stared at her in awe as the sun streaked across her body and she smiled down at me. "Take off your clothes," she commanded with a twinkle in her eye, and her mere presence shot electrical charges through me.

I leapt to my feet and stripped faster than a firefighter. "Marry me!" I yelled into the wind, unable to contain myself.

She knelt on the blanket and I knelt beside her. "I have. I will. I do."

Amid the mysticism of this sacred place, we made love in a beautifully primal way, inside one another, coupling and uncoupling like the great red stones that come together and pull apart over centuries. And in the heat of passion, our bodies wet and souls throbbing, I caught sight of something blowing over the edge of the mesa, a two-legged kite sailing away.

"My pants," I panted.

"You won't be wearing them now, darling," she said and kissed me deeper, and for a moment I wondered if she meant that literally—simply because they'd blown away—or figuratively, because she would be wearing the pants in this relationship.

But I quickly wiped those earthly thoughts away, because love was all that mattered now—Callie Rivers belonged to me.

About the Authors

Andrews & Austin operate several large entertainment business ventures but still find time for one of their biggest passions—writing. Their strong lesbian characters, witty storytelling, and distinctive style derive from years of writing for television and film. Their goal is to help lesbian fiction be appreciated and embraced by everyone. They were 2007 Golden Crown Literary Award winners for debut author with their first work, *Combust the Sun*.

Visit their website at www.andrewsaustin.com.

Books Available From Bold Strokes Books

Deeper by Ronica Black. Former homicide detective Erin McKenzie and her fiancée Elizabeth Adams couldn't be any happier—until the not so distant past comes knocking at the door. (978-1-60282-006-7)

The Lonely Hearts Club by Radclyffe. Take three friends, add two ex-lovers and several new ones, and the result is a recipe for explosive rivalries and incendiary romance. (978-1-60282-005-0)

Venus Besieged by Andrews & Austin. Teague Richfield heads for Sedona and the sensual arms of psychic astrologer Callie Rivers for a much needed romantic reunion. (978-1-60282-004-3)

Branded Ann by Merry Shannon. Pirate Branded Ann raids a merchant vessel to obtain a treasure map and gets more than she bargained for with the widow Violet. (978-1-60282-003-6)

American Goth by JD Glass. Trapped by an unsuspected inheritance and guided only by the guardian who holds the secret to her future, Samantha Cray fights to fulfill her destiny. (978-1-60282-002-9)

Learning Curve by Rachel Spangler. Ashton Clarke is perfectly content with her life until she meets the intriguing Professor Carrie Fletcher, who isn't looking for a relationship with anyone. (978-1-60282-001-2)

Place of Exile by Rose Beecham. Sheriff's detective Jude Devine struggles with ghosts of her past and an ex-lover who still haunts her dreams. (978-1-933110-98-1)

Fully Involved by Erin Dutton. A love that has smoldered for years ignites when two women and one little boy come together in the aftermath of tragedy. (978-1-933110-99-8)

Heart 2 Heart by Julie Cannon. Suffering from a devastating personal loss, Kyle Bain meets Lane Connor, and the chance for happiness suddenly seems possible. (978-1-60282-000-5)

Queens of Tristaine: Tristaine Book Four by Cate Culpepper. When a deadly plague stalks the Amazons of Tristaine, two warrior lovers must return to the place of their nightmares to find a cure. (978-1-933110-97-4)

The Crown of Valencia by Catherine Friend. Ex-lovers can really mess up your life…even, as Kate discovers, if they've traveled back to the 11th century! (978-1-933110-96-7)

Mine by Georgia Beers. What happens when you've already given your heart and love finds you again? Courtney McAllister is about to find out. (978-1-933110-95-0)

House of Clouds by KI Thompson. A sweeping saga of an impassioned romance between a Northern spy and a Southern sympathizer, set amidst the upheaval of a nation under siege. (978-1-933110-94-3)

Winds of Fortune by Radclyffe. Provincetown local Deo Camara agrees to rehab Dr. Nita Burgoyne's historic home, but she never said anything about mending her heart. (978-1-933110-93-6)

Focus of Desire by Kim Baldwin. Isabel Sterling is surprised when she wins a photography contest, but no more than photographer Natasha Kashnikova. Their promo tour becomes a ticket to romance. (978-1-933110-92-9)

Blind Leap by Diane and Jacob Anderson-Minshall. A Golden Gate Bridge suicide becomes suspect when a filmmaker's camera shows a different story. Yoshi Yakamota and the Blind Eye Detective Agency uncover evidence that could be worth killing for. (978-1-933110-91-2)

Wall of Silence, 2nd ed. by Gabrielle Goldsby. Life takes a dangerous turn when jaded police detective Foster Everett meets Riley Medeiros, a woman who isn't afraid to discover the truth no matter the cost. (978-1-933110-90-5)

Mistress of the Runes by Andrews & Austin. Passion ignites between two women with ties to ancient secrets, contemporary mysteries, and a shared quest for the meaning of life. (978-1-933110-89-9)

Sheridan's Fate by Gun Brooke. A dynamic, erotic romance between physical therapist Lark Mitchell and businesswoman Sheridan Ward set in the scorching hot days and humid, steamy nights of San Antonio. (978-1-933110-88-2)

Vulture's Kiss by Justine Saracen. Archeologist Valerie Foret, heir to a terrifying task, returns in a powerful desert adventure set in Egypt and Jerusalem. (978-1-933110-87-5)

Rising Storm by JLee Meyer. The sequel to *First Instinct* takes our heroines on a dangerous journey instead of the honeymoon they'd planned. (978-1-933110-86-8)

Not Single Enough by Grace Lennox. A funny, sexy modern romance about two lonely women who bond over the unexpected and fall in love along the way. (978-1-933110-85-1)

Such a Pretty Face by Gabrielle Goldsby. A sexy, sometimes humorous, sometimes biting contemporary romance that gently exposes the damage to heart and soul when we fail to look beneath the surface for what truly matters. (978-1-933110-84-4)

Second Season by Ali Vali. A romance set in New Orleans amidst betrayal, Hurricane Katrina, and the new beginnings hardship and heartbreak sometimes make possible. (978-1-933110-83-7)

Hearts Aflame by Ronica Black. A poignant, erotic romance between a hard-driving businesswoman and a solitary vet. Packed with adventure and set in the harsh beauty of the Arizona countryside. (978-1-933110-82-0)

Red Light by JD Glass. Tori forges her path as an EMT in the New York City 911 system while discovering what matters most to herself and the woman she loves. (978-1-933110-81-3)

Honor Under Siege by Radclyffe. Secret Service agent Cameron Roberts struggles to protect her lover while searching for a traitor who just may be another woman with a claim on her heart. (978-1-933110-80-6)

Dark Valentine by Jennifer Fulton. Danger and desire fuel a high stakes cat-and-mouse game when an attorney and an endangered witness team up to thwart a killer. (978-1-933110-79-0)

Sequestered Hearts by Erin Dutton. A popular artist suddenly goes into seclusion; a reluctant reporter wants to know why; and a heart locked away yearns to be set free. (978-1-933110-78-3)

Erotic Interludes 5: *Road Games* eds. Radclyffe and Stacia Seaman. Adventure, "sport," and sex on the road—hot stories of travel adventures and games of seduction. (978-1-933110-77-6)

The Spanish Pearl by Catherine Friend. On a trip to Spain, Kate Vincent is accidentally transported back in time...an epic saga spiced with humor, lust, and danger. (978-1-933110-76-9)

Lady Knight by L-J Baker. Loyalty and honour clash with love and ambition in a medieval world of magic when female knight Riannon meets Lady Eleanor. (978-1-933110-75-2)

Dark Dreamer by Jennifer Fulton. Best-selling horror author, Rowe Devlin falls under the spell of psychic Phoebe Temple. A Dark Vista romance. (978-1-933110-74-5)

Come and Get Me by Julie Cannon. Elliott Foster isn't used to pursuing women, but alluring attorney Lauren Collier makes her change her mind. (978-1-933110-73-8)

Blind Curves by Diane and Jacob Anderson-Minshall. Private eye Yoshi Yakamota comes to the aid of her ex-lover Velvet Erickson in the first Blind Eye mystery. (978-1-933110-72-1)

Dynasty of Rogues by Jane Fletcher. It's hate at first sight for Ranger Riki Sadiq and her new patrol corporal, Tanya Coppelli—except for their undeniable attraction. (978-1-933110-71-4)

Running With the Wind by Nell Stark. Sailing instructor Corrie Marsten has signed off on love until she meets Quinn Davies—one woman she can't ignore. (978-1-933110-70-7)

More than Paradise by Jennifer Fulton. Two women battle danger, risk all, and find in one another an unexpected ally and an unforgettable love. (978-1-933110-69-1)

Flight Risk by Kim Baldwin. For Blayne Keller, being in the wrong place at the wrong time just might turn out to be the best thing that ever happened to her. (978-1-933110-68-4)

Rebel's Quest, Supreme Constellations Book Two by Gun Brooke. On a world torn by war, two women discover a love that defies all boundaries. (978-1-933110-67-7)

Punk and Zen by JD Glass. Angst, sex, love, rock. Trace, Candace, Francesca...Samantha. Losing control—and finding the truth within. (1-933110-66-X)

Stellium in Scorpio by Andrews & Austin. The passionate reuniting of two powerful women on the glitzy Las Vegas Strip where everything is an illusion and love is a gamble. (1-933110-65-1)

When Dreams Tremble by Radclyffe. Two women whose lives turned out far differently than they'd once imagined discover that sometimes the shape of the future can only be found in the past. (1-933110-64-3)

The Devil Unleashed by Ali Vali. As the heat of violence rises, so does the passion. A Casey Family crime saga. (1-933110-61-9)

Burning Dreams by Susan Smith. The chronicle of the challenges faced by a young drag king and an older woman who share a love "outside the bounds." (1-933110-62-7)

Fresh Tracks by Georgia Beers. Seven women, seven days. A lot can happen when old friends, lovers, and a new girl in town get together in the mountains. (1-933110-63-5)

The Empress and the Acolyte by Jane Fletcher. Jemeryl and Tevi fight to protect the very fabric of their world: time. Lyremouth Chronicles Book Three. (1-933110-60-0)

First Instinct by JLee Meyer. When high-stakes security fraud leads to murder, one woman flees for her life while another risks her heart to protect her. (1-933110-59-7)

Erotic Interludes 4: *Extreme Passions* ed. by Radclyffe and Stacia Seaman. Thirty of today's hottest erotica writers set the pages aflame with love, lust, and steamy liaisons. (1-933110-58-9)

Storms of Change by Radclyffe. In the continuing saga of the Provincetown Tales, duty and love are at odds as Reese and Tory face their greatest challenge. (1-933110-57-0)

Unexpected Ties by Gina L. Dartt. With death before dessert, Kate Shannon and Nikki Harris are swept up in another tale of danger and romance. (1-933110-56-2)

Sleep of Reason by Rose Beecham. While Detective Jude Devine searches for a lost boy, her rocky relationship with Dr. Mercy Westmoreland gets a lot harder. (1-933110-53-8)

Passion's Bright Fury by Radclyffe. Passion strikes without warning when a trauma surgeon and a filmmaker become reluctant allies. (1-933110-54-6)

Broken Wings by L-J Baker. When Rye Woods meets beautiful dryad Flora Withe, her libido, as hidden as her wings, reawakens along with her heart. (1-933110-55-4)

Combust the Sun by Andrews & Austin. A Richfield and Rivers mystery set in L.A. Murder among the stars. (1-933110-52-X)

Of Drag Kings and the Wheel of Fate by Susan Smith. A blind date in a drag club leads to an unlikely romance. (1-933110-51-1)

Tristaine Rises: Tristaine Book Three by Cate Culpepper. Brenna, Jesstin, and the Amazons of Tristaine face their greatest challenge for survival. (1-933110-50-3)

Too Close to Touch by Georgia Beers. Kylie O'Brien believes in true love and is willing to wait for it, even though Gretchen, her new boss, is off-limits. (1-933110-47-3)

100th Generation by Justine Saracen. Ancient curses, modern-day villains, and an intriguing woman lead archeologist Valerie Foret on the adventure of her life. (1-933110-48-1)

Battle for Tristaine: Tristaine Book Two by Cate Culpepper. While Brenna struggles to find her place in the clan, Tristaine is threatened with destruction. Second in the Tristaine series. (1-933110-49-X)

The Traitor and the Chalice by Jane Fletcher. Tevi and Jemeryl risk all in the race to uncover a traitor. The Lyremouth Chronicles Book Two. (1-933110-43-0)

Promising Hearts by Radclyffe. Dr. Vance Phelps arrives in New Hope, Montana, with no hope of happiness—until she meets Mae. (1-933110-44-9)

Carly's Sound by Ali Vali. Poppy Valente and Julia Johnson form a bond of friendship that becomes something far more. A poignant romance about love and renewal. (1-933110-45-7)

Unexpected Sparks by Gina L. Dartt. Kate Shannon's attraction to much younger Nikki Harris is complication enough without a fatal fire that Kate can't ignore. (1-933110-46-5)

Whitewater Rendezvous by Kim Baldwin. Two women on a wilderness kayak adventure discover that true love may be nothing at all like they imagined. (1-933110-38-4)

Erotic Interludes 3: *Lessons in Love* ed. by Radclyffe and Stacia Seaman. Sign on for a class in love…the best lesbian erotica writers take us to "school." (1-9331100-39-2)

Punk Like Me by JD Glass. Twenty-one-year-old Nina has a way with the girls, and she doesn't always play by the rules. (1-933110-40-6)

Coffee Sonata by Gun Brooke. Four women whose lives unexpectedly intersect in a small town by the sea share one thing in common—they all have secrets. (1-933110-41-4)

The Clinic: Tristaine Book One by Cate Culpepper. Brenna, a prison medic, finds herself drawn to Jesstin, a warrior reputed to be descended from ancient Amazons. (1-933110-42-2)

Forever Found by JLee Meyer. Can time, tragedy, and shattered trust destroy a love that seemed destined? Chance reunites childhood friends separated by tragedy. (1-933110-37-6)

Sword of the Guardian by Merry Shannon. Princess Shasta's bold new bodyguard has a secret that could change both of their lives. *He* is actually a *she*. (1-933110-36-8)

Wild Abandon by Ronica Black. Dr. Chandler Brogan and Officer Sarah Monroe are drawn together by their common obsessions—sex, speed, and danger. (1-933110-35-X)

Turn Back Time by Radclyffe. Pearce Rifkin and Wynter Thompson have nothing in common but a shared passion for surgery—and unexpected attraction. (1-933110-34-1)

Chance by Grace Lennox. A sexy, funny, touching story of two women who, in finding themselves, also find one another. (1-933110-31-7)

The Exile and the Sorcerer by Jane Fletcher. First in the Lyremouth Chronicles. Tevi and a shy young sorcerer face monsters, magic, and the challenge of loving. (1-933110-32-5)

A Matter of Trust by Radclyffe. When what should be just business turns into much more, two women struggle to trust the unexpected. (1-933110-33-3)

Sweet Creek by Lee Lynch. A celebration of the enduring nature of love, friendship, and community in the heart-warming lesbian community of Waterfall Falls. (1-933110-29-5)

The Devil Inside by Ali Vali. The head of a New Orleans crime organization falls for a woman who turns her world upside down. (1-933110-30-9)

Grave Silence by Rose Beecham. Detective Jude Devine's investigation of ritual murders is complicated by her torrid affair with pathologist Dr. Mercy Westmoreland. (1-933110-25-2)

Honor Reclaimed by Radclyffe. Secret Service Agent Cameron Roberts and Blair Powell close ranks to find the would-be assassins who nearly claimed Blair's life. (1-933110-18-X)

Honor Bound by Radclyffe. Secret Service Agent Cameron Roberts and Blair Powell face political intrigue, a clandestine threat to Blair's safety, and the seemingly irreconcilable differences that force them ever farther apart. (1-933110-20-1)

Innocent Hearts by Radclyffe. In a wild and unforgiving land, two women learn about love, passion, and the wonders of the heart. (1-933110-21-X)

The Temple at Landfall by Jane Fletcher. An imprinter, one of Celaeno's most revered servants of the Goddess, is also a prisoner to the faith—until a Ranger frees her by claiming her heart. The Celaeno series. (1-933110-27-9)

Protector of the Realm, Supreme Constellations Book One by Gun Brooke. A space adventure filled with suspense and a daring intergalactic romance. (1-933110-26-0)

Force of Nature by Kim Baldwin. From tornados to forest fires, the forces of nature conspire to bring Gable McCoy and Erin Richards close to danger, and closer to each other. (1-933110-23-6)

In Too Deep by Ronica Black. Undercover homicide cop Erin McKenzie tracks a femme fatale who just might be a real killer…with love and danger hot on her heels. (1-933110-17-1)

Erotic Interludes 2: *Stolen Moments* ed. by Radclyffe and Stacia Seaman. Love on the run, in the office, in the shadows…Fast, furious, and almost too hot to handle. (1-933110-16-3)

Course of Action by Gun Brooke. Actress Carolyn Black desperately wants the starring role in an upcoming film produced by Annelie Peterson. Just how far will she go for the dream part of a lifetime? (1-933110-22-8)

Rangers at Roadsend by Jane Fletcher. Sergeant Chip Coppelli has learned to spot trouble coming, and that is exactly what she sees in her new recruit, Katryn Nagata. The Celaeno series. (1-933110-28-7)

Justice Served by Radclyffe. Lieutenant Rebecca Frye and her lover, Dr. Catherine Rawlings, embark on a deadly game of hide-and-seek with an underworld kingpin who traffics in human souls. (1-933110-15-5)

Distant Shores, Silent Thunder by Radclyffe. Dr. Tory King—along with the women who love her—is forced to examine the boundaries of love, friendship, and the ties that transcend time. (1-933110-08-2)

Hunter's Pursuit by Kim Baldwin. A raging blizzard, a mountain hideaway, and a killer-for-hire set a scene for disaster—or desire—when Katarzyna Demetrious rescues a beautiful stranger. (1-933110-09-0)

The Walls of Westernfort by Jane Fletcher. All Temple Guard Natasha Ionadis wants is to serve the Goddess—until she falls in love with one of the rebels she is sworn to destroy. The Celaeno series. (1-933110-24-4)

Erotic Interludes: *Change Of Pace* by Radclyffe. Twenty-five hot-wired encounters guaranteed to spark more than just your imagination. Erotica as you've always dreamed of it. (1-933110-07-4)

Honor Guards by Radclyffe. In a wild flight for their lives, the president's daughter and those who are sworn to protect her wage a desperate struggle for survival. (1-933110-01-5)

Fated Love by Radclyffe. Amidst the chaos and drama of a busy emergency room, two women must contend not only with the fragile nature of life, but also with the irresistible forces of fate. (1-933110-05-8)

Justice in the Shadows by Radclyffe. In a shadow world of secrets and lies, Detective Sergeant Rebecca Frye and her lover, Dr. Catherine Rawlings, join forces in the elusive search for justice. (1-933110-03-1)

BOLD
STROKES
BOOKS